SAFETY LAST

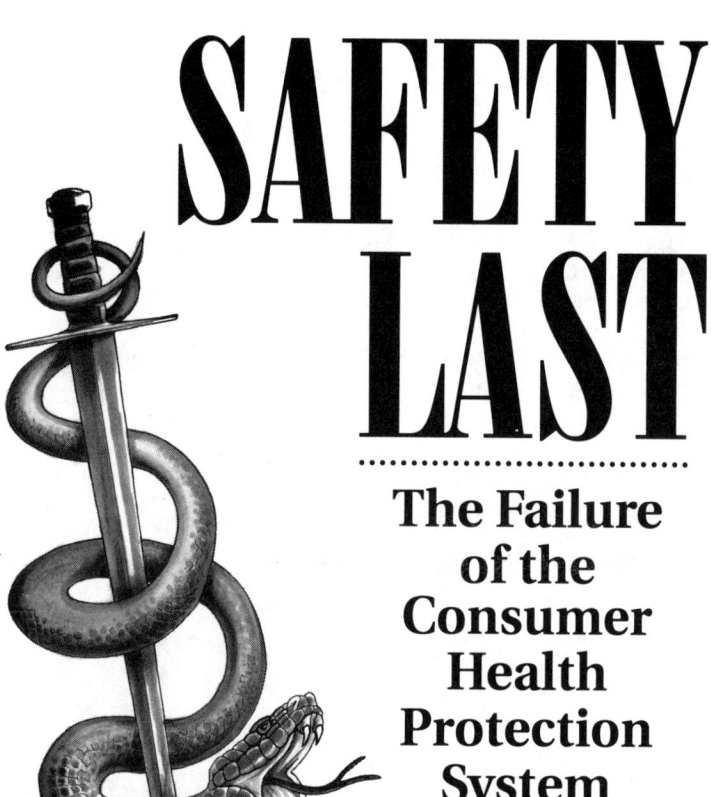

SAFETY LAST

The Failure of the Consumer Health Protection System in Canada

Nicholas Regush

KEY PORTER BOOKS

Copyright © 1993 by Nicholas Regush

All rights reserved. No part of this work covered by the copyrights hereon may be reproduced or used in any form or by any means—graphic, electronic or mechanical, including photocopying, recording, taping or information storage and retrieval systems—without the prior written permission of the publisher, or, in case of photocopying or other reprographic copying, without a licence from the Canadian Reprography Collective.

The publisher gratefully acknowledges the assistance of the Canada Council and the Ontario Arts Council in the publication of this work.

Canadian Cataloguing in Publication Data

Regush, Nicholas M., 1946-
    Safety last

ISBN 1-55013-462-0

1. Drugs — Canada — Testing.   2. Implants, Artificial — Canada — Testing.   I. Title.

RM301.27.R44   1993   354.710077'84   C92-095708-0

Key Porter Books Limited
70 The Esplanade
Toronto, Ontario
Canada M5E 1R2

Design: Annabelle Stanley
Printed and bound in Canada

93 94 95 96 5 4 3 2 1

For the commitment and all-round stellar support on the Meme breast-implant investigation and other stories, this book is for *Gazette* editors Ray Brassard, Catherine Wallace, and Alan Allnutt.

It is also dedicated to Barbara Moon, editor-at-large at *Saturday Night* magazine, a superb and very, very patient teacher.

CONTENTS

Acknowledgements / ix
Introduction / 1

Part One: Say Goodbye to the Health-Safety Net

1. A Time to Remember: Thalidomide and the Dalkon Shield / 9
2. History Repeating Itself: Thirty Years after Thalidomide / 15
3. Halfway Revolution: Out of Control on Medical Devices / 35
4. Drug Connect-the-Dots: The Drug Industry and the New World Order / 49
5. Disgrace South of the Border: The FDA Follies / 59

Part Two: Big Trouble

6. Sins of Omission: The Meme Breast Implant / 73
7. Too Good To Be True: Migraine Headaches and Imitrex / 107
8. Those Halcion Nights: Sleep on a Tightrope / 123
9. A Case of Mistaken Identity: Toradol for Pain Relief / 129

Part Three: Storm Warnings

10. Woman as Guinea Pig: Pills for Menopause / 139
11. Nuts and Bolts: The Orthopaedic Hardware Store / 149
12. Software Safety: The Neglect of
    Computer-Controlled Medical Devices / 155
13. The 5-Per-Cent Acne Solution:
    The Saga of Benzoyl Peroxide / 161

Part Four: Options

14. The Political Option: Swift Kick and New Think / 171
15. The Personal Option: Become Street Smart on Drugs and
    Medical Devices / 181
16. Final Word: Looking Ahead / 187

Appendices / 189
Index / 207

ACKNOWLEDGEMENTS

I've worked at *The Gazette* in Montreal since 1980 with some of the best people in the newspaper business. At the top of the list are Ray Brassard, Catherine Wallace, and Alan Allnutt. Others at *The Gazette* who handled my copy and made life easier and more enjoyable are Matt Radz, Russ Peden, John Simpson, Frank Mackey, and Marv Zivitz. A special thanks also to Joan Fraser for the encouragement and supervision of stinging editorials on Health and Welfare's handling of the Meme breast implant. My colleague and friend William Marsden, Canada's best investigative reporter, was always around to offer suggestions and support. And for the life of me, I can't figure out how crack feature writers Janet Bagnall and Mark Abley (who sit nearby) put up with my huffing and puffing on the Meme for so long—and even offered a boost when times were tough. Thanks also to Robert Walker, *The Gazette* ombudsman, who handled a litany of complaints from Health and Welfare and breast-implant manufacturers about my stories with fairness, humour, and grace. Walker is one of the most savvy people in the newspaper business—anywhere. Thanks to colleagues Kate Dunn, Sarah Scott, Phyllis Beaulieu, Page Woodward, and Elizabeth Thompson for their support. And likewise to editor Norman Webster, former editor Mark Harrison, publisher David Perks, and former publisher Clark Davey.

Thanks also to *The Gazette*'s David Pinto whose endless hours spent in scanning wire copy, old journals, and anything under the sun helped enormously in my research.

The work of a reporter involves daily interaction with library staffers. A special thanks (especially for handling those last-minute requests) to Agnes McFarlane, Donna MacHutchin, Elizabeth Ferguson, Pat Duggan, Pat Onofrio, Mike Porritt, and Yvette Dailey.

As for *The Gazette*'s switchboard personnel, these are the folks who are like family. Millie Thompson, now retired, was as good a den mother as a reporter could have. Bertha Daigneault, holder of the night flame and now semi-retired, kept the lines to Ottawa and elsewhere busy until late each night. Jackie Collin's warm sense of humour and all-round help and Johanne Poissant's mischievous antics and snap-to-it assistance have often turned a scowl on my face into a smile. Thanks also to Maralyne Fisher, Marie Collin, and Gaby Hogan for putting up with my late-night and weekend telephone requests.

I would also like to take this opportunity to thank scores of federal public servants who provided me with details of the inner workings of the federal Health department. They did so at risk of losing their jobs. I am deeply grateful to them.

Thanks also to Sybil Goldrich, staunch consumer advocate and new friend, for help in navigating a path through the minefield of breast-implant politics. And to Denise Dunleavy, Diana Zuckerman, Marella Tardiff, Joy Langan, Beryl Gaffrey and especially Linda Wilson for the good fight.

Ottawa chemist Pierre Blais deserves the nation's gratitude for his courageous battle against the sale of the Meme.

And thanks to Pierre Binon, professor of pharmacology at the Université de Montréal for his conscientious drug tracking.

Without the good humour, encouragement, and patience of Susan Renouf, editor in chief of Key Porter Books, you wouldn't be reading this book. Susan also chose Charis Wahl, the perfect editor, to shepherd in the manuscript. Charis prepared me for her expert blue-pencilling by telling me time and again how much fun she was having reading my late-arriving chapters.

Last, but not least, my wife, Barbara Lewis, as always, kept me from falling off the edge.

Nicholas Regush
Montreal, Quebec, and Rochester, Vermont
February 1993

INTRODUCTION

Montreal, November 21, 1991.
A conference room at The Gazette

Sound the trumpets. Bang the drums. There was Margaret Catley-Carlson, deputy minister of Health and Welfare Canada, the nation's largest government department. Walking dutifully behind his "Maggie" was Marcel Chartrand, the department's chief of media relations. They had come to see me at the deputy's request. She had also invited Raymond Brassard, then my editor, and *Gazette* ombudsman Robert Walker.

The Health department was not enthralled by my manner of reporting; several months earlier it had banned me from interviewing its employees. Catley-Carlson and Chartrand were here to explore ways to break the "impasse." In other words, they had come to question my credibility.

The hostilities were related to my reporting on the Meme breast implant. One of the Health department's senior scientists had expressed strong concerns about the potential harm of the implant. Other scientists in Canada and the United States were questioning the department's decision to allow the sale of a poorly tested silicone-gel implant with a polyurethane cover that released a potential carcinogen into the body. The department had dug itself a hole, declaring the Meme safe until proven otherwise, rather than requiring proof of its safety. The hole deepened when U.S. government research led to the decision by the Meme's manufacturer to suspend sales in April 1991.

My chronicle of the Meme saga began in November 1988 and

continued after the implant's withdrawal from the market. Catley-Carlson's elected boss, Benoît Bouchard, had taken over the Health department and its tortured policy on the Meme from Perrin Beatty in May 1991. My ongoing stories irritated the minister, although he appeared more concerned with constitutional issues and Quebec's economy than with running his department. Catley-Carlson was ordered to "fix it," meaning me.

Here's the fix: whenever I require information or comment from the Health department, I must dictate my questions to Carole Peacock, director of communications, who eventually sends them up the chain of command. Often after my story is published. Peacock faxes me the department's reply, which frequently bypasses the question or amounts to gibberish. Perhaps the person wording the replies needs a refresher course in Basic English, but I assume the bafflegab is part of a sophisticated strategy to protect government secrets. Whatever the purpose, the exercise violates official government policy. On November 23, 1984, the Prime Minister's Office issued guidelines to encourage open communications between public servants and the media. By closing official channels to me, Bouchard, in effect, forced scores of concerned public servants to speak with me in secret. More sought me out after the department sent around a memo reminding managers and their employees that they were not to speak to me.

I didn't take the ban personally—it was business, as the Godfather would say—but having to listen to Catley-Carlson rant on that *Gazette* coverage on the Meme was unfair was boring and silly. Chartrand, whom I had come to know prior to the ban to be both decent and competent, if somewhat cowed, said little and looked embarrassed. I'm sure he knew the score: the department's Health Protection Branch, responsible for the protection of Canadians "by identifying, assessing and managing risks to human health," was a mess.

The branch had begun its decline during the late 1970s. Tough economic conditions led to government cutbacks. Programs that reviewed the safety of drugs and medical devices did not broaden according to plan. Staff shortages caused discontentment among overworked scientists and friction between them and their managers. By the early 1980s, government safety reviewers were under increasing pressure from their managers and industry representatives to speed up pre-market evaluations.

When the Tories took power in 1984, they chipped away at government regulation. Their trust-industry philosophy has shredded a safety net that, at the best of times, has been delicate.

By the time Catley-Carlson arrived at *The Gazette*, two words summed government policy: "Safety last."

For Catley-Carlson, one word summed me up: "obso," short for "obsolete," or "reformer." When we first met on September 20, 1990, to discuss the Meme, she had referred condescendingly to people who take up issues.

She had also detailed her vision of a new partnership between government and industry: Industry really wanted to do good because it was in industry's best interest to do so. Think partnership, not conflict. Crusaders who would keep industry in check were obso.

As she spoke—she had actually asked me not to interrupt—I pondered whether she and I were from the same planet. Her suggestion that the drug industry does not require aggressive monitoring seemed evidence of an active fantasy life.

True, government and industry are developing a familial bond in Canada and elsewhere. Indeed, they have become brother and sister, in some instances of the marrying kind. Such family values will no doubt be enhanced by international trade agreements, now in the making, to "harmonize" governments' regulations for industry. The multinational drug companies are looking to the day when they will no longer be required to jump through different regulatory hoops before their drugs are approved for market. They had been nagging Canada and other nations to agree on a single standard for drug-safety review. This, the companies claim, will save them bushels of money, which they will then shovel into research and investment. That will grow more jobs and better drugs for consumers.

As someone once said, "I should live so long to see that work so nice."

Unless you believe in the Tooth Fairy, it is clear that the push to harmonization is moving regulatory standards in Canada and other nations to a lower common denominator. Lowered standards for drug-safety review are already in play. The result is less safety protection for consumers, and even less on the way.

And Catley-Carlson's vision of a partnership between industry and government? It's not an equal partnership, and it never will be. The multinational dominatrix roams the planet, choosing the friendliest conditions for investments and profits. Desperate governments aching for capital submit.

When I left Catley-Carlson's office in September 1990, I resolved to uncover the daily workings of her department, to unmask the lie that policy made there is in the best interests of Canadians.

By the time we met again at *The Gazette* in November 1991, Catley-Carlson and Bouchard knew how deep my information ran. Only a week earlier, *The Gazette* had published my story about how visible-minority scientists at the Health department had been blocked from advancement to managerial positions by a group of British-born managers. This had been going on for twenty years. I had also found that many scientists in the Health department, regardless of race, feared for the safety of Canadians, and all expressed concern that the situation was worsening. In most cases, however, it was the documents I obtained that told the story.

The meeting ended without resolution. Catley-Carlson made it plain that the department didn't trust me, and that Brassard would have to accompany me to Ottawa if I wished to conduct official interviews. In days of yore, that would have amounted to a slap across the face with a glove. I watched Chartrand swollow hard. Walker grimaced. I knew that Brassard was already planning for the duel. I couldn't hold back a smile. Over the past year, it broadened into a book.

Safety Last is divided into four parts. Part One explores and analyses how and why the Canadian safety net is being stripped, and draws a comparison with the situation in the United States. Part Two investigates how the Health department has dealt with the Meme breast implant and three major prescription drugs. Part

Three warns of looming difficulties with drugs and medical devices, and Part Four examines possible ways of alleviating the safety crisis, with particular emphasis on how you can arm yourself for better health protection in an era of deregulation.

One final note: the Health department recently issued a report recommending speedier drug review. Bouchard's promise to implement the suggested changes to the system has pleased drug companies. It is a clear sign that Tory health policy will continue to play to the interests of multinationals.

The department, under fire for its handling of the Meme breast implant, has also issued a report on medical devices, vowing to implement recommendations that call for stronger safety checks. But a government bent on pleasing multinationals cannot be trusted to serve the health interests of Canadians first. Had Bouchard really wanted important changes, he would have instructed the report's authors to dissect the bureaucratic quagmire that has for twenty years blocked effective monitoring of medical devices. The report does not address this issue.

So, don't hold your breath. It's still safety last.

1

SAY GOODBYE TO THE HEALTH-SAFETY NET

1

A TIME TO REMEMBER:

Thalidomide and the Dalkon Shield

TWO PRODUCTS—ONE A DRUG AND ONE A MEDICAL device—are synonymous with injury and sorrow. The first calls to mind individuals who have flipper-like arms and legs, missing fingers and toes, and/or organs in the wrong places. These are the Children of Thalidomide, the hundred or so Canadians whose mothers were among thousands of Canadian women who used the drug, brand-named Kevadon or Talimol, as a sleeping pill or as a remedy for morning sickness during the late 1950s and early 1960s.

Thalidomide was first marketed in West Germany as Contergan. (The animal trials of the day indicated the drug was safe, but didn't test for birth defects.) An effective non-prescription sleeping pill and anti-nausea treatment for early pregnancy, it was also added to neuralgia, asthma, and cough medicines as a sedative.

In 1961 West German doctors linked frequent and long-term use of thalidomide with muscle disorders, tingling in the hands, and wasting of thumb tissue. Moreover, these side-effects could become permanent with long-term use of the drug: to control its use, thalidomide was first made a prescription drug and was ultimately banned in 1962, when it was strongly implicated as causing damaging effects in the foetus in early pregnancy. Manufacturers used the drug's popularity in Germany to whisk it through regulatory agencies in many countries, including Canada, Britain, Australia, The Netherlands, and Japan. All told, some

8,000 thalidomide children were born worldwide. The U.S. Food and Drug Administration, in the person of Frances Kelsey, an FDA drug reviewer, refused to approve thalidomide. The safety data didn't satisfy Kelsey and she held firm.

In February 1990, twenty-eight years after Canada finally banned thalidomide, War Amputations of Canada finally won $7.5 million in federal compensation for individuals affected by the drug. The government stressed that the settlement was not an admission of regulatory negligence; indeed, it held that Health officials had kept distribution of the drug in check. The War Amps task force, however, concluded in its report of February 14, 1989, that Health officials ignored early warning signs and were slow to act. The Canadian ban, in March 1962, came some three months after action by the West Germans and the British. At that time, J. Waldo Monteith, the federal Health minister, said: "It is our job to ensure that these victims are cared for in the best possible manner, that their needs are met to the fullest extent."

Maybe, but that's not what happened. Some of the Canadians affected by thalidomide relied on friends and family; others made modest deals with the manufacturer, the William S. Merrell Company. The Children of Thalidomide waited for the Canadian government for twenty-eight years.

In the world of medical devices, the Dalkon Shield is the ranking tragedy. About four million women worldwide used the simple, plastic contraceptive device that fit into the uterus. To make removal easy, the device had a thin three-inch string that extended from the uterus into the vagina. The string, made of hundreds of tiny filaments, was covered by an open-ended sheath.

The device was developed by the Dalkon Corporation, which conducted no safety tests on the shield, but sold 27,000 of them anyway, claiming without a scrap of proper scientific evidence that their product was safer than and as effective as the birth-control pill.

Lacking a network to market the IUD effectively, Dalkon sold the product in 1970 to the A.H. Robbins Company, which had no experience in the contraceptive field.

The facts surfaced less than one year later: the Dalkon Shield caused serious pelvic infections, sterility, and miscarriages. Thousands of women were infected; some died. Robbins finally halted sale of the shield in June 1974. Thousands of lawsuits followed.

The culprit was the filament structure of the string. Bacteria harboured in the vagina ascended the string ladder to the uterus, causing serious pelvic inflammatory disease. Court records show that Robbins ignored warnings by its own staff that there was potential for infection. Even after it stopped selling the shield, Robbins argued it was safe.

Thalidomide and the Dalkon Shield were the wake-up call for regulators and prompted changes in federal safety review, such as the introduction of stiffer requirements for proving that a product is safe for use on animals, and safe and effective for use by humans.

But that was a long, long time ago for a planet on fast-forward.

Maybe George Santayana was really thinking of our health-protection system when he wrote, in *The Life of Reason*: "Those who cannot remember the past are condemned to repeat it."

And he might well have been pointing the finger at Canadian politicians who confuse the promise, on paper, of the health system with its performance. Who hasn't heard some of our representatives in Ottawa say it: "Canada has one of the best health-care systems in the world." Or the variation on that theme: "Our review of drugs is one of the most stringent in the world."

These utterings are often used to counter criticism of government handling of a health matter, or in support of a colleague under fire. Three federal Health ministers, whom I have interviewed face to face—Monique Bégin, Jake Epp, and Perrin Beatty—have been very quick to sing this Canadian refrain. So has the incumbent, Benoît Bouchard.

You may be wondering, "Well, isn't it true? Are we not among the best and toughest?" There are several answers: Yes, Canada's regulatory record compares very favourably with those of developing nations, and pretty well with those of industrial nations. So far, good for us. However, on a scale of ten, the highest score among industrial nations is about five. Being one of the best is not so terrific.

Moreover, politicians are often not able to judge performance. They rely on briefings from assistants or bureaucrats, and these can be embarrassingly thin on substance, context, and insider information.

On paper, Canada's drug-safety review system sparkles. Anyone reading up on how drugs are developed and tested by pharmaceutical companies and then reviewed by Health and Welfare Canada might feel assured that the system is totally dedicated to the protection of the consumer. To be sure, it's considerably more elaborate than it was at the time of thalidomide. Let's run through the process quickly to see some of the finer theoretical features. Later, we'll compare what's on paper with what really goes on.

On Paper

Drug companies say it costs them considerably more than $100 million to bring a new drug to market. No company has ever produced a public accounting in support of that claim, but, what the hey, we'll trust them. This expensive process begins in the company laboratory, where compounds are screened in tissue cultures or on small animals to determine their effect and potential therapeutic value. One in about five thousand might merit further consideration.

Preliminary animal tests investigate how the compound is absorbed, metabolized, and eliminated from the body. They also hint at how it will affect vital organs, the reproductive and immune systems, and behaviour. The company then tests at least two mammalian species—one a non-rodent—to determine the dose range, from non-toxic to lethal.

The test data and manufacturing information are then sent to Health and Welfare Canada for review; the company also encloses an application to test the product on humans. First, safety tests—to determine if the drug causes excessive side-effects—are conducted on healthy volunteers. Next, small controlled pilot studies and then larger "clinical trials," usually with hospital patients, are undertaken. Patients in these randomized, double-blind trials are assigned, on the basis of chance, to one of two groups: one is a control group, which is given a placebo; the other receives the new treatment. The code telling the researchers who has received the experimental treatment is revealed at the completion of the study.

It then rests with Health department reviewers to examine all the test data on the new drug, which the company provides in the form of a comprehensive summary, including tables listing all studies. The review determines whether the drug's benefits outweigh its risks. (All drugs have risks: the reviewer's job is to decipher—on the basis of the data supplied by the company—the benefit-to-risk margin.)

When a drug "passes" its review, the company receives a notice of compliance, proof that it has complied with laws and regulations governing the sale of drugs in Canada. Technically, the government doesn't actually "approve" the drug for market; it merely checks that the company has gone about its business correctly. (Might this be a legal distinction made only by government? You bet—we'll call it "drug approval" from now on.)

Before a drug receives final approval for sale in Canada, the company and Health department must agree on the content of the "product monograph," an executive summary of benefits and risks of the drug. This document serves as the prescribing information for doctors.

Should new information (such as unexpected side-effects) become known as the new drug is used, the product monograph may be updated. The companies must report side-effects of their drugs within fifteen working days to the Health department. The revised information may come from new studies of the drug or reports sent to the company voluntarily by health professionals. The government also receives voluntary reports, mainly from doctors and hospitals.

This is an elaborate system. It appears to work efficiently and smoothly; it seems to have your best interests at heart. So what's the problem? Maybe there isn't one—on paper.

2

HISTORY REPEATING ITSELF:

Thirty Years after Thalidomide

In my first major effort to understand Canada's drug-review system, I was fortunate to meet Dr. Ian Henderson, then head of the Health department's Bureau of Human Prescription Drugs. It was 1982, twenty years since thalidomide.

Henderson is honest, pleasant, and informative. He headed an 80-member team, whose job it was to review new-drug submissions—about 100 each year—in addition to about 180 requests annually for review of products already on the market. Since 1971, the bureau's workload had increased at least 10 per cent annually; the number of staff had remained the same. Senior management at the Health department had declared it a time for economic restraint. Work harder. Be happy.

Henderson said there was better all-round productivity, but people were getting edgy. The backlog was building—the average waiting time for response to a submitted request was about five months. Drug companies were huffing and puffing at the door.

Back then, the vast majority of new drugs were minor molecular modifications or copies of older products. (A 1981 U.S. Food and Drug Administration report concluded that, of the more recent 112 new drugs given market approval in that country, only 17 [15 per cent] offered any important therapeutic gain over existing drugs. Dr. Sidney Wolfe, head of Public Citizen's Health Research Group in Washington, D.C., a consumer watchdog organization, reported that fewer than 5 per cent of the approximately

15

800 or so new drugs in the development pipeline in the United States had the potential for important therapeutic gain.

Meanwhile, the companies were whining about how consumers were suffering as a result of the long waits for approval, and taking pot-shots at one another for clogging up the drug market with confusing products.)

Back in 1982, Henderson was feeling the heat from his bosses, who were being pressured by the drug companies to speed up approvals of their drugs, many of which were probably unnecessary. He feared his reviewers would soon cut corners in evaluating submissions, to the detriment of Canadians.

Henderson was remarkably courageous to speak so openly, but then, unlike some of his successors, he ran the place with real concern for consumers. Henderson paid for this and similar remarks he made to me, and to Joan Hollobin and Dorothy Lipovenko of *The Globe and Mail*. His superiors gagged him by making him a medical adviser to the Drugs Directorate. Today, Henderson is retired—or about to retire—from public service.

Henderson had more than just new drugs to worry about in 1982. The bureau had a mandate to review all drugs that had entered the market prior to 1963. About 450 of 7,000 medications available by prescription were suspected to be completely lacking in meaningful medical benefits. Some of these medications were bizarre compounds purporting to treat coughs, colds, asthma, and urinary infections without ever having been evaluated adequately. Henderson was particularly concerned about those containing barbiturates, which are addictive. Not surprisingly, his understrength troops were overrun.

(The obvious question was: why weren't drug companies voluntarily pulling these products from the market? You know the answer, but I did pop the question to Guy Beauchemin, then head of the Pharmaceutical Manufacturers Association of Canada, a multinational lobby. Beauchemin looked a tad embarrassed and essentially replied that some of PMAC's members were more forward-looking than others.)

Henderson was also concerned that clinical tests sponsored by drug companies were not subject to government monitoring.

Doctors who run tests on behalf of drug companies are required to follow directions approved by the Health department. Henderson, a physician, didn't trust his colleagues to get it right every time, and he had little faith in drug companies to weed out the slouches and botchers.

More worrisome was the lack of surveillance by companies and the Health department of drugs in the marketplace. Relatively few individuals take part in clinical tests; many use a drug once it is available for sale. Unexpected side-effects will often not appear until doctors prescribe a drug widely. In 1982, Henderson proposed that drug companies be required to monitor their drugs as a condition of sale. Dr. Edward Napke ran the department's drug-monitoring unit; it examined about 4,000 voluntary reports of side-effects submitted by doctors and hospitals each year—a tiny fraction of the side-effects that likely occur. Napke had been fighting since the thalidomide ban (and continued to do so until his recent retirement) for a "real" surveillance system that would collect, collate, and evaluate drug data and feed back the information to the medical profession and the drug industry. In 1982, Napke had a shoestring budget of $21,000. (Ten years later, a 1992 federally sponsored review of the drug-approval process recommended major improvements in drug surveillance.)

Instead of listening to Henderson and Napke, the Health department became increasingly preoccupied with politically driven measures that would help speed drugs through the approval process.

All Eyes on the Drug Backlog

Psychiatrists might describe the fuss made about the drug-review backlog as "shared psychopathology." Roughly deconstructed, it means: "Some people got an idea in their heads and couldn't let it go: they infected other people with it, and support for it grew exponentially—even though the idea was as useful as a prune pit."

The prune pit was gobbled up in 1985 by the Eastman Commission of Inquiry into the Pharmaceutical Industry, and the Ministerial Task Force on Program Review; even the Auditor General's Report in 1986 bit. All these busybodies were strongly concerned that drugs were not getting out to Canadians quickly enough.

The Auditor General noted that, in 1982, the drug backlog was 243; by 1986, it had jumped to 1,112. Lest figures be deceiving, the audit explained that there was "an influx of submissions due to anticipated changes in the Patent Act": the vast majority of these submissions were copies and near-copies, "me-too" drugs.

In 1987, a federal Working Group on Drugs argued that delays in drug approval led to low investment in Canadian research, and that doctors were robbed of early experience with new drugs.

Maybe, but did this have significant bearing on public health?

A senior Health department manager on the committee and the representative from the Canadian Public Health Association held that it did not. The other five committee members, three of whom were from the drug industry, disagreed, and called for urgent action on the drug backlog and bureaucratic inefficiency. It also lamented that the drug backlog was souring government-industry relations: The drug industry saw the department's drug reviewers as unresponsive to change; the drug reviewers saw industry as motivated primarily by profit. Such tensions, the report claimed, were not good, particularly for investment in Canada.

In response, the Health department put a work plan on paper in June 1988. It vowed to streamline its internal procedures, hire new managers to whip the scientific troops into shape, contract-out submissions to outside "experts," and rely much more on the drug-approval decisions of foreign regulatory agencies. The department also pondered dinging the drug companies for part of the costs of an accelerated review system. (By the time of the report, however, the flow of company submissions had returned to normal, helping the backlog to shrink to 596. Cursory reviews of generics and submissions requesting approval for the use of existing drugs for new medical purposes also brought down the numbers.)

Health minister Jake Epp promised to increase efficiency by 20 per cent over three years, and to eliminate the remaining backlog. He concluded that, yes sir, this improved efficiency would mean "faster access to new drugs and a better health-care system for Canadians."

Perhaps the minister sounded so cheerful because his concept of reality was based on the briefing papers provided by his officials. A particularly uplifting one, dated November 1, 1989, and signed by Albert Liston, an assistant deputy minister, and Emmanuel Somers, the department's drug-approval czar, unintentionally unmasks speeded-up drug approval for what it really is: a sham.

In a preamble of sorts, the briefing refers to a concerted effort by the Health department to ensure that Canadians are not denied access to breakthrough drugs. It informs the minister that there is a backlog of 241 submissions for new drugs—those not yet on the market—awaiting evaluation. The two senior managers then inform the minister that the press has been yammering on about a backlog of 1,000 submissions. Of course, the dummy reporters are referring "to a vast variety of submissions at least half of which are concerning amendments to previously approved drug submissions." They chose not to remind their boss that the department's own definition of backlog, according to a policy statement of May 5, 1988, includes amendments to previously approved drug submissions.

Nice. They snow the minister on the extent of the backlog, take a shot at reporters, and make themselves out to be shrewd backlog-eaters by assuming the minister does not recall that, eighteen months earlier, there were 596 submissions in the backlog, including amendments. It's enough to make you sorry for the politicos.

The more instructive segment of the briefing follows, in which Liston and Somers inform the minister that strategies are in place to speed up the approval of important drugs:

Breakthrough drugs are delayed somewhat by the queue system in which a drug must take its turn as it comes up for evaluation. This system is being augmented by a "fast track system" for priority drugs.

The fast track system allows new "breakthrough drugs" to be evaluated as soon as a submission is presented to the [Health Protection Branch]: development and implementation of the fast track system is undertaken at present for AIDS *therapy and is likely to extend soon to therapies for other life threatening and serious illnesses.*

Moreover, Liston and Somers point out, the minister oughtn't to forget the Health department's Emergency Release Program, which gets some drugs to folks before evaluation: "A Canadian patient in urgent need of the life saving breakthrough drug may receive the drug, at the request of his own physician and the cooperation of the manufacturer."

Well done: So, why does the entire drug-approval system need revamping, when even the "breakthrough drugs," which patients can get before they are approved, are far and few between?

Ah, but have the NDPers and Liberals grasped this point? No, they have not. Their health critics have joined the call for faster approval, not noticing the difference between new, run-of-the-mill drugs, of which there are very many, and new and important drugs, of which there are very few.

In December 1992, I interviewed NDP health critic Jim Karpoff and Liberal health critic Rey Pagtakhan, a medical doctor, about the suspicious rush by the Health department in December 1991 to approve Imitrex, a new anti-migraine drug. (The sad saga of Imitrex is recounted in Chapter 7.) Typically, they criticized the rush on Imitrex but supported quick drug approvals.

Not to worry, a speed-up was in gear. A memo to his managers, from Somers, dated August 22, 1991, might have been entitled "How Proud I Am." It certainly speaks well of changes in the drug-approval system under his command since the Working Group on Drugs reported in 1988. The backlog, Somers announces, is down to 186. The response time of the Bureau of Human Prescription Drugs to a submission has gone from 682 days (as of April 1990) to 429 days. New drugs will now become old drugs after seven years. Old drugs don't require submissions for labelling changes. Watch that backlog shrink! Streamlining of internal procedures are well underway, Somers coos: twenty guidelines and twenty-five reports have been issued to assist the drug industry and other interested parties to address government drug procedures.

Then comes the real eyebrow-raiser in the memo: As of August 1991, 129 contracts had been issued to external experts for review of submissions, 66 of them prescription drugs. "Early difficulties [not described] were encountered with the introduction of contracted reviews. These have been largely overcome."

Wait a minute! Let's have more detail here on contracting-out—the lynchpin of the speed-up. Somers began to nurture the development of that new program in June 1988, and some fifteen months later, new drug submissions began to be contracted-out to non-government "experts."

A careful inspection of the bundles of Health department documents on external review (which had arrived in the mail from "Capital Friends of Nicholas Regush") strongly suggested, again, that the department's official line didn't run parallel to what was really happening.

The official line, which hasn't changed much to date, appears in a very hopeful briefing paper for Perrin Beatty, signed by Liston and Somers on November 1, 1989. It advised Beatty on how to respond to the question: "Is the practice of contracting out of drug submission evaluation putting Canadians at risk?"

The suggested response: "The contracting out of drug submission [evaluation] is being conducted in a carefully organized supervised manner in which well qualified individuals who satisfy Conflict of Interest Guidelines evaluate drugs according to the same methods as internal evaluators within the Health Protection Branch."

Beatty might also reassure his questioner that a close link is to be established "between the external reviewer conducting the primary review and the internal staff who will evaluate and challenge the findings of the first review."

The briefing ends on the upbeat: "Far from putting Canadians at risk, this innovative and carefully conducted method of bringing new external expertise to the review process will help to reduce the existing backlog of new chemical entities awaiting evaluation, thus bringing useful therapies to Canadians in a more timely way."

Well, like I mentioned, that was the official line. Here's another perspective:

The contractors were academics, former Health department employees, and scientists and doctors who had banded together for the purpose of reviewing drugs on contract. The program had attracted considerable attention. The money isn't bad—up to

$70,000 a review, about $100 an hour, plus travel and overhead expenses. For example, the fifty-five reviews commissioned by the Bureau of Human Prescription Drugs between November 1989 and the end of August 1991 cost $1,854,586.05. That's about $34,000 per review, about two months of forty-hour weeks. It's six months' salary for an experienced government drug reviewer.

Prospective contractors have to jump through a few hoops. The first is evaluation, being judged on the basis of credentials, overall scientific track-record, and experience in working with drugs. The successful candidate's area of specialization is noted on the file. Presumably the idea is to match expertise with disease categories, but that wouldn't explain why a retired assistant director in the Bureau of Human Prescription Drugs, with expertise in endocrinology, but only a smidgeon of hands-on drug-review skills was given $18,000 to review a cancer drug. One drug reviewer in the Health department wondered, "Think of how you would feel if you were a cancer patient and learned that the man who reviewed the safety and effectiveness of the drug you are taking was incompetent to do so. And that he got the job because the government wanted to get rid of him and juiced up the incentive by allowing him to review drugs."

That numerous external reviews were inadequate and had to be reworked was not surprising, given that external reviewers were provided with only one or two days' training and that there was very little contact between internal and external reviewers. It was a far cry from the buddy system that Liston and Somers had described in their briefing to Perrin Beatty. Chris Turner, who worked in the Bureau of Biologics, which reviews vaccines and other bioproducts, said, "Not once in about ten to fifteen cases that I know about was anyone inside assigned to work with an external reviewer."

On paper, the internal reviewer is supposed to look over the review when it comes in from the external reviewer and, if necessary, request clarification and more information. This wasn't always happening. Sometimes there was a time delay, and when the internal reviewer finally made contact with his outside buddy, the final government cheque had already been sent. That is what happened, for example, with an acne drug called Acnidazil—and as it turned out, the external review had been deficient. The external reviewer, who had been fully paid, requested an additional fee for answering late questions.

The poor quality of external review became a major concern of scientists and doctors who review drugs in the six clinical divisions of the Bureau of Human Prescription Drugs. They viewed the program as costly and time inefficient, and questioned the impartiality of some external reviewers.

This brings us to the second part of the evaluation of prospective external reviewers: conflict of interest.

The Health department's conflict-of-interest guidelines are your easygoing common or garden variety. They exclude as reviewers those who have done original research on the drug to be reviewed. They also exclude those whose professional reputation is associated with the drug's manufacturer or the manufacturer's competitors, and those who received more than 15 per cent of their income from the drug's manufacturer or its major competitors in the twelve months before a contract begins. (The same rule applies for twelve months after the contract ends.)

Now, here's how easy the going can get. Hun-Medipharma Research Inc., a Kirkland, Quebec, firm, reviewed both prescription and non-prescription drugs for the Health department. The firm also did research for drug companies and helped them to submit drugs for government approval. The company's executive director, Atilla Fazekas, a physician, was married to the company's medical director, Anne-Kristin Nickel, a physician. She was also medical director of ICN Canada Ltd., a subsidiary of ICN Pharmaceuticals, a large U.S. drug company. Hun-Medipharma had a contract to conduct "some clinical research" for ICN, according to Fazekas, but it has not reviewed ICN drugs for the Health department. The company was, Fazekas stated, free of drug-industry influence. When told that some government scientists thought Hun-Medipharma's ties to industry were too close for comfort, Fazekas replied: "This view is unfounded and malicious. I am associated with independent experts at universities and my wife works for a company that is independent of ours." Had he not noticed that his wife had two jobs?

Fazekas also said that he would be willing to cancel Hun-Medipharma's research work for drug companies if the Health department offered the firm a substantial contract to review drugs on an ongoing basis. However, he didn't like his chances because of "the arbitrary methods the government uses in selecting scientists to conduct reviews."

When I asked the Health department whether it was in error in allowing Hun-Medipharma to review drugs and would it no longer do so, this sublime fax was the department's response: "The Department has qualified many outside reviewers. Contracts are issued according to individual expertise, and availability of contractor. Many reviewers have not yet received a contract from the Department."

I'm glad I asked.

So glad, in fact, that I also asked Carole Peacock, my conduit for questions to the Health department, about Dr. Robert Nelson, a neurologist at the Ottawa General Hospital. Had the department hired Nelson to review the product monograph for the new anti-migraine drug Imitrex, on which he had conducted clinical tests for Glaxo Canada Ltd.?

Here was the departmental oracle's reply by fax:

> *Dr. Robert Nelson is the chairman of the Division of Neurology at the University of Ottawa and the Director of Neurology at the Ottawa General Hospital. He was one of the Canadian clinical investigators who studied Imitrex. The Bureau of Human Prescription Drugs was pleased to obtain his comments on the Product Monograph, to provide prescribing information which would maximize safety for the Canadian public. Dr. Nelson's comments on the Product Monograph were secondary to an extensive in-house review of the entire New Drug submission by a medical officer.*

Okay, fine: Nelson carried out tests on the drug. Next, he approved the data that he and others collected on the drug. Finally, he assisted in the promotion of the drug for Glaxo.

Gee, Dr. Nelson, is this right? During my telephone conversation with him, he seemed like a decent type, who hadn't much thought about the possibility of being in conflict. "My feeling about it was that they wanted someone who would have experience with the drug," he explained.

Ah well, water off a duck's back—especially in the bold new era of drug approval awaiting us. Somers can therefore wax philosophical in his memo to managers that "the world is moving at an accelerating pace towards international harmonization of regulatory standards. Drug regulation is a front-runner in this race." The greatest impact on drug approval, he predicts, will "probably result from the international efforts in 1993 for harmonized technical and regulatory standards."

Somers ends his memo on this hopeful note: "Many of the concepts can be integrated into the current regulatory system—enhancing the system in a planned, progressive manner to gain immediate benefits while establishing the framework that will ease the transition to the revised regulatory system."

Be that as it may, but Health minister Benoît Bouchard was still looking for outside help—a benediction—to politically consolidate a new era of speedy drug approval. On January 7, 1992, he announced that he was giving the job to Dr. Denis Gagnon, Vice-Rector of Research at Laval University. Gagnon was given six months to produce a report on how best to continue to revise the drug-approval system.

While Gagnon did his survey, I thought that I would check out real life in the drug-review trenches at Health and Welfare.

Palace Revolt

When one or two individuals speak out against the boss or workplace procedures, it's easy to write them off as malcontents. When scores of the scientists and doctors who review drugs at the Health department say they fear for the safety of Canadians, folks should pay attention. In an ideal world, I suppose, some bigwig would also pay attention and then call in the investigators to sniff out the truth. Should the truth be unpleasant, you might expect the guilty to be banished to government basements to sharpen pencils. But the Health department works in mysterious ways.

There, scientists and doctors used to sneak up to bulletin-boards as if they were the Democracy Wall. They posted newspaper articles that discussed their safety concerns. They pinned up the Nuremberg Code of Ethics in Medical Research and the 1975 revisions to the Declaration of Helsinki, which guide medical doctors in biomedical research involving human subjects. The scientists and doctors did this as a reminder that they still cared about how they approved drugs for human tests, even though they are often too rushed by their superiors to ask drug companies important follow-up questions about test data. They posted "Values" that described their work conditions and their mandate—at least on paper. Here's one more reminder of how things have gone sour—particularly drug reviews, which are rushed by strong industry pressure to get drugs on the market quickly.

On February 27, 1992, Jacques Messier, like China's old guard, ended the practice of protest by poster. A veterinarian, who was director of the Bureau of Human Prescription Drugs, Messier decreed that posting such materials constituted a labour violation: use of bulletin-boards were to be limited to official notices and announcements of social and recreational events. All other postings were to be approved by Messier himself.

The scientists and doctors had viewed the bulletin-boards as a viable, if narrow, avenue of free speech. Without them, they began to talk to me. (Some of these confidences appear in Part Two, which includes cases of what can go badly wrong in a drug-review system that is on fast-forward for no good reason.)

On April 27, 1992, twenty-one of the twenty-four medical doctors who review drugs at the Bureau of Human Prescription Drugs wrote a terse two-page letter to their boss, veterinarian Messier. It expressed their concern about the lack of medical representation at junior- or senior-managerial levels in the bureau. The "increasing erosion of in-house medical expertise will interfere with the Bureau's mandate to ensure the safety and efficacy of drugs prescribed by physicians to the Canadian public," the doctors warned. "It may also jeopardize the health of Canadians participating in clinical studies required to develop new drugs."

The immediate impetus for the letter was Albert Liston's decision to eliminate the post of assistant director—medical, a post then held by Dr. Michelle Brill-Edwards since December 1, 1988. (Brill-Edwards's courageous battle to hold up the rushed approval of the anti-migraine drug Imitrex is described in Chapter 7.) The medical post had been created by then director Gordon Johnson, a pharmacist, to ensure that medical expertise was available at a senior level. (Johnson was succeeded on an acting basis by Claire Franklin, a pesticides expert; then by veterinarian Messier, and then by Franklin. The last real medical doctor to head the bureau was the pesky Ian Henderson.)

The doctors' letter to the vet explained the drug-review process in very basic terms:

> *The drug review process is an essential public service that requires expertise in many biomedical disciplines. The fundamental purpose of the process is to ensure the safety and efficacy of drugs used to treat human diseases. The drug development process itself involves extensive input from highly qualified medical researchers. An independent and clinically sound evaluation of new drug data must also involve the knowledge and experience of medically qualified individuals who are intimately aware of clinical trial design, clinical pharmacology and current medical diagnosis and therapy as well as regulatory law. It is therefore essential that such advanced medical expertise be represented at the highest decision and policy setting levels.*

The letter then points out that not only has the director's job been taken over by non-doctors, but the jobs of those reporting directly to the director, the chiefs of divisions, have as well. Of six divisions geared to review drugs targeted at various body systems (cardiovascular, central nervous, and so on) only one is headed by a medical doctor.

The letter concludes this way: "In our judgement an organizational structure lacking advanced medical expertise at a senior level is less than adequate to ensure the safety of Canadians with respect to new drugs."

Messier told an *Ottawa Citizen* reporter that twenty-four doctors on staff constituted sufficient medical expertise, that there was no need for doctors to take senior positions. And—can't you hear it coming?—"Canada's drug review and approval process is one of the best in the world."

Messier was clearly lip-synching his master's voice: Bouchard's position taken on the advice of senior bureaucrats was that doctors are not necessary at higher levels.

The veterinarian told *The Ottawa Citizen* that his bureau had been having problems finding qualified doctors to take senior posts. True, some doctors were shying away from the Health department. (Wouldn't you, if the word around Medical Town was that the job was more painful than the end of extra billing even if the pay per annum—as much as $130,000—was adequate?) However, several medical specialists of solid reputation had, for whatever reason, shown an interest in top jobs during the department's recruitment drive in 1990 and 1991. After they were given only lukewarm attention, their interest faded.

There are several possible explanations for the Health department's shift from medical to non-medical management. A recent study of the federal bureaucracy by Barbara Wake Carroll, a political scientist at McMaster University in Hamilton, finds that the federal trend is towards managers without formal expertise in the areas they govern. This preference for managerial abilities over technical competence stems from the philosophy that "it is the management skills that count, not necessarily knowledge of that department. That can be learned."

Wake Carroll concludes that the lack of technical knowledge is likely to be detrimental to the development of policy: senior bureaucrats who lack area-specific skills "may be less able to comprehend or evaluate the technical activities and information they must manage and assess."

Just ask the twenty-one doctors who wrote to their boss, The Vet.

A second explanation has it that doctors are being bypassed because they ask too many questions. MDs are likely to be more aware of the shades and nuances of how drugs affect patients than are their colleagues, the PHDs. In an era of drug-review speed-up, you can't have too many people asking too many questions.

"Non-medical managers in the Health department are less likely to take patient interest into consideration and more likely to respond to pressure from a drug company. This has been my experience." That's the view of Chris Turner, a doctor who worked as a drug reviewer for close to five years until he couldn't stomach the system any longer. He moved on to be assistant national director for Blood Services at the Canadian Red Cross Society in Ottawa.

Explanation number three holds that the Somers-run drugs sector is awash in cronyism. There is also some reluctance to appoint members of visible-minority groups. This means that less than the brightest and the best are achieving the senior posts as we'll see later in this chapter.

The drug industry has taken to the cronies, however. It even helped to appoint a Somers protégée, pharmacist Mary Carmen-Kasparek, to head the Bureau of Non-Prescription Drugs in June 1991.

In December 1991, Judy Erola, president of the Pharmaceutical Manufacturers Association of Canada, the chief lobbyist for the drug industry in Canada, sat on the three-member board—with Somers and Francine Krueger, a staffing officer in the Public Service Commission—that chose Carmen-Kasparek. Erola had been proposed for the seat on the board by Somers.

Erola told me that there was "no direct conflict of interest" in her "healthy" appointment. Carmen-Kasparek had a proven track-record of meaningful academic and scientific credentials and she "was clearly the leading candidate."

The official Health department position was that Erola's association deals mostly with prescription drugs. Because Carmen-Kasparek's appointment was to the body overseeing non-prescription drugs, there was no conflict of interest.

Maybe I'm Emmanuel Somers's grandfather.

The fact that prescription drug companies sell non-prescription products is a mere bagatelle. What in hell is the drug industry doing helping to select our public regulatory officials? (The same board interviewed and subsequently selected Len Ritter, formerly in narcotics, to head the Bureau of Veterinary Drugs. No, of course, he's not a vet.)

So why are doctors being bypassed in the drugs sector for senior-management posts?

My explanation of choice is cronyism, even though the other explanations also have merit.

The following case raises questions about the way Somers runs his sector, and crystallizes our understanding of why the twenty-one doctors who wrote to Messier fear for our safety.

The Tell-Tale Case of Shiv Chopra

Fifty-seven-year-old Shiv Chopra has been employed with the Health department for twenty-three years. He holds a Bachelor's degree in veterinary science from Punjab University and a Master's and doctorate in microbiology from McGill. In 1969, he began working in the Health department as a scientific adviser on drugs. Between 1977 and 1980, he served as a management consultant to Liston, then head of the drugs sector. Between 1980 and 1986, he was a scientific adviser in the Bureau of Human Prescription Drugs. Then he became scientific adviser in the Bureau of Veterinary Drugs, where he continues to work.

In September 1990, Chopra learned that the job of director of the Bureau of Human Prescription Drugs was vacant. He applied to Somers, who told him that a medical degree was required. He next heard from Somers in a letter, dated October 4, 1990, informing him that Claire Franklin would become acting director.

Franklin, like Chopra, has a doctorate, not a medical degree. Nor was she bilingual, as was required. Her primary area of experience is pesticides; she had previously worked in the Health department's Environmental Health Directorate, which Somers had headed before coming to the drugs sector. In the early 1970s, Franklin was director of the Thunder Bay School of Medical Technology at McKellar General Hospital. She also chaired the medical-laboratory sciences program at Lakehead University. After Franklin's appointment, the job classification and description were changed to better reflect her managerial duties.

Taken aback by Franklin's appointment, Chopra wrote to Somers on October 10, 1990, asking him to explain how he had failed to meet the qualifications for the position. Somers telephoned

Chopra about two weeks later. "Some get it, some don't," he said.

The Public Service Commission held that Chopra had not been given a fair chance to compete for the job. Chopra filed his appeal on July 9, 1991. Twenty-four hours before the appeal was heard, the department reclassified the job from bilingual to English only.

Ten days later, the appeal board decided that the Health department had not demonstrated that Franklin was fully qualified for the job: "I cannot conclude from this evidence that [Franklin] had the required knowledge of marketed drugs available for human use or the actual knowledge of existing programs and activities relating to the scientific and medical appraisal of drugs." The board also ruled that Somers had the discretionary power to judge Chopra as lacking in managerial skills, and to disqualify him as a candidate on that basis.

Chopra was angry. He had never been made a manager in the department, even though his yearly evaluations tagged him as having management potential. He was also ticked off that senior managers have the power to appoint people to acting positions for the short term without competition.

He was therefore not pleased to see Franklin remain bureau director after he won his appeal: the department simply ignored the board's decision and hustled Franklin off for intensive French-language tutoring. Chopra complained to the Public Service Commission, which got the department to end Franklin's appointment on September 20, 1991, but Franklin stayed on the job.

Next, the Professional Institute of the Public Service (PIPS) of Canada, Chopra's union, complained in writing to the commission, only to learn on October 11 that Franklin had been reappointed on an acting basis "until completion of the formal selection process for the acting appointment."

Because this appointment was for a period of less than four months, Chopra did not have any right of appeal.

Meanwhile, the department changed the job description of director to match Franklin's qualifications. The job now required a doctoral degree "in a related field and experience in conducting pharmacology, toxicology, or clinical investigations."

In December 1991, Chopra asked the Federal Court of Canada

to revoke Franklin's appointment. PIPS issued a press release, which quoted its president, Iris Craig, as saying: "The merit principle is at stake and in this case the presence of an unqualified senior manager places the public at risk. . . . Must we wait for another Thalidomide crisis before management at Health and Welfare stop compromising professional expertise in favour of personal patronage appointments?"

Dr. Michelle Brill-Edwards filed an affidavit on Chopra's behalf. She had also applied for the job as bureau director, having served as Franklin's medical assistant for about one year (and had tangled with her on at least one drug approval, as you will see in Chapter 7). In her affidavit of January 13, 1992, she says of Franklin: "She does not have substantive medical knowledge of drugs for use in humans. She also does not have substantive knowledge of the design of clinical trials in humans. Nor does she have substantive knowledge of the medical aspects of the appraisal of drugs for use in humans."

On the eve of Chopra's day in court, the Health department was "pleased" to announce that Franklin had accepted a special assignment involving a review of potential reforms in drug approval. Her successor was Messier, The Vet.

On February 13, the Federal Court issued an order to endorse the agreement. The department asked the Public Service Commission to conduct a new competition for the job of bureau director; Somers was barred from involvement. Franklin won the competition and is now bureau director.

Chopra's persistence cast a light on hiring practices in the Health department that have a strong bearing on public health. It also revealed that Franklin's appointment was merely the shadow of the beast.

India-born Shiv Chopra is just one of many scientists with roots in India, Pakistan, the West Indies, and elsewhere who saw the Health department of the 1960s as an opportunity ladder for good income and social standing. They signed up soon after the thalidomide crisis, when the department was recruiting scientists to usher in a new and supposedly more sophisticated era of drug review. Most, including Chopra, have been bitterly disappointed.

Today roughly 10 per cent of the department's Health Protection Branch's 1,048 scientific and professional staff are visible minorities; yet fewer than 1 per cent of the branch's managers come from this group. In Somers's sector, for example, there are a total of eight British-born scientists; five are managers. Somers is also white and British-born.

Chopra views this as a form of apartheid. "Are so few visible minorities considered good enough to be managers for the development and regulation of Canadian science?" he asks.

PIPS receives a disproportionate number of grievances against management from visible minorities in the Health Protection Branch. "These are not malcontents, not whiners," says Carmel Kasper, a union vice-president. "They are people who have felt genuinely that they have been discriminated against."

Concerns about discrimination are obviously not unique to the Health department—racism thrives in Canada. But the lack of social equity in the Health department has blocked the flowering of considerable human talent, which could have served the public very well.

Take Dennis Awang, who was given his walking papers at age fifty-four in February 1992. Awang had worked in the drugs sector since 1969; he was let go ostensibly because of budget cuts. Awang is an internationally respected authority on herbal medicine. He was born in Trinidad. He is black. There was a time when Awang was routinely called " blackie" by a British-born Health department colleague and had to remove adhesive labels from South African imported fruits from his telephone receiver, reading lamp, and office door. Most damaging was the bitterness and hurt inflicted by his white-skinned bosses who did little to find him another job worthy of him in the bureaucracy. Canadian and U.S. scientists wrote letters to the Health department, expressing disbelief that a scientist of Awang's calibre would be so casually discarded.

Combine this shallow—if not racist—management with cronyism, unchecked conflict of interest, chronic understaffing, a lack of doctors at senior levels to check drug submissions, a drug-review system on fast-forward to please the drug industry, an abysmal monitoring system of drug side-effects, and know-little or -nothing politicians, and you have a drug-safety net hanging by a thread.

3

HALFWAY REVOLUTION:

Out of Control on Medical Devices

When I'm away from *The Gazette* for more than a few days at a stretch, my mail box runneth over. Usually there's something from public-relations companies flogging the latest medical-technology "breakthrough"—an artificial ear or a gizmo for heart surgery, or a computer-driven "imaging" machine that probes the depths of the body for signs of illness.

The purpose of all the PR hype is to inspire people like me to pitch a gee-whiz story on the device to an editor, who can gee-whiz it at the editorial meeting, where the dictum is given to present it in "gee-whiz style" to you, the reader.

Pick up any newspaper, especially on the weekend, and you are likely to see a gee-whiz story on some new device that uses sound waves to blast apart kidney stones, or an experimental robot-assisted surgical unit, or an electronic ear that purportedly allows the deaf to hear. TV reporters lap up "breakthroughs" like blue jays gorging on sunflower seeds. Radio talk shows corral the appropriate medical guest, typically a doctor shilling for the "breakthrough" manufacturer, and gee-whiz it ad nauseam.

"Super-gee-whiz" PR hype is very expensive. Last December, for example, I received a book entitled *Medicine: A New Vision*, trumpeting the achievements of radiology. We naturally think of x-rays, but the book demonstrates, with its full-colour photos, that radiology is also computer-guided diagnostic technology—body-scanning devices commonly referred to as PET, MRI, CT, and

Ultrasound. The book commemorates the seventy-fifth anniversary of the Radiological Society of North America and sets out to raise public awareness of what radiologists do. As the author was commissioned by the society, he produced a snow job on radiology, without voicing a note about health professionals' concerns about the costs-benefit ratio of this technology.

High-tech radiology saves many lives, as early diagnosis can often lead to effective treatment. But health economists and some doctors worry that excessive use of this technology jacks up health-care costs to little benefit. Some of these machines cost well over $1 million, not to mention their high operating costs.

There is also concern about the safety of these highly complicated devices. For example, the lack of proper safe-proofing of the computer software can cause therapeutic radiation to misfire, seriously injuring patients. (This disturbing subject is taken up in Chapter 12.)

All this PR hype works. If it didn't, thousands more people would be out selling shoes or writing for newspapers or advising politicians. Over time, steady gee-whiz contributes to our acceptance of newness as a virtue, and of makers of miracles, namely the manufacturers of gee-whiz products and the doctors who use them.

The result is an increased demand for these products, which often don't measure up to expectations: the artificial heart needed to be overhauled; the kidney-stone smasher raises blood pressure in some patients; and a new laser that uses radiation to reshape eyes for 20/20 has produced blurred vision. But as old "breakthroughs" fall, new ones are raised up in a rhythmic balancing of overreaching high-tech ventures. Now hold that image as we turn our full attention to the safety issues surrounding medical devices.

With so much emphasis on the benefits of medical devices, Canadians generally expect them to be safe. A recent Angus Reid Group poll found that Canadians have overwhelming confidence in the safety and effectiveness of medical machinery. This misguided confidence, is, at least in part, based on a gross misconception of how devices are reviewed for safety. In fact, only 5 per cent of medical devices are assessed for safety by federal reviewers. (Thousands of Canadians have been killed, mangled, crippled, burned, and otherwise injured because medical devices have messed up.)

Behind the PR hype is a medical arms race, grossly inadequate federal evaluation of the safety and efficacy of devices, and ad hoc monitoring of harm caused by these products.

As more devices appear on the market, safety concerns are mounting: the regulators have lost control.

There are at least 400,000 different medical devices available in Canada. By the end of the century, there will be tens of thousands more.

This population explosion of devices ranges from the practical and exquisitely simple tongue depressor to a brain scanner. When you think about it, our lives are bracketed by medical devices: from the foetal monitors tracking our first heartbeats to life-support systems making the beat go on when the body says die.

In Canada, roughly $4 billion is spent annually on such devices, about 80 per cent of which are made elsewhere, usually in the United States, whence the multinationals supply half the world's market. Most of these devices are found in hospitals or doctors' offices; but they are increasingly finding their way into the home, in the form of blood-sugar monitors, blood-pressure machines, and home kidney-dialysis units. As home care gains momentum, some hospital-like equipment will become as ubiquitous as the VCR: special beds, intravenous stands, oxygen and even vital-sign monitors. We can visualize a future in which a robot-controlled medical unit in our own home does a complete blood workup and diagnosis in minutes. Soon, surgery, minor and advanced, may be coming to the kitchen table near you. Tough on doctors, right?

While on this Great Adventure, it's good to know that someone is watching out for us, someone able to evaluate whether the machines in our lives put out properly. You wouldn't want to step into your surgical unit for a blister puncture and receive a vasectomy—or a penis—instead.

Those who watch over medical devices are scarcer than donor organs. Sixty or so scientists at Health and Welfare Canada's Bureau of Radiation and Medical Devices are all that ensure those thousands of medical devices are safe and effective.

Here's the official government definition of a medical device:

Any article, instrument, apparatus or contrivance, including any component, part or accessory thereof, manufactured, sold or represented for use in: the diagnosis, treatment, mitigation or prevention of a disease, disorder, or abnormal physical state or the symptoms thereof, in man or animal. Restoring, correcting or modifying a body function of the body structure of man or animal. The diagnosis of pregnancy in humans or animals: or the care of humans and animals during pregnancy and at and after birth of the offspring, including the care of the offspring, and that includes a contraceptive device but does not include a drug.

Quite a mouthful! Manufacturers are required to present basic information about their devices—including directions for use, purpose of the device, and the address of its Canadian distributors—to the bureau within ten days of the product being for sale in Canada. The bureau has the right to call in more information—such as testing methods and results—from the manufacturer and to order the manufacturer to stop selling the device until the information is reviewed. Registration, however, should not be confused with evaluation of safety and efficacy. It merely informs the bureau of products that are for sale.

The actual review of safety and efficacy is limited to a small number of registered devices. During a "pre-market" review, bureau scientists check out animal and human test results and manufacturing data supplied by the manufacturer. If they are deemed satisfactory, the manufacturer is awarded a "Notice of Compliance" (as is the case with approved prescription drugs). Medical devices that must be reviewed are those to be implanted in human body tissue or cavities for thirty days or more, contact lenses for long-term wear, menstrual tampons, and test kits for signs of AIDS-associated retroviruses. (Intrauterine contraceptive devices, intraocular lenses, and pacemakers are no longer reviewed.)

The bureau's research and standards division has also devised voluntary standards for such devices as contraceptives, pacemakers for the heart, portable emergency oxygen inhalers, disposable insulin syringes, evacuated blood-collection tubes, ozone-emitting devices, and colour-coding of medical gas-handling devices.

Aiding the two technical divisions are clinical advisers who evaluate the application of devices to humans.

Another group in the bureau is responsible for following up on problems with medical devices voluntarily reported (mainly by hospitals). These reports—about four hundred each year—represent a tiny portion of the problems that occur.

It doesn't take a Pythagoras to figure out that our federal Health department gives little weight to the review and tracking of medical devices. Rather, it is content to rely on a largely voluntary reporting system based on the manufacturers' word that they build safe and effective devices and monitor their own performance. To put it mildly, we could have done better.

Off to a Difficult Start

The Bureau of Medical Devices was created in 1974, the year that the Dalkon Shield was withdrawn from the market. The dangerous contraceptive demonstrated to regulators why they couldn't rely on manufacturers to monitor themselves. So did the infant incubators whose oxygen concentrations could damage eyesight in newborns. Such demonstrations and the subsequent pressure for protection against faulty medical devices became hard for even the federal government to ignore.

Creation of the bureau was no Manhattan Project. Even the appointment of a physicist, Agit Das Gupta, to head the bureau seemed arbitrary. He was yanked from the Bureau of Radiation, where he enjoyed a good reputation. Das Gupta wasn't particularly interested in medical devices and quickly concluded that the government wasn't either; his bureau was given four staffers and minimal office space, and was made accountable to the Environmental Health Directorate, where existing bureaus (Radiation, and Chemical Hazards) were engaged in combat over scarce funds and resources.

Das Gupta warmed to the job. By 1976, he had boosted his staff to fifteen, and accomplished his original task of developing regulations (in the form of an amendment to the Food and Drugs Act) that gave his team some powers to police manufacturers. Included in the regulations was the requirement that manufacturers register their products with the bureau.

Inevitably, some products were seen to be higher risk than others and therefore requiring more of the bureau's attention, in the form of pre-market review of their safety and efficacy. First on the list were intrauterine devices and pacemakers. Next came intra-ocular lenses, prolonged-wear contact lenses, and tampons. In October 1982, all new implants were added to the list. Medical devices had become a growth industry that was drowning the bureau's reviewing capacity.

I began tracking how Das Gupta dealt with his burden in 1982 and continued until he retired five years later. It was like watching someone trying to push a giant boulder across a football field.

Two of his efforts merit special attention.

As Das Gupta sees it, he couldn't get the staff he required because his boss, Emmanuel Somers, the directorate's head, was focused on environmental issues and downplayed the importance of medical devices. In late 1982, when Somers was dispatched for six months to the World Health Organization in Geneva, Das Gupta convinced the Treasury Board to add thirty person-years to the bureau. When Somers returned, he reallocated more than a dozen of the new recruits to other parts of the directorate. When the new regulation requiring pre-market review of implants came into force in April 1983, a tidal wave of more than five hundred applications arrived in the first year alone. But Somers considered Das Gupta just a typical government manager who was never satisfied.

Das Gupta then launched his second major effort to bolster the bureau by improving the small program that tracked problems associated with medical devices. He reasoned that better reporting of problems would result in quicker feedback to health professionals: lives could be saved and injuries prevented. Because doctors and hospital officials might be more comfortable reporting problems to fellow health professionals than to the government, Das Gupta convinced the Canadian Medical Association (CMA) to set up a twenty-four-hour bilingual problem-reporting hot line. The project boosted the bureau's reports to 522 in 1985–86, from 324 in 1984–85.

In the face of such success, the Health department axed the program just before the contract with the CMA was to expire. Albert Liston, the assistant deputy minister, told me that the department couldn't afford the $74,000 needed to fund the program for another year. Medical devices just didn't rate. The doctors at the CMA were obviously none too pleased. Their hard work to set up the program, which showed every sign of gathering steam, had gone up in smoke.

A few months earlier, Das Gupta had suffered a heart ailment. Upon his return to the job he had learned of plans to merge the Radiation and Medical Devices bureaus. The proposal spoke volumes about the low priority the government assigned to medical devices. Das Gupta despaired—and retired.

Problems

Das Gupta was frank about the extent of problems linked to medical devices. During his tenure at the bureau, he could account for more than two hundred deaths and eight hundred injuries, documented cases culled from voluntary reports from hospitals and doctors and coroners' reports. Given the erratic nature of medical studies and problem-reporting patterns, he estimated that anaesthesia-equipment malfunction alone probably accounted for two hundred deaths annually in Canada in the early to mid 1980s. He knew that anaesthesia gas lines in a number of major hospitals in Canada were patched together with masking tape: the hospitals were too poor to purchase new lines.

One way of warning health professionals about problems associated with medical devices was to issue warning bulletins, known as "alerts." From 1977 to Das Gupta's resignation from the bureau, eighty-five alerts were issued about deaths or potentially life-threatening conditions related to medical devices. They included faulty cranial drills used in brain surgery, disconnections of patients from ventilators, lamp holders on infant incubators that could cause explosions, insulin pumps that broke down, faulty electrosurgical equipment, poorly designed safety restraining vests, a blood warmer that did not maintain a patient's blood at the correct temperature during surgery, defective heart valves, defibrillator-battery failures, catheters that perforated the heart, malfunctioning hospital beds, and the explosion of a regulating device that monitors oxygen concentration at a patient's bedside.

Getting these alerts issued and out to the public was no easy task. Das Gupta had to consult his boss, Emmanuel Somers, who, in turn, had to consult his boss, Albert Liston. The next step was even stranger: permission had to be obtained from the product's manufacturer and the final wording of the alert agreed upon. A strong draft warning was often greatly diluted by the time it was published. Das Gupta grew uncomfortably accustomed to the unstated Health department rule that the bureau should not displease manufacturers. Alerts were usually issued only in the case of death or the clear potential for death.

There is no better example of a watered-down alert than that of the sixty-degree Convexo-Concave (C-C) heart valve, manufactured by Shiley Inc. of Irvine, California, a subsidiary of Pfizer Inc., the giant multinational drug company. The C-C was introduced in 1976, before pre-market review legislation and scrutiny for safety and efficacy.

Heart valves, which regulate blood flow, are obviously essential to the working of a heart: defective valves can lead to fatigue and heart failure. The C-C artificial valve was promoted as capable of reducing the risk of blood clots, a major problem of artificial heart valves, and soon became popular.

In early 1980, Das Gupta's scientific "star," bureau chemist Pierre Blais, spotted major problems with the C-C. Two Alberta women had died following implantation of the heart valve, and Blais discovered that heart tissue could get trapped in the device unless the surgeon positioned it very precisely. Several months later Blais found that one of the device's welded struts could break under the repeated stress of opening and shutting with each heart beat. (This finding was confirmed when Blais was asked by the Saskatchewan government to investigate two deaths apparently caused by C-C failure.) Blais informed Das Gupta in a memo that "this valve is conceptually faulty."

By August 1982, when Das Gupta had finally run the alert on heart valves through the bureaucratic gauntlet, it had turned into a compendium of problems detected in various valves—the C-C valve was not singled out. Nor was it in another alert, issued four months later, that warned of difficulties encountered in implanting various heart valves.

Blais's findings were effectively ignored. In September 1984, he was convinced the strut problem in the C-C "could be a surgical disaster." Das Gupta concurred, but by the time the final wording of the alert was settled, there was no longer any mention of the welding problem in the C-C; rather, the alert focused on ways to implant the valve with greater precision.

By 1986, when Shiley stopped making the C-C, the company was already marketing its successor, a new valve without a welded strut. A year later, on October 2, 1987, it was deemed "correct" for the bureau to issue an alert advising hospitals against the implantation of the C-C and similar heart valves. The evidence? Seven Canadian deaths associated with the C-C had been confirmed. Between 1,500 and 2,000 Canadians, and about 21,000 Americans had received the valve. Out of an approximate total of 86,000 implantations, 460 fractures have occurred, resulting in about 310 deaths worldwide.

In August 1992, Pfizer settled a suit on behalf of 50,000 patients, agreeing to pay $300 million in compensation for valves that break and cause illness or death. The company also agreed to make a one-time payment of $4,000 to each claimant to cover anxiety-related medical expenses and to establish a research fund to develop screening tests for faulty valves and to replace them.

Late in 1988, I began to investigate the safety issues related to the Meme breast implant. (You can learn about some of the untold dynamics of all this in Chapter 6.) Work on the Meme focused my attention anew on medical devices in the post–Das Gupta era.

Despite the barriers and problems that he had encountered, Das Gupta had kept the bureau treading water with his energy and integrity. As I expected, the bureau declined rapidly after his departure.

Das Gupta's replacement, Ernest Létourneau, a medical doctor no longer in practice, made it clear that he had arrived to chummy up the bureau to industry. In a British trade journal, he co-wrote of the "perceptible, positive shift in the bureau's relationship with regulated industry." Létourneau's boss, Albert Liston, had already declared publicly, soon after being appointed assistant deputy minister and head of the Health Protection Branch in 1985, that he favoured a change in the government's "big-stick mentality" regarding health protection.

Létourneau and Liston, champions of a conservative, laissez-faire approach to the regulation of medical devices, brought in like-minded managers: Roy Hickman succeeded Somers at the Environmental Health Directorate (Somers went to work his magic as head of the Drugs Directorate). And the arrival in 1989 of Margaret Catley-Carlson as deputy Health minister ensured that the times were a changin'.

The bureau lost interest in sending out alerts in July 1988. Evidently the bureau did not consider it a hazard to the safety of health professionals that fifteen brands of medical and surgical gloves tested during the summer of 1988 had failed to meet standards. Or that during the same period, there were breakdowns in anaesthesia equipment and resuscitation machines, and defects in devices used to stabilize the heart before and after heart surgery.

When I asked Hickman why the alerts had stopped, he explained it like this: The alerts were supposed to be a rapid mechanism, but delays were caused by internal bureau procedures. Because the system was faltering, it was decided to phase out the alerts.

Hmmm, I replied, what then would serve as a replacement for the alerts? Hickman didn't know.

Here's what was actually happening: When Das Gupta left, Létourneau and company built up layers of bureaucracy so thick that they were impenetrable to scientists who wanted to respond to problem reports. In Das Gupta's day, all problem reports and plans to deal with them were discussed at weekly meetings. Létourneau's bureau cancelled the meetings and substituted procedures that required numerous signatures and mountains of paper. A problem report was automatically stalled because of the time the paperwork took to drift around for signatures. Some of the reports got lost in the shuffle; others were filed away and never heard of again. Naturally, hospital officials and doctors, remembering better days, complained that they waited months for an answer to a report.

Even Germain Houle, the anaesthetist from Montreal's Royal Victoria Hospital who headed the expert advisory committee to the bureau, complained bitterly to me about "the collapse of the warning system." He had learned during a meeting with bureau officials that they had been sitting on the medical- and surgical-glove test data for months. "I felt like getting up and leaving, I was so mad," he said. "It didn't seem to even occur to these people that health professionals should be warned." Houle vowed that he would "read the riot act" to Catley-Carlson during a scheduled meeting, but months later told me that he hadn't.

Catley-Carlson dismissed alerts as mere leftovers of bygone days. Not sufficiently briefed on problem reporting for our meeting on September 20, 1990, she referred my questions to Liston who roused himself sufficiently to assure me that an effort was under way to find better communications procedures in the Environmental Health Directorate. A consultant had been hired to help forge better rapport between Houle's group and the bureau, and better response to reports of problems associated with medical devices.

While this change was being heralded, I discovered in the summer of 1992, the bureau was taking some short cuts with medical-device reviews. Somers's tactic of body snatching Das Gupta's staff had created a long-term critical backlog in the reviewing process. And, as we have already seen, when the Health department finds backlog (in this case, of nearly two hundred medical devices), it tries to make it disappear lest industry be displeased.

Take but one example: A letter dated March 8, 1988, written to Létourneau by William Welsh, head of the pre-market division, states that, in future, "minor deficiencies" of "simple" devices will be disregarded. If the department had questions, the manufacturer would be required to reply within a reasonable time—after the device went on sale.

According to microbiologist Nirmala Chopra, who reported to Welsh at the time and ran the unit that conducted reviews, there were hundreds of devices that were simply "signed off" as reviewed even though no review had occurred. More than a dozen implants that release drugs into the body were approved on one day in 1988. "These had been assigned for review, but then the word came down from management that they were to be collected and signed off, and they were," she said.

The Health department response when I raised these charges was a faxed admission that Welsh had gone too far in his memo and that the practice of disregarding "minor deficiencies" in "simple" medical devices had been curbed. No, the fax from on high didn't state when the "direction to cease this practice" had been issued.

When in Doubt, Commission a Report

By February 1991, the heat on medical devices had risen to the top—to Minister of Health Benoît Bouchard. The minister appointed a committee to figure out how to improve things. Give him credit: he chose the right person to chair it—Ambrose Hearn, executive director of the Canadian Council on Health Facilities Accreditation. There were eight other appointees, drawn from the health professions, industry, and the public.

Now, we all know that committees get appointed to put off political decisions and then fade away. We have seen millions of dollars spent on committees to review provincial health-care systems, only to see these often cumbersome reports stashed on shelves to gather dust. So when Hearn wrote to ask whether I would be interested in stating my views before the committee, I was too discourteous to reply.

The report was completed (without my help) in April 1992 and released the following October.

I find that most reports on health matters reveal a frightening lack of understanding of the day-to-day workings of bureaucracy. They usually ignore the personalities and political context of those who run things and therefore miss important opportunities to understand how conditions go wrong, and stay wrong, despite all the fine recommendations.

Hearn told me that it was not part of his mandate to examine closely how the medical-devices bureaucracy functions. Nor did he focus on specific problems such as the Meme breast implant. That's too bad, because this analysis of particular snafus and incompetence is necessary to gauge how changes can be implemented. In this sense, the Hearn Report is a failure; it is also superficial and so cautiously worded that it won't make waves. But—and it's a big *but*—seen in the context of similar adventures, the report smacks of considerable independence and integrity, and it offers strong recommendations for change. At the very least, it reports that things have indeed gone wrong.

The committee listened to many presentations and read many briefs. It commissioned a comparison of regulatory systems, and some surveys by the Angus Reid Group. The committee's overall assessment of the Medical Devices Bureau can be boiled down to the following: The program "has evolved by crisis not design, by organizational expediency rather than a well-articulated strategy." Recent changes in medical technology are making matters worse, and the regulatory system is losing ground. This system must be given higher priority. In other words, we must reverse history.

The scores of recommendations cut a wide path. The key ones included: Develop closer cooperation with the United States and other countries in processing devices. Strengthen the enforcement powers of the bureau by making violations of the law and the accompanying penalties, convictions, seizures, and recalls public. Subject all high-risk medical devices to a full pre-market review. Make greater use of expert advisory committees and external contracting-out for submission evaluation. Strengthen the system that tracks problems associated with medical devices. Phase-in mandatory problem reporting by companies and health professionals. Set up device registries for high-risk devices. Develop a communication plan that will properly inform health professionals and the public about the risks and benefits of medical devices. And so on.

What's to argue—except, perhaps, that submissions should be contracted-out for review. It hasn't worked well for drugs, and it is not likely to work well for medical devices, unless great caution is taken to avoid conflict of interest.

Ah, but what of the implementation of the report! Nothing yet, but we'll have to wait and see. After all, among Hearn's colleagues on the implementation committee are Létourneau and Hickman.

Meanwhile, I'll just go on snooping around, keeping in mind a story Agit Das Gupta told me in the fall of 1991. Now where had I heard it before?

In the late 1970s, Das Gupta said, eight visible-minority scientists in the Bureau of Medical Devices concluded that some of them were losing their jobs because of their colour. According to Das Gupta, Emmanuel Somers was inclined to replace visible-minority scientists with others who were British-born. He took advantage of government cutbacks to get rid of people he didn't want in 1978. "You should be able to go higher and get justice. But you can appeal all you want and it seems that, both then and now, they only laugh at you," Das Gupta said sadly.

Das Gupta contends he lost his own job after twelve years of service through a favourite Somers manoeuvre: the staff reorganization.

"This . . . [style of management] runs very deep at Health and Welfare and it won't be easy to excise," Das Gupta said.

Emmanuel Somers refused to comment on these allegations.

4

DRUG CONNECT-THE-DOTS:

The Drug Industry and the New World Order

Hi there, boys and girls, it's time to play "Drug Connect-The-Dots."

The object of the game is to link up as many pharmaceuticals issues as you can. The overall connect-the-dots pattern that you find must not be obvious to most people, but must shed light on international drug-industry trends. My turn. My turn.

Dot number one: the intriguing idea that Canada spends far too much money treating illnesses rather than preventing them. Join this dot with the evidence that spending on drug prescriptions to treat illnesses is rising.

Look. We've re-created a fundamental question:

Is Spending More Money on Drugs Worth It?

Spending on drugs in Canada increased from roughly $2 billion (8.9 per cent of health-care costs) in 1980 to an estimated $8.5 billion (14.1 per cent of health-care costs) in 1990. Roughly 45 per cent of drugs sold are prescription drugs. (They number about 3,500.) Forty-seven per cent are non-prescription, and 8 per cent are veterinary.

Now to answer our question: We don't know if spending more money on drugs is worth it, because we know far too little about the impact of drugs on the health of Canadians, as very few population studies on drug therapy have been done.

Considering how much drugs cost provincial governments, it

is little wonder that they are nervous about any rise in use and cost. Equally unsurprising is the fact that they are paying attention to the idea of preventing illness, rather than serving up potions and surgery once illness strikes.

There is growing evidence that factors other than medical care, such as income, education, and social relationships, play an important role in determining the quality and length of life. Multiple deprivations, including poverty and lack of social support, appear to predispose people to illness. One recent U.S. study showed that giving pets to people over age sixty-five appears to help them live longer. Jonathan Lomas, a health economist at McMaster University, told me that spending on such unorthodox things should be considered by health-care managers as seriously as paying for a new drug that fights cholesterol. Health-care policy in Canada, by and large, is still very much focused on improving medical care: according to Robert Evans, a health economist at the University of British Columbia, such attitudes encourage health managers to consider favourably any new medical treatment, test, or drug perceived to contribute to health.

At a meeting of the Royal College of Physicians and Surgeons held in Montreal in September 1992, University of Montreal sociologist Marc Renaud raised a few eyebrows (and hackles, no doubt) when he suggested that some medical research may have diminishing returns. He noted that gains in life expectancy were tapering off in Canada even though billions of dollars were being spent on biomedical research. He was rightly irked about the lack of research on diet when so much money was being thrown at drugs and medical devices.

What's really under the microscope these days is the value of medicine itself. Numerous studies of surgery show that as many as one-third of procedures may be inappropriate or unnecessary. It has been found that doctors' practice styles rather than illnesses account for the differences in treatment from region to region. Wide variations have been found in such procedures as coronary bypasses, hip replacements, hysterectomies, tonsillectomies, and cardiovascular surgery. One Manitoba study found that five times as many hysterectomies were performed in one area of the province as in another.

Similarly, studies on whether physicians prescribe drugs appropriately yielded varying results. For example, in some hospital studies, 50 per cent of antibiotics and ulcer drugs were inappropriately prescribed.

In other words, we are likely not getting the best overall value for the $65 billion—or roughly 9 per cent of our gross national product—that we spend annually on health care in Canada.

Let's now connect the idea that we know little about how drugs affect the health of Canadians with a third dot—the assault by drug companies on doctors to prescribe their products.

These three dots produce this picture:

Prescribing Drugs by Russian Roulette

The drug industry in Canada sells about $9 billion worth of drugs each year to Canadians. It also spends about $700 million a year on marketing and promotion aimed at doctors. Any medical journal contains full-colour ads that rival in sophistication and cost those that tout perfume and booze. Back in January 1989, Judy Erola, then chief lobbyist for the Pharmaceutical Manufacturers Association of Canada (PMAC), the trade group for brand-name drug companies, conceded that some of its sixty-five member companies might try a little restraint in their advertising. They seem to have resisted.

Recently in the United States—where the drug industry spends $350 million a year just on advertising in medical journals—a study concluded that the public is at risk because the ads are so misleading. The study published in June 1992 in the *Annals of Internal Medicine* found deficiencies in 100 of 109 typical ads. Forty failed the "fair balance" test set by the U.S. Food and Drug Administration (FDA), requiring advertisers to inform doctors adequately about both benefits and risks. Thirty ads cited statistics from poorly designed studies. The remaining thirty misled doctors through inappropriate graphs or tables. The FDA hasn't helped matters: it screens only a small percentage of ads.

In Canada, such corporate behaviour is purportedly kept in check by the high-mindedness of the Pharmaceutical Advertising Advisory Board, a multidisciplinary body that reviews ads. Given the extent to which advertising was botched on the drug Toradol (see Chapter 9), and is still operating under the same lack of rules, I have my doubts. Also, lest we forget, U.S. medical journals are read by Canadian and other non–U.S. doctors.

Doctors like to think their prescribing habits are immune to the effects of advertising. They often cite other sources of influence, such as journal articles and their own experience. But, when quizzed about certain drugs, as they are in decade-long research at Harvard Medical School, their opinions more closely resemble drug-company hype than the scientific facts on these drugs presented in journal articles.

The drug industry's assault on the prescribing consciousness of doctors doesn't end with full-colour, multipage ads. Thanks to the army of about four thousand salesmen or detail men—roughly one for every eighteen doctors in Canada—the corporate message has a good chance of sticking in the brain cells of doctors. Drug companies also sponsor research—in fact, they sponsor most clinical research—as well as symposia, medical meetings, and continuing-education conferences. True, you find few corporate logos stamped on pencils these days, what with medicine's recently heightened sensitivity to "ethics," but the pharmaceutical giants score big with image advertising, as in "this talk/award/public-television show/etc. is sponsored by Blah Blah Company."

A couple of years back, almost anything went—trips to Hawaii, free toasters, you name it. It was open season on doctors, and many complained bitterly as they pocketed their hundred-dollar money orders (to buy books) or gorged on twelve-course meals. I attended a "dinner meeting" at a fashionable Toronto Chinese restaurant to hear what birth-control pilldom had to say to young general practitioners, who were obviously starving and in need of exotic sustenance while they learned effortlessly.

Some of this excess has been curbed, of late, because the Canadian Medical Association (CMA), after years of waffling on physician ethics, finally established voluntary guidelines in February

1992. They suggest that, despite what they deduced while at medical school, doctors are not obliged to accept gifts from strangers.

The last straw for the CMA, according to John Williams, the association's director of Medical Ethics and Legal Affairs, was the infamous Squibb computer affair of 1989. Squibb Canada Inc. played two thousand doctors for complete fools, giving them computers to track their patients on the drug Capoten, a pill to control blood pressure. Hey, this was research: the doctors just happened to get to keep the computers on a kind of long-term loan after the "study" was completed. This foolery was even too much for PMAC—the brand-name-drug lobby—and Squibb asked for their computers back.

The CMA's guidelines politely request that doctors not allow personal benefit to get in the way of the well-being of their patients. This rule is obviously wide open to interpretation, as Williams concedes.

I mentioned to him that I'd been seeing a blizzard of media-related drug promotion of late, in which doctors or "product champions" extol the virtues of a particular drug. The idea is that lazy reporters will pass on the product champion's expertise to Mr. or Ms. Public, who, in turn, will then ask his or her family doctor for "that new superpill written about yesterday in *The Globe and Mail*."

And what did the CMA have to say about doctors endorsing products? And being paid to do so?

"This is a grey area," Williams replied, "and it isn't really covered specifically by the guidelines."

The CMA is considering more detailed guidelines. They may take another year or so to finalize. Then they have to go through the various CMA committees at the association. And . . .

Let's pause to sum up our drug connect-the-dots thus far. The emerging picture looks like this: We know little about how drugs affect the health of Canadians, so we don't know if spending more on drugs is really the route we want to take. The way doctors learn about drugs they prescribe and their cosy relationship with the drug industry raises further troubling questions about our rising drug bill and the side-effects of the drugs on the nation's health.

Hold that picture as we connect one more dot: the drug industry-inspired idea that long-term patent protection for drug companies is in the interests of every Canadian. Hmmm.

Does Long-Term Patent Protection Serve the Interests of Every Canadian?

Bill C-91, which has just become the law of the land, will give brand-name-drug companies twenty years of patent protection before a generic-drug company can market a copy of the brand-name product. As it takes about ten years to develop a drug, Bill C-91 grants the brand-names ten full years on the market without competition, about three years more patent protection than that provided in Bill C-22. Passed in 1987, Bill C-22 allowed a generic to be licensed (for a royalty to the developer of 4 per cent of sales) after seven years.

The brand-name-drug industry contends that added protection will enable them to invest more in Canada—more jobs and funds for Canadian medical researchers. The 65 PMAC–associated companies, largely situated in Quebec and Ontario, say they are an important force in the Canadian economy, employing some 18,000 people. In 1991, they spent $376.4 million on research and development, much of it clinical research.

PMAC has certainly received a lot of support from scientists who rely on drug-company funding. The star-studded Ottawa-based Canadian Society for Clinical Investigation announced in a June 23, 1992, letter to its membership that a new bill (Bill C-91) was about to be introduced. The group asked members to use letters, faxes, and phone calls to lobby for the new bill. "Together we can protect the future of medical research by doing our part," the letter exhorted.

The same day, in Ottawa, the Canadian Federation of Biological Societies, representing six thousand biomedical and biological researchers across Canada, also spoke up on behalf of the new bill. And why not? They strongly depend on drug-company money, especially as the Tories have been cutting back funding, thereby entrenching both the need for and the power of corporate funding of R&D.

Industry financing of research is taking new turns. Marion Merrell Dow Canada Inc. recently put up $1.3 million to create the Cardiac Prevention Research Centre of Nova Scotia at Dalhousie University in Halifax. Research will focus on smoking cessation and exercise, as well as dietary and drug projects. PMAC companies have also set up an educational foundation that, in 1991, in conjunction with the Medical Research Council, a Health department medical-science funding agency, awarded 125 students and young researchers grants totalling $1.5 million. Glaxo Canada Inc. recently set up a program for four Quebec medical schools that will assist students to select medical specialties.

Such grants do not come entirely free—loyalty to the drug industry is being indirectly purchased, although some scientists and doctors argue they are not compromising themselves.

The companies, you see, need the outside researchers to carry out their R&D projects. Most drug companies have not invested in good research laboratories in Canada, and rely on such close collaboration. But the companies hold all the aces, as they can simply do their R&D elsewhere should economic conditions become unfavourable for investment in Canada. So it is no surprise that Canada's biologists and clinical investigators rushed to support Bill C-91.

The critics of the bill, naturally led by the nineteen firms producing generics, aren't bound by the same economic considerations. Their assault on the bill focused on the increased costs of extended patent protection to provincial health plans. Depending on the source, estimates of the increase Canadians will pay range from $25 million to $1 billion a year. If you believe consumer crusader Ralph Nader, the bill also signals the end of Medicare because it will make it more difficult for the provinces to provide adequate health care.

PMAC's counter-argument is that price increases won't get out of line—that is, above the rate of inflation—because the Patented Medicine Prices Review Board can roll them back. As the Consumers' Association of Canada points out, however, the review board discovered that 34 per cent of new drug products exceeded its pricing guidelines, but has no mechanism to recover the extra costs.

PMAC boasts that extra dough in the coffers of its members will ensure that Canadians have the earliest possible access to new drugs. But what does this really mean? That many new laboratories will be built in Canada to develop new drugs? Not likely. Bill C-22 certainly didn't bring on a building boom. Does it mean that more money will be available for Canadian doctors to test new drugs developed elsewhere? Perhaps, but Canada already does a fair share of clinical testing of new products.

All right, let's assume that bushels of money will become available for drug development in Canada. Does this mean that important new drugs will jump from the lab to the pharmacy shelves?

Of the three hundred medications that PMAC says are now in development in Canada and around the world for such conditions as heart disease, cancer, and Alzheimer's, relatively few are likely to be "breakthroughs" should current trends continue. Given the uncertainty, it's not possible to claim that more drug profits will somehow bring real benefits to Canadians. A distinction must be made between what is important for the health of Canadians and what is healthy for Canada's industrial drug strategy.

And just what is driving Canada's industrial drug strategy? Connect another dot and we find that:

International Trade Agreements are Driving Canada's Industrial Drug Strategy

Is this emerging industrial strategy detrimental to our health? Patent extention is a symptom of what's in store for Canada in the rapidly growing global market-place. Drug companies, like other multinationals, can pick and choose where they spend their cash. If the economic or political climate in one country becomes unfavourable, they simply move to a sunnier one. This is the bottom line. The companies know it. Governments know it, too, and dance to the companies' tune. Extending patent protection for PMAC companies was such a jig. The climate for the drug industry had improved in Canada since Bill C-22, but it didn't go far enough. Bill C-91 brings Canada close enough to other nations' chorus line to compete for drug-industry investments.

Patent protection, however, is merely the forward picket on this international drug battlefield. New international trade agreements in the making, such as GATT (General Agreement on Tariffs and Trade), which involves 108 nations; NAFTA (North American Free Trade Agreement) involving Canada, the United States, and Mexico; and the EEC (European Economic Community), are ensuring that national regulations, including those involving health matters, become subsumed by industry's global interests. The mechanisms that some nations, such as Canada and the United States, have set up to protect their citizens from untested and/or dangerous drugs may be deemed an impediment to trade, i.e., "protectionist" of the market, if not of the population. Trade agreements may build roads for capital and goods by bulldozing protections against the sales of potentially dangerous goods.

The drug industry has been preparing the roadbed for years. It has successfully lobbied nations to speed up their drug-review procedures. (We saw what this speed-up is doing to Canada's drug-safety net in Chapter 2.) And it is pressuring them to agree on common—and less strict—standards. It appears we are being herded onto a bold new industrial playing field that is already endangering the structures put in place after the thalidomide tragedy. In the next chapter, we'll examine the result of this pressure on the safety net in the United States. But first, the one dot that completes the drug picture: the report on drug review penned by Denis Gagnon, Vice-Rector of Research at Laval University.

Gagnon didn't play connect-the-dots; instead, he played:

Speed Up the Drug System

Gagnon was asked in January 1992 by Health minister Benoît Bouchard to advise him on ways to improve drug review. He completed his task in June, and Bouchard released the report on November 30. Bouchard might as well have asked PMAC to conduct the inquiry.

The only bit of evidence Gagnon reported that suggested some drugs were not getting out fast enough was a fleeting reference to some drugs for breast cancer. The rest of his 192-page tome is premised on the notion that we'd better speed things up so that the drug industry will provide us with more timely drugs.

Gagnon envisions a new drug-review agency reporting to the Health minister. How he would ensure that it would be independent of influence is never made clear. Nor is his definition of "experts" to head the agency and be on his council of doctors and scientists, which would recommend rejection or approval of drugs to the Health minister.

And the current backlog? Send in the Swat team. Gagnon recommends that a special task force dispose of it as quickly as possible. Nowhere in his report does he mention what's in the backlog or why these drugs are so important to Canadians.

Some of Gagnon's recommendations—there are 152—are motherhood issues that have been floating around for years, with no one bothering to tie them down. His classic is a nod to a strong drug-monitoring system.

He's keen on external drug review, which is already in high gear and heading for the brick wall, as discussed in Chapter 2. As a placebo to consumer groups, Gagnon suggests that product monographs, compiled by the drug companies, should become public property. Sure. Why not? I feel better already, I'm sure of it.

There's not much more to capture the imagination in the report, except for some technical stuff on how bureau scientists can be organized differently to review drugs.

And, of course, Gagnon would like to see his recommendations implemented immediately.

5

DISGRACE SOUTH OF THE BORDER:

The FDA Follies

It was a dark and cold day in January 1992—perhaps even stormy. The mighty *New York Times* asked me to write an opinion piece on the new American folk hero Dr. David Kessler, commissioner of the U.S. Food and Drug Administration.

The *Times* editor was very pleasant. He had noticed my reporting on the Meme breast implant. I agreed to do the piece. Stupid, stupid me. I knew the *Times* would never publish it, but I fell victim to Canadian Inferiority Syndrome. The idea of being published in *The New York Times* was too great a temptation for this Canuck.

Kessler had spit in the eye of thousands of plastic surgeons hellbent on remodelling every small breast in sight. Unlike his silicone-friendly predecessors at the FDA, he had taken the lead in removing from the market inadequately tested breast implants and greatly limiting the use of the remaining devices. The *Times* interpreted this action as a sign that a major housecleaning of consumer health products was in the works. As I had contacts at the FDA, would I probe Kessler's mind and predict his next moves on behalf of the wronged U.S. consumer?

"Sure," I said. Then I suggested a modified approach to the subject. I could include inside dope on how Kessler was getting pressured by Dan Quayle and his infamous Council on Competitiveness, a White House recipe for making tapioca of regulations to curb industry's greed. The council championed deregulation in all areas—the environment, transporation, health, etc.

"Just be sure that you give us a strong sense of what Kessler will do next," the *Times* editor said.

All the signs were there. The Op-Ed brains trust didn't want an analysis of Kessler's chances of accomplishing significant change at the FDA. But I merrily set out to Op-Ed my way.

The Quayle Factor

Kessler was at a crossroads. After sixteen months on the job, he had rattled some cages. He had taken a bead on inadequately tested breast implants, misleading food labelling, and excessive drug promotion by the drug industry. But Kessler had caved in to the White House on other matters of pivotal importance, such as backing off on a bill that would give the FDA greater enforcement powers and agreeing to speed up drug review. When the *Times* approached me, Kessler was caught between Dan Quayle, who wanted to pin his whatsits, and more progressive souls who were urging him to pull Excalibur from the bureaucratic stone.

In late 1990, Kessler was new on the job. Not impressed with procedures to keep industry in line, he vowed publicly to beef up the FDA's powers: regulations can be solid as bedrock but unenforceable.

Kessler knew that the FDA was getting no respect: some manufacturers of medical devices didn't even bother to report to the agency deaths and serious injuries related to the use of their products, although required to, by law, within five days. In 1989, the Washington-based Public Citizen's Health Research Group reported that thirty-five companies had not reported problems on seventy-six devices since 1985. This in-your-face attitude extended to pacemakers, respirators, and breast implants. At least seven deaths and more than a hundred injuries had gone unreported. Take Aequitron Medical Inc. of Plymouth, Minnesota. It didn't bother to report four deaths and four serious injuries associated with its infant respirators. When the FDA discovered the problems during a routine inspection of the manufacturer, it took five months to send Aequitron Medical a slap on the wrist.

Also in 1989, congressional committees reported that makers

of devices had recalled problem products from the market from 1983 through 1988 without notifying the FDA, as required by law. Among the products yanked were pacemakers, heart valves, paediatric cribs, anaesthesia machines, and dialysis units.

To his credit, Kessler recognized the need for federal regulatory-agency clout in recalling medical devices and prescription drugs, inspecting imports, and gaining access to company documents, if necessary by subpoena. He supervised the creation of a legislative package; got the approval of his boss, Louis Sullivan, secretary of Health and Human Services; and received indications of support from the White House. The package was circulated among politicians, and a bill incorporating the FDA's package was introduced in Congress.

Kessler assured a congressional committee in March 1991 that he endorsed the proposed legislation; but four months later, when he returned to testify, he astonished committee members by holding that the FDA was still thinking about its enforcement needs. By this time, the medical-devices lobbyists had worked up a frontal assault on the proposal for granting the FDA subpoena power, and the White House had turned chicken.

Kessler had been telephoned on the eve of his July testimony by a member of Quayle's council, who suggested that he be a loyal soldier. When a member of the congressional committee asked Kessler whether the council had interfered, he replied that "the administration must speak with one voice."

Kessler paid the price several months later. When he was considering action on silicone breast implants, he was faced with a practical lesson on how the lack of subpoena power can handcuff a regulatory agency. The FDA had, at long last, required makers of the implants to submit their data on the safety and efficacy of their products. The companies submitted such poor-quality safety data that FDA scientists had judged the information inadequate. This didn't stop an advisory committee on breast implants from recommending to the FDA that the implants be allowed to remain on the market because they satisfied a genuine demand for image and body reconstruction.

But then word leaked out, so to speak, from a lawsuit involving silicone implants, that Dow Corning, a leading manufacturer and purveyor of silicone to other companies, had withheld product information from the FDA by placing documents under a court seal. When Kessler asked Dow Corning for the information, the company essentially told him to take a hike.

The late Ted Weiss was a Manhattan Democrat who headed the congressional committee that monitors the FDA. Weiss and his expert assistant, Diana Zuckerman, had been hounding Kessler for months that breast implants were unsafe. A blunt letter from Weiss to Kessler cuts straight to the issue of the Dow Corning documents and puts Kessler on further notice that someone is monitoring his actions:

> *These documents . . . are convincing evidence that, for more than 20 years, Dow has falsely claimed that their breast implants were proven safe when in fact their own research indicated they could be dangerous.*
>
> *In addition to memoranda that clearly indicate that Dow officials knew they were making false statements about safety to the physicians who were buying and implanting the product, we have documents describing animal studies which show that Dow did not include information about potentially serious medical complications caused by implants in their published study or their recent pre-market approval (PMA) application to FDA. It is particularly outrageous that the company started studies of new implant models in women even before they had completed the necessary tests in animals. In addition, the company continues to refuse to provide those documents to the FDA, despite your recent demands that they do so.*

Weiss then gives the screw a turn:

> *On December 20, I wrote to you regarding similar concerns and urged you to refer this matter to the Department of Justice for investigation. To date, the FDA has failed to do so. I am now enclosing the documents referred to above, which*

I believe require you to expedite a thorough investigation of possible misbranding as well as scientific misconduct in the cover-up of research results.

Then there is this reminder:

As you know, I have strongly supported your efforts to restore confidence in the FDA during the past year. I recognize your commitment to require manufacturers to prove their products are safe and effective, in order to be sold in this country. However, the FDA's repeated failure to exercise its regulatory responsibilities regarding breast implants sends the wrong message to American industry, and will relegate the FDA to the role of paper tiger rather than protector of consumers and enforcer of the law.

Three days later, despite protestations by Dow that their products were safe, Kessler banned the unrestricted sale of all silicone-gel breast implants.

So score one for the commissioner, with a big assist from Weiss and Zuckerman.

Kessler also felt the heat from women's groups wanting the implants banned. And when *The New York Times* and the rest of the U.S. media discovered the issue, the public saw and heard little but breast implants for weeks. Better late than never.

More Quayle, Kessler?

Kessler also got his ears pulled on drug review. This time, Quayle played a visible role. On November 13, 1991, he and Health secretary Sullivan announced that the FDA was reforming procedures to evaluate the safety and efficacy of prescription drugs. Sullivan was just window-dressing. The proposal, from Quayle's council, was aimed at speeding up the procedures. Among their other ill-conceived recommendations, the council wanted new drugs to be reviewed by experts outside the FDA; drugs approved in other countries to be automatically given clearance; and hospital review boards, rather than the FDA, to decide on when to allow human drug trials once animal research is completed.

Good soldier Kessler said he would give the new ideas a try, although his agency didn't even have copies of the proposals—the White House controlled the press conference.

It would have been difficult for me to list Kessler's next targets for FDA scrutiny in the *Times* without including some reservations, given Kessler's capitulation on key issues. And who knew how much more was in store, with Quayle's council out for blood and publicity. After all, George Bush had created the council in 1989 to pressure agencies to delay or kill proposed regulations. Although some people see regulation as protection of the public from the excesses of industry, the council viewed regulation as a death hold on free enterprise.

Now, the FDA not only is vulnerable to political interference, but also has a long history of incompetence and negligence that rivals that of Canada's Health Protection Branch. In April 1991, a fifteen-member panel headed by Charles Edwards, president of Scripps Clinic and Research Foundation of La Jolla, California, and a former FDA commissioner, concluded that the agency's problems were so severe that they posed a threat to Americans' health. The FDA required stronger enforcement powers, better management, better-trained employees, more funds, better laboratory equipment, and more authority in government.

During twelve years of Ronnie, George, and Dan, the FDA had the stuffing knocked out of it. The commissioner's power to issue regulations was cut in 1981; since the late 1970s, the agency's seizures, injunctions, and prosecutions slowed to a trickle. The FDA treated industry as a partner and became increasingly vulnerable to drug-industry lobbying. It tarnished its reputation further in 1989 when some of its drug reviewers were discovered to have taken gratuities. By the time Kessler took over, senior agency managers didn't even have proper records of the regulations they had proposed: some four hundred—ranging from the size of type on drug packages to standards for defibrillators—had never been acted upon.

One of my key FDA sources, who has worked in the agency for many years, has complained that managers often do not listen to warnings about medical devices from the agency's own scientists.

He wasn't exaggerating. A congressional hearing held on June 3, 1992, produced evidence that medical-devices reviewers were often undercut or ignored when they recommended non-approval of a product. Some managers viewed non-approval as jeopardizing their goal—a high approval rate.

Committee chairman and Michigan Democrat John Dingell stated "that there existed within some divisions an informal and undocumented process to override reviewers' recommendations by constructing an informal appeal process bypassing the reviewer, or by subtly or directly indicating to the reviewer that their reluctance indicated that they were not team players." Reviewers who asked too many questions would have promotions and/or bonuses held back. Some reviewers told the committee that documentation was removed from files or destroyed.

Reviewers told the committee that their managers were technically incompetent to assess the quality of reviews. My FDA source has described the agency as "directed by a whole bunch of managers who are undereducated and not technically oriented. This is particularly the case in medical devices. They often can't grasp the technical debates and are mesmerized by industry scientists. This has contributed to one crisis after another, one mess after another."

My source was referring in part to the FDA's slow action on the Convexo-Concave heart valve, which remained on the market for five years after the first reports of breakage and deaths. (Canada, you'll recall, messed up on this one as well.)

Another reference was to insufficiently tested jaw implants buried in about 70,000 Americans, some whom have suffered extreme pain and damage to facial and skull bones. Some of the devices had a failure rate of almost 100 per cent. The FDA finally recalled devices from the two manufacturers of the implants in May 1992. (Another company had withdrawn its version in 1988.) These products, like breast implants, were marketed prior to 1976 and therefore were exempt from safety and efficacy checks. "Jaw implants are an example of the kind of product we should have been looking carefully at years ago, but we either didn't have the manpower or the will to do it," my source said.

There are about 130 pre-1976 devices still waiting for FDA review and still being put into human beings, although it is not known if they are safe or effective. They include artificial testicles, penis implants, saline breast implants, tooth implants, knee and shoulder replacements, centrifugal pumps used in heart bypass, and electrical stimulators. The manufacturers have been notified that they must come up with test data equivalent to that required for high-risk products. The FDA is legally bound to complete these reviews by December 1, 1995. Good luck! Then they can start on the hundreds of so-called medium-risk devices for which there are no performance standards.

The FDA is playing catch-up on yet another front. For years, consumer advocates have been suggesting that registries be established for patients with implants. This way, should something go wrong with a product, patients could be traced and warned efficiently. In March 1992, the FDA finally required manufacturers to register patients with any one of twenty-five implants and ten other devices such as infusion pumps, respirators, defibrillators, and breathing monitors. Again, better late than never.

The Real Backlog

You would think that after all the holler about the FDA's deplorable record, the proponents of fast-speed safety review would shut up and let Kessler get on with overhauling agency procedures. But no. A surprised Kessler received a harshly worded letter in September 1992 from Congressman Dingell, suggesting that the FDA had become too conservative and was taking its own sweet time in approving medical devices. Yes, this was the same Dingell who chaired the congressional committee and was in favour of improved reviews of medical devices.

The Dingell letter is a sign of things to come. Industry wants its products out there now, and astute politicians can sense the changing tide.

Kessler's dilemma is the one also facing Canada's protection system for medical devices: years of neglect of consumer safety and kowtowing to industry have produced an infrastructure not geared to modern industrial demands, let alone consumer safety.

And such demands are growing just when past neglect is due back to haunt us. (Breast implants should be seen in this context, as should the many orthopaedic devices that look good for a few years and then deteriorate. We'll pick up on this issue in Chapter 11.)

In short, industry growls that new devices are waiting to be reviewed, yet hundreds of thousands of people are dealing with potential time bombs in the form of implants and other medical devices. This is the real backlog. And only recently have there been some modest signs of catch-up.

The Drug Speed-Up

Since his first day on the job, Kessler has been lobbied by the drug industry and its favourite politicians for faster drug review. Then he got goosed by Quayle and became a spokesman for speed-up rather than an independent voice. In October 1992, Congress gave him approval to hire an army of drug reviewers: approval time is to be cut in half, to six months from twelve, by 1997. Industry agreed to shell out about $330 million over five years in fees to the FDA—enough to hire six hundred reviewers.

The FDA has been understaffed for years, but the potential of a few life-saving drugs that may huddle in the blizzard of new products this decade does not call for a Manhattan Project on drug approval.

One argument for having many reviewers is that, by the end of the decade, some 1,200 new biotechnology products a year will be in need of approval. But the extra profits that a company will earn with a faster approval time will not necessarily translate into significant or even modest health benefits.

Surely, the FDA, like any other regulatory agency, can fast-track those products that show the greatest potential for treatment. Short cuts are also possible in certain circumstances, as we have seen with some drugs for treatment of AIDS.

The big question remains: how will industry financing of the review process affect independence? Will review decisions be subtly influenced? Will reviewers take care not to bite the hand that feeds them?

Meanwhile, the FDA is pushing ahead on other speed-up

procedures. Potentially life-saving drugs may be approved quickly, even in months, on the evidence of short-term signs of effectiveness. For example, researchers could consider the reduction of a tumour to be an indication of a cancer drug's efficacy rather than waiting for a more detailed understanding of the drug's effect on the body, including whether the patient's life is extended. Such a drug, once approved, would be further tested and closely monitored for side-effects by the drug company. Should problems become significant, the drug could be withdrawn.

This proposal will undoubtedly provide terminal patients who have little to lose with one more chance. But where will the line be drawn? There are many diseases and many lobbies in the wake of AIDS activism. In the worst-case scenario, many junk drugs will be whizzed through the system under pressure from lobbyists, bringing harm, not relief, to patients. The other danger is that the fast track might gradually be opened to drugs that do not merit such attention: if there's money to be made, drug companies will be trying.

Another FDA plan makes even less sense. The agency plans a pilot project to farm out some new drug submissions to outside reviewers. Some FDA reviewers surveyed by the Public Citizen's Health Research Group were concerned about the possibility of conflict of interest.

Then there's "safety-testing harmonization." The FDA has reached agreement with Japan and the European Community on guidelines for animal drug testing. Tests in one country will be accepted by the others. No more duplication of animal tests for review purposes. Long-term testing is to be reduced by at least six months. In fact, some toxicological testing will last only six months, which may not be long enough to adequately screen for such effects as cancer.

Why bother to be thorough when everyone is clamouring for the newest and the best? Besides, long-term animal tests are very expensive and cut into drug company profits.

What next?

But wait! You really want to know what happened to me at *The New York Times*, right? I went through the exercise. Actually,

I went through it twice. The editor said my first effort was not the list of issues that Kessler would tackle next. I reminded him of my hope to include some details of the commissioner's indecisiveness about being a free-thinking spirit at the FDA. The editor then suggested that I might include some of this, but that I should focus more on Kessler's future targets in my second attempt.

It was rejected, too, but the editor informed me that the newspaper's Science section had decided to take on the issue of the FDA's difficulty to protect the public. Kessler's concerns about better enforcement powers for the FDA would likely be included.

He spoke truth.

There it was. Page One on January 26, 1992. *The New York Sunday Times*.

I was impressed. And jealous too.

2

BIG TROUBLE

6

SINS OF OMISSION:

The Meme Breast Implant

IN THE EARLY 1970S, I TEAMED UP WITH NEW YORK WRITER and friend Richard Altschuler to pen a book entitled *Open Reality*. We shared the view that industrialized societies had dug themselves a big hole called consumerism and fallen into it. *Open Reality*, published in 1974, focused on the extent to which the corporate world's advertising had turned us into believers that happiness was only a purchase away. Not surprisingly, our buy-something way of life led to a permanent state of confusion and anxiety. The research for the book left me acutely aware of how much our consciousness is made up of corporate messages that define every aspect of our lives—sex, leisure, politics, marriage, religion, and so on. I think now, as then, that women have been especially victimized by this tactical onslaught, particularly by corporate-produced imagery of eternal youth and beauty.

In 1980, while serving as a commentator on health issues for CBC radio in Montreal, I came across ads for breast implants in local newspapers. The implants were essentially plastic bags filled with silicone gel. The agencies' sales pitch offered to refer women to plastic surgeons who would do the procedure in private clinics. There was nothing illegal in this, but it made me question the ethics of doctors who were using this scheme to side-step professional rules forbidding them to advertise. I decided to look into it.

The agencies I visited scored high on the sleaze scale—one owner displayed pictures of bare-breasted actresses all around his office. He explained that women were valued more for their looks than men were—nudge, nudge, wink, wink. When it is so easy for a woman to change her breasts, why disappoint her man? I began to understand why some women have such contempt for men.

A couple of days at the McGill University Medical Library also proved unnerving. Breast implants were not a new idea: at the turn of the century, doctors injected women with paraffin, vegetable oil, lanolin, or beeswax; in the 1930s, they inserted glass balls. By the 1950s, they had switched to various plastics, and then—ta dum!— in 1963, Dow Corning Chemical Corporation, the world's largest supplier of silicone, developed the silicone-gel implant.

By 1980, some half-million women had undergone the surgery, which involved fashioning a pocket under the real breasts and inserting the implants. The procedures required a general anaesthetic, meaning it was real surgery; but some fashion magazines were making it seem no more involved than trying a new perfume. It struck me as revealing of our culture and its sexual priorities that penis size had not enjoyed the same attention in the world of fashion.

The dozen women who consented to interviews for my radio report all equated larger breasts with greater self-esteem. They all had one other thing in common: their doctors had given them the impression that there was a solid body of scientific evidence showing breast implants to be safe.

Combing through the medical journals, it quickly became apparent to me that these doctors were, well, lying. There was very little serious safety research on breast implants and even less understanding of their short- and long-term physical effects. The obvious questions were: What forces did the body unleash to protect itself against these foreign objects, and with what results? What harm could be caused to surrounding and distant tissue if silicone leaked through the bag? The data in the medical literature amounted to a mere shrug.

Nor was it entirely clear why so many implanted women eventually developed hard breasts. (The process involves the contraction and then hardening of scar tissue around the implants.) Some studies showed as many as 74 per cent of patients affected to some degree. The more common reported figure was between 10 and 40 per cent.

To "treat" hardened breasts, doctors used the "squeeze technique," applying pressure to the breasts until the scar tissue popped like a balloon. This was not only extremely painful but, according to some medical reports, forced some silicone from the implant into surrounding tissues. Yet, little was known about the migration of the gel and its effects.

Over the years, implanted women also reported persistent aching of the breasts; a loss of feeling, particularly in the nipples; poor positioning of the implants; and a loss of breast symmetry.

The plastic surgeons I interviewed had two types of responses. The wafflers acknowledged the high rate of breast hardening and the lack of solid scientific investigation of breast implantation. Some even dared to suggest that a moratorium on breast implants might be in order until the questions were answered. But all intended to continue to make good money, about $2,500 an implantation, until that moratorium day dawned.

During one interview, a waffler pulled out a silicone-gel implant sample that had been sitting in his desk drawer for several weeks. It had turned sticky and yellow just from exposure to air. The surgeon shook his head, as if to ask, "Can't they make a better product than this?" and continued to book appointments.

The other group of plastic surgeons, the bioethicists, emphasized the importance of explaining what was known about breast implants to their patients and letting them decide. One doc admitted that scientific data on breast implants were sparse and that manufacturers were irresponsible in not funding the proper studies. Yet, he seemed content to relate his own clinical experience—without controlled follow-up of his patients—by way of informing prospective newcomers of the benefits and risks of the surgery. Medical arrogance was entering the danger zone.

I'd like to report that my radio piece had some impact, but the only person I heard from was the owner of a referral agency, who thanked me for the publicity.

I swore off the subject.

Eight Years Later

I joined *The Gazette* in 1980. Two years later a new Canadian federal regulation came into force, requiring manufacturers to submit safety and efficacy data on any new device—including breast implants—to be implanted in a human body for thirty days or more.

In 1982, the U.S. Federal Drug Administration classified breast implants as potentially risky as there was insufficient evidence of their safety and efficacy.

I took quick note of both actions and assumed breast implants would receive the regulatory attention they deserved. I was wrong.

Six years later, complaints about breast implants led the FDA to call a public meeting of its advisory panel on medical devices. The agency wanted the panel's help in determining the types of safety and efficacy studies that manufacturers of breast implants should be required to submit for review.

Just days before that November meeting, the Washington-based Public Citizen's Health Research Group had released worrisome study data from Dow Corning: injections of silicone caused highly malignant cancers in more than 23 per cent of rats tested. Health Research Group had also documented FDA concerns about the experimental findings. One of the reviewers, for example, wrote a memo, asking that a public alert be issued to warn of the potential long-term cancer risk of breast implants. He wrote: "While there is no direct proof that silicone causes cancers in humans, there is considerable reason to suspect that it can do so." Neither the memo nor the data, however, convinced the FDA's advisory panel that the removal of breast implants was warranted. But the ensuing controversy made international headlines—and prompted me to ask a few questions.

Jacques Papillon was one of the bioethics-school surgeons I had interviewed for my radio report, and I had spoken to him on occasion since: once to discuss the treatment of burns, on which he is a widely acknowledged expert, and a few times on health-care policy issues that concerned him and his colleagues at Hôtel Dieu Hospital. I had been troubled by his laissez-faire views on breast implants, but, at least, he wasn't a waffler. So, when

Health Research Group made noise in the United States, I made an appointment with Papillon.

Now I might have caught him on a bad day, but he began with typical complaints about breast implants: The companies don't spend a damn penny on proper studies. They have no ethics. They should do follow-up with patients. Then he turned his attention to the Meme, a silicone-gel implant with a polyurethane foam covering: Plastic surgeons were implanting it without knowing what happens to the foam in the body. The manufacturer doesn't know where the foam goes and what happens to it after it separates from the implant. Then he added rather sternly: "You should look into this."

Papillon was turning away patients who requested a Meme implant. He was probably losing business—and money—to his colleagues.

As I left his office, Papillon handed me an article on polyurethane-covered breast implants, written by Pierre Blais, a federal government scientist. Blais drew attention to the lack of scientific data on the implants and questioned their safety. Papillon would later regret ever mentioning the Meme to me.

Pierre Blais was slim and drawn, and very cerebral. Over the years I had asked him questions about medical devices—contraceptive devices and high-tech sensory equipment, including the so-called electronic ear. He had always responded with surprising energy and a torrent of information, some relevant and some not. Not your typical close-mouthed federal scientist, always looking over his shoulder to see if the boss is in hearing range. The Health department's media-relations office said Blais "ran off at the mouth."

His article in the September 1988 issue of *Transplantation/Implantation Today*, a Canadian journal, was an eye-opener: Various polyurethanes were known to deteriorate in the body. For instance, cardiac pacemaker leads insulated with this type of plastic often had to be replaced. So did in-dwelling catheters. So why design a breast implant of such unstable material, particularly one that gets tangled up with breast tissue, and is therefore difficult to remove when necessary? Moreover, deteriorated polyurethanes could release toxic chemicals.

There was a subtle undercurrent to the article—something was rankling Blais. That something, I would learn later, was his employer. As we have seen, Health and Welfare's response time to concerns raised by scientists, politicians, or the public about medical devices was as speedy as a porcupine waddling across a country road.

My first task in following up on Blais's concerns was to review the way the Health department dealt with breast implants in general. As I scrutinized statements made in the House of Commons, and internal Health department memos that had come my way, a pattern began to emerge.

The Historical Context

In 1988, most of the breast implants on the Canadian market had been available prior to October 1982 and were therefore exempt from legislation requiring manufacturers to submit test data on their safety and efficacy. Thousands of Canadian women had no way of knowing if their implants were the products of good science and appropriate manufacturing procedures. (You will recall that the exemption of these "old" devices was not meant to give tacit approval of their safety and efficacy. Rather, it was a matter of priority: eventually these old products might be scrutinized more closely—if anyone found the time.)

On December 4, 1985, Tory MP Suzanne Duplessis of Quebec City voiced her concerns in the House of Commons. Research by chemist Robert Guidoin at Laval University showed that implants were subject to a build-up of mineral deposits, which could change the positioning of the implant and contribute to hardening. Duplessis pointed out that the Health department had made no provision to monitor silicone-gel implants.

A fellow Tory, Health minister Jake Epp, replied that requests for further studies were under consideration. This did not appease Duplessis. On December 10, she rose in the Commons to insist that a strong research program be established. She also called for stronger control of breast implants.

Monique Landry, pinch-hitting for Epp, retorted that Health and Welfare was re-evaluating the need for research "with a view to improve the quality and safety of breast implants in Canada."

That so-called re-evaluation was composed largely of the opinion of plastic surgeons on breast-implant risk solicited in an April 1986 letter from the Health department. Not surprisingly, doctors agreed that risk of complications was low, if reasonable surgical care was exercised (although there was very little good science to back up this conclusion).

Asking the fox to assess the safety of the chicken coop gave birth to a federal strategy. The feds would assist the plastic surgeons in preparing and publishing a patients' guide that would explain the benefits and risks of implantation.

It was a clever move: not only did it categorize implants as a consumer rather than a medical problem, but it also allowed the department to claim for months that a major education effort was under way.

But Duplessis wasn't prepared to back off. In February 1987, she pushed Epp for better monitoring of the safety and efficacy of all breast implants. Epp didn't think this would be feasible; increased regulation meant more reviewers and paperwork, which took dollars that his department could not afford. The cost of producing the guide to breast implants, however, would be modest. Epp did claim to be willing to explore alternatives—and the job of preparing a list of possible options was given to Blais, the department's resident expert on breast implants.

On May 1, 1987, a memo incorporating some of Blais's ideas was sent through channels to Epp. Two key proposals would force better medical follow-up of patients: placing all breast implants in an "investigative" category, and creating provincially operated implant registries.

The idea of a registry was "considered" at a federal-provincial meeting of deputy ministers of Health, according to a Health department briefing memo, dated November 5, 1987, but nothing came of it.

In fact, the Health department's policy on breast implants amounted to encouraging doctors to provide women with scientifically incomplete information about inadequately tested devices to be inserted in their bodies.

And that was the good news.

Meme Irregularities

As a matter of course, I rang up Health and Welfare to ask about the history and legal status of the Meme breast implant in Canada. Papillon had spoken of the Meme as "new," so I assumed the government had reviewed the manufacturer's test data. A thorough check should shed light on Papillon's concerns about the polyurethane cover.

I asked for Blais, but the media-relations office prescribed David Johnson, then head of the research and standards division of the Bureau of Radiation and Medical Devices. Even in those heady days before the government blacklisted me from conducting interviews, I had to beg to talk to a specialist. Blais was the expert on breast implants, but Blais was loose-lipped. Johnson's expertise was mainly in radiation, but Johnson was tight-lipped. Therefore Johnson was the spokesman on breast implants.

Johnson told me on the phone: "The company says it is exempt from the [safety and efficacy review] regulations, but I've asked that this be looked into." Two samples of the Meme were to be analysed to determine whether the implants were in any way different from pre-1982 versions. (Some changes would have qualified the product as "new.")

Wait a minute. He was telling me that the Meme had never gone through federal safety checks. According to his facts, it had been exempt from the new safety-review legislation, but now the Health department appeared to be having second thoughts about the "old" implant.

The obvious questions were: Who decided to exempt the implant? On what grounds? When? And why, then, was the government getting its ear again?

Johnson's answers were less obvious. He merely repeated that the department was investigating the Meme's regulatory status. He even announced that he was about to repeat himself, as in, "I repeat, the department is investigating the Meme's regulatory status."

More enlightening were late-night telephone conversations and packages delivered by special messenger. The "Meme's regulatory status," as Johnson put it, was mired in muck.

On February 21, 1985, about four years before my non-conversation with Johnson, a complaint was filed at the Health department about the Meme's regulatory status. Bryant Medical Products Inc. of Mississauga, a distributor of medical devices, including competing breast implants, noted that the Health department had never reviewed the Meme and another polyurethane-covered implant called the Replicon. Why not? Both were being sold in Canada by the same distributor.

The complaint prompted an immediate investigation, but lo and behold, there was no federal record of the Meme or Replicon being marketed in Canada. That's because neither the owner, Natural-Y Surgical Specialties of Los Angeles, nor the Canadian distributor, Silimed, Inc., of Montreal, had notified the Health department.

As we know, Canadian law requires a manufacturer of medical devices to notify the department within ten days of a product's being for sale. It's not an onerous demand—only basic information must be provided, such as the name of the product, its manufacturer and distributor, its purposes and labelling. Registration enables Health department regulators to acquaint themselves with the existence of a suburban double garage engaged in the manufacture and sale of a "Cosmic Energy Pain Neutralizer." Registration can also flush out a manufacturer of a "new" implant who lacked the good sense to submit product test data for review.

On March 28, 1985, Sylvain Boucher, a federal inspector, visited Silimed, Inc. (later Réal Laperrière, Inc.) He was advised by vice-president Richard Laperrière, brother of company president Réal, that the implants had been sold for about ten years in Canada and that his company had become distributors for the manufacturer in February 1984.

About two weeks later, on April 16, Boucher wrote to Réal Laperrière, Inc., asking that the company formally register its products. Boucher also wanted information on the sales histories of the Meme and Replicon, to determine whether a safety review was legally required.

The next letter written by Boucher to the company reveals how the matter would be settled. On August 23, he informed Réal Laperrière that, according to the department's information, Natural-Y implants had been sold exclusively by Weck, a division of Squibb Canada, since March 30, 1976. Therefore the implants didn't require safety reviews. But Boucher urged Laperrière to register the products. The entire matter would then be closed.

Fortunately, Boucher and his superiors in the department's regulatory enforcement division are not everyone's idea of a medical-devices safety net for products that remain in the body for long periods. Some scientists at the Health department were not simply going to take the word of the seller that two products are the same.

Microbiologist Nirmala Chopra, who headed the product-review unit, repeatedly asked the enforcement division to obtain real evidence, such as the company's manufacturing data on the implants, to qualify the Meme for an exemption.

Internal Health department documents show that Pierre Blais had also been tracking the Meme's regulatory status, including Laperrière's neglect to register the product until forty-four months after Boucher's first request. Blais had also become increasingly concerned about the Meme's potential dangers. Indeed, David Johnson was still asking questions about the Meme in early November 1988, largely because Blais wouldn't leave the file alone.

First Story

My first report on the Meme was published on Boxing Day, 1988. It filled the "Discover" page of the D-section of *The Gazette*. This is an odd place for an inquiry that raised important questions about the stability of the Meme's polyurethane foam and the implant's legal status. Some 7,500 pairs of the Meme had already been implanted, mostly in Quebec women. Female colleagues remarked that my report would have made headlines had it been about testicular implants.

I'm not exactly the silent type and howled at Raymond Brassard, who was then my editor. (It wasn't his doing, but you have to fight for your stories at a newspaper.) Ray's sensible response was to encourage me to follow the story.

There were four excellent reasons for doing so. First, case

reports on problems with polyurethane implants were worrisome. In one case, removal of the implants for medical reasons necessitated the removal of muscular and glandular tissue as well, as the polyurethane foam had tangled up with the breast tissue. In another, bits of the polyurethane had been left behind when the implant was removed, and had caused infection. How often would these things happen as more and more implants were removed?

Second, several plastic surgeons were becoming concerned about the Meme, although perhaps not as concerned as they ought to have been. Jacques Bouchard, then head of the Association of Plastic Surgeons of Quebec, said studies pointed to potential problems. "When we started putting in this implant several years ago, the studies on it made it seem like a miracle," he told me. "But now that more studies are appearing, we don't really know where we stand with this implant."

"Then why put it into women?" I asked.

Bouchard danced around the question, saying that women were demanding the Meme and that, so far, there didn't appear to be any problems among his patients.

Was this plastic surgery's new hip approach to the modern consumer? "If the patient demands something, let her have it. It's her decision." It was certainly worth watching.

The third reason to pursue the Meme story had to do with that much-touted patient's guide to breast implants. Bouchard had been on the committee that had prepared it, so I asked him for a copy. After a long look around the office, he found one. The only one. In French. It had been jointly published only months earlier by the Health department, the Canadian Association of Plastic Surgeons, and Bouchard's Association of Plastic Surgeons of Quebec.

Didn't Bouchard have copies in French and English to distribute to all his breast-implant patients? Weren't thousands published? The first printing was practically gone and the Health department had withdrawn its support. He had received a letter indicating that the government would no longer finance and distribute the guide.

Really? Why not?

He didn't know.

(I flip through the guide.) It says here that breasts can become hard in 40 per cent of cases. Isn't the figure as high as 74 per cent?

Well, 40 per cent is sort of the average.

Hmm. I see there is no mention that there is little knowledge of the long-term effects of silicone-gel implants. Why not?

The guide's contents were arrived at by consensus, so naturally some of the risks were watered down. Plastic surgeons have different opinions about the risks. But the guide is only a first step—it is not mandatory that our members give it to patients. But we like to think that the information at least represents a standard for the profession.

Leaving Bouchard's office, I thought, "So this is the government's major action on breast implants, a poorly distributed 'first-step' guide."

The Meme had much better marketing plans, which was the fourth reason to keep going. According to Réal Laperrière, 117 out of 126 plastic surgeons in Quebec and the Maritimes had used the implant. Plans were in the works to begin distribution in Toronto.

Four reasons were more than enough. I'd take a closer look at the Meme.

2-4 *Toluene Diamine*

My report on the Meme was buried deep in the newspaper, but some people found it. *The Gazette* library received calls for copies and I was called by Meme users for more detailed scientific information, particularly about potential side-effects.

I also received a phone tip that Chris Batish, an organic chemist at the University of Florida in Gainesville, had detected the presence of 2-4 toluene diamine, a potential carcinogen in the Meme's polyurethane cover.

Toxicology textbooks revealed that 2-4 toluene diamine causes liver cancer in rats and is suspected of causing cancer in humans. The chemical is also widely known to Canadian and U.S. occupational health and safety experts. Variable amounts of exposure to the chemical on the job can cause liver damage, central-nervous system problems, blindness, and skin blistering. Workers involved in preparing the chemical for industrial polyurethane foams, or for the dyes used in textiles, leather, and furs, wear protective clothing. Back in 1971, the United States banned its use in hair dye. The U.S. Environmental Agency considers it hazardous waste. So what was 2-4 toluene diamine doing in women?

Chris Batish had been amazed to find that 2-4 toluene diamine was among the building blocks of the Meme cover. He later conceded that he had used harsh laboratory conditions to break down the polyurethane, but also emphasized that the original composite material, toluene diisocyanate, was too unstable to be used in the body and likely to break down over time.

Surgitek of Racine, Wisconsin, was the Bristol-Myers Squibb subsidiary that had acquired the Meme in December 1988. Its spokeswoman was Jacqueline Markham. Markham had been president of Natural-Y, the original owner of the Meme. She said the company had not detected any sign of 2-4 toluene diamine on the basis of urine samples from women with the implant.

What did Batish think about the urine samples? Because 2-4 toluene diamine reacts or combines with other chemicals, he thought it wouldn't be easy to detect in the body without special tests.

Next, I had to know how much the biomaterials scientists knew. For instance, had there been warnings in the scientific literature about the breakdown potential of polyurethanes? Indeed there had. Testing to detect breakdown products from plastics began in the 1960s. During the 1960s and 1970s, researchers implanted a wide range of polyurethanes in rats and had recorded variations among the samples in cancer rates and types of cancer. They suggested that the polyurethanes were breaking down; some of their products were acting as "chemical carcinogens." A rat isn't a human, but the results beg for attention. In this context, the Batish test on the Meme, however preliminary, sent up a red flag.

Next, a biology lesson.

Consultation with several biomaterials experts shed some light on what the human body is capable of doing to an implant. This natural process isn't pretty.

It begins as soon as the immune system spots an invader. When implanted, the device sits in the body's own natural bath of rich proteins; within hours these proteins coat the device's surface and begin to interact with the implant. This sets off new and complex immune reactions that cause scar tissue to form around the implant. Another component of the immune system causes inflammation in the area and, sometimes, pain in response to the surgery. Then along come potent immune scavenger cells, which begin to feast on the implant. They can interact with the proteins involved in the inflammation and set off destructive forms of oxygen, known as "free radicals," thought to attack cells.

Okay, but let's come to the point. What bodily ills can result from all this internal violence? Studies suggested that the breakdown of implant materials could cause chronic inflammation, bone erosion, diseases of the connective tissue, and, possibly cancer; but tests were too few to be persuasive. This was an area badly in need of scrutiny, which meant this was a job for the Health department, watchdog of the Canadian public.

To get a sense of how the Health department was dealing with the Meme, I requested interviews with Pierre Blais; his boss, Irwin Hinberg; and Tightlips Johnson. The media-relations office, after some hemming and hawing, agreed, on condition that I interview Blais and Hinberg together. I could be alone with Johnson.

Media relations also informed me that interviews would be taped. Such a precedent-setting move could mean only that breast implants were giving the department pain, and my arrival had added to the discomfort. My sources hinted that Blais was stirring things up. A suit involving the Meme filed against a doctor in British Columbia might be giving the Health department shortness of breath regarding the implant's exemption from safety and efficacy reviews. The lawyer for the plaintiff, Linda Wilson, a secretary in Delta, had told me that he intended to raise questions about the Meme's legal status.

The interviews went badly. Johnson was cordial, but stiffer than advanced rigor mortis. His answers to my questions amounted to this: We are looking into the Meme breast implant.

What was I supposed to do? Slap him around? Is that why they left us alone together? The tension between Blais and Hinberg could have deflected lightning. Blais, looking gaunt, tired, and put upon, scarcely glanced at Hinberg, who acted very much in charge and did most of the talking. Hinberg's most animated remark about the Meme was: The lack of knowledge about how long it takes the foam coating to completely decompose and the potential long-term effects of the resulting chemical mixture in the body are very worrisome.

During a lull in this high drama, I suggested to Blais and Hinberg that a group of researchers had detected 2-4 toluene diamine in the Meme. (I hadn't bothered to mention it to Johnson because it was outside his area of expertise.) Blais's eyes brightened; Hinberg appeared surprised and concerned. Was this a hopeful sign?

One would suppose that a government department, hearing that a carcinogen was detected in a popular implant, would immediately get to the heart of the matter. But this was the Health department.

A few weeks after my story on 2-4 toluene diamine was published (in the A-section) on January 29, 1989, I was pleased to receive a modest package of government documents related to the Meme. Included were some revealing briefing memos—the type of documents that members of the Cabinet rely on to answer questions from the Opposition or reporters. One briefing, dated January 29 and signed by Hinberg, indicated, that following my visit, his group ran a simple test on an intact Meme implant to check for any surface sign of 2-4 toluene diamine. "Very clever," I thought. They had not looked for the chemical in decomposing polyurethane, as they should have. So, not surprisingly, the result was negative. So what? The test had nothing to do with the potential of the polyurethane to break down in the body and release the chemical. But this near-useless test did provide the Health department, and Perrin Beatty, with a public-relations stunt to convince the public that the department was on the job.

The package of leaked documents was not all bad news, for stuffed in among the briefing notes was a report on the Meme penned by none other than one David Johnson. It described a meeting held on January 6, at which he and other scientists in the department had recommended that "distributors," namely

Laperrière, be asked to establish the safety and effectiveness of polyurethane implants. Federal regulations empower the Health department to make such demands when the situation warrants. The report concludes with this statement: "The group also recommended in the interim, distributors be asked to voluntarily stop sale of PU [polyurethane] coated breast implants."

This meeting had been billed as a "consensus conference" and included Blais and Hinberg among the eight participants. The group had reviewed the available information on the implants and agreed that action had to be taken.

Ah, but would management listen to its scientists? As we've seen, the Health department has a long history of ignoring scientific concerns detrimental to industry. So, not surprisingly, it was assistant deputy minister Albert Liston, self-declared champion of the "be nice to industry" approach, who rejected the consensus group's advice.

One internal memo showed that Liston—a manager rather than a working scientist for most of his thirty-odd years with the department—had claimed that there was insufficient reason to pull the Meme from the market. Instead, he wanted Réal Laperrière, Inc. to "voluntarily" submit proof that the implant was safe and effective.

Liston's move, however, smelled worse than a decaying corpse at an autopsy. By being true to his "hands-off" style, he was asking Laperrière to walk on water. Anyone bothering to review the available information on the Meme would have had to conclude that the company could not prove the implant safe and effective: the long list of appropriate studies that were part of a safety and efficacy review simply had not been done. This fact was out in the open—the consensus group had raised it. And that was why they recommended an interim ban.

So what? Who would ever find out what the department's scientists really thought?

Cover-Up

With David Johnson's report on the consensus conference staring me in the face, I interviewed him on the phone. I could hear him fiddling with his tape recorder as we dispensed with the preliminaries and got on to his group's recommendations for regulatory action.

Johnson seemed less cordial and more nervous than usual, perhaps because I had learned about the meeting. Why he lied to me was more puzzling.

He insisted that the scientists had asked only that the implant's manufacturer supply the bureau with documentation of the implant's safety and efficacy. "There were no stronger recommendations," he said. Wrong. But give him credit, he's consistent. Several weeks later, he told the same lie on the CBC-TV program *Marketplace*. The reporter, who also had obtained a copy of Johnson's report, asked him to read the recommendation that he was disavowing. Amazingly enough, he read it, looking very embarrassed. Damn good television!

The attempts to conceal the truth about the meeting didn't end with those two episodes. The office of Ernest Létourneau, Johnson's boss and head of the Bureau of Radiation and Medical Devices, had stamped "received" on a copy of Johnson's report. When I first interviewed Létourneau about the report, he said that he had only "vague recollections" the meeting had taken place. A few days later, presumably after refreshing his memory, he said: "Johnson is right. . . . Such a plea [to withdraw the Meme] was never made." He then suggested that his copy of Johnson's report was "an early version."

There were more shenanigans. Johnson and Hinberg did reconnaissance around Health department offices to locate all copies of the report. (The search-and-seizure mission was called a "memo recall.")

Why? Part of the answer arrived in the next package of documents I received.

Blais Takes a Stand

The late philosopher Alan Watts once wrote that people tend to suck their fingers rather than watch where they point. That's the image that came to mind of Liston, Johnson, Hinberg, and Létourneau as I read the most dramatic government memos I had ever laid eyes on. No kidding—more than a hundred pages and not a dull one among them. Covering a six-week period, beginning in late January 1989, they reveal how Pierre Blais tried to warn his bosses about the potential dangers of the Meme, and how they, in response, challenged his credibility.

On January 27, Blais warned Hinberg that the Meme was "unfit for human implantation and potentially hazardous to users" because, "in effect, the coating is a packaging material."

Three days later, Hinberg sent back a memo demanding further evidence. The next day, Blais informed Hinberg that he had run some tests on the Meme's foam and found it to be similar to a polyurethane packaging material. He concluded that "it is unquestioningly a packaging and general purpose foam" and appended two pages of more technical detail to the memo.

Bear in mind that, while this correspondence was shuttling back and forth, my story of 2-4 toluene diamine had been published and the Health department was telling the Canadian public that it was addressing the safety of the Meme. (Remember that PR test for surface 2-4 toluene diamine that Hinberg had his scientists run?)

While reading through the stack of memos, I naturally wondered if it was possible that Hinberg or some higher-level manager hadn't convened a scientific meeting on Blais's findings. Surely the very idea that an industrial packaging foam might be serving as the cover for a breast implant should command serious attention in the department. Silly me—I had been assuming that public safety was a priority.

In fact, it took two full weeks for Hinberg to do anything at all, and then he wrote Blais to ask for more information. This time, Hinberg wanted "all the evidence." And if he didn't receive it from Blais within a week, he would "take appropriate disciplinary action."

Blais was only down the hall. Hinberg could have dropped in to chat about his findings. But he obviously wasn't interested in findings—his memos were "for the record."

Blais was pretty good at memos for the record, too. On February 20, he wrote Hinberg. Included was this reminder:

In late January 1989, I reported to you that the prosthesis coating is made from a common class of commercial polyurethane foam available from various vendors for assorted consumer product applications. Industrial (nonspecific) applications of such foams allow broad compositional variations, elevated impurity levels and the incorporation of reactive intermediates of unknown biocompatibility. The safety, efficacy and quality assurance levels of a medical implant based on these foams therefore cannot be demonstrated without testing each implant.

The memo included the following: "I remain available at all times to discuss any area that may need clarification or elaboration."

A four-page, single-spaced technical report was attached.

But wait! What have we here? Someone is changing the scientific record for the government's record. It's David Johnson editing Blais's February 20 memo and appended report. One of his many deletions was Blais's reference to the consensus conference of January 6.

In a March 3 memo, Hinberg ordered Blais to accept Johnson's changes. On March 6, Blais wrote that he would comply with the order, but objected that "the contents of the original documents is significantly altered," citing the deletion of his references to the consensus conference, including the fact that the group recommended an interim ban of the Meme. These changes "of particular concern to me" were now in the record.

Finally, Hinberg's memo of March 9 ordered Blais to destroy all copies of his original February 20 memo and the appended report, as well as his memo of March 6.

On March 29, the day that my story outlining this rewrite of Meme history appeared in *The Gazette*, Liston signed a briefing intended for Beatty. It included the following description of Blais's February 20 memo: "The original memo did require significant alterations. It contained a collection of unsubstantiated personal opinion from a scientist, which would have been worthless and unacceptable unless supported by fact. Drs. Johnson and Hinberg rightly refused to accept this from Blais."

By this time, however, the Liberals and NDP were beginning to take a keen interest in the Meme. So were the media. The Health department had bungled the Meme file, and Beatty couldn't live on briefing notes alone. So what did the Health minister do? He appointed a plastic surgeon, who used the Meme in her own practice, to conduct an "independent" review of the Meme's safety. Meet—

Carolyn Kerrigan

After all of seven weeks on the job, Carolyn Kerrigan of the Royal Victoria Hospital in Montreal submitted her fifty-two-page report.

It was based on the opinions of Meme-using plastic surgeons and a review of poorly controlled studies, conducted mainly by plastic surgeons.

She spent at least $15,000 of our tax money to conclude that (a) there is no evidence that the Meme is unsafe, and (b) because scientific data on the Meme were inadequate, she couldn't pronounce it safe either. (Which, of course, is what Blais had been saying all along.) For example, Kerrigan reported that she wasn't certain if the polyurethane cover really broke down and if the implant placed women at higher risk for cancer.

To hire a plastic surgeon to go through this exercise was bad enough, but to trumpet her conclusions as a vindication of the Health department's behaviour was a gross disservice to Canadian women. Kerrigan concluded the department was "responding appropriately" to concerns raised about the Meme "through a continuing review of current uncertainties surrounding all types of breast implants."

Beatty praised Kerrigan's report, saying it put to rest concerns raised by the media. It didn't.

The Health department wielded the Meme report as a weapon to try to silence Pierre Blais. It didn't.

Neither did firing him.

The Health department's three-page dismissal letter, dated July 17, 1988, and signed by Liston, referred to his "unsuitability for employment in the Public Service." It cited him for being persistently at odds with the department's assessment of the Meme and for insubordination on three occasions, including his breach of Hinberg's orders to destroy memos, which he had kept on file in his office. It also claimed that Blais had, "on the balance of probability," leaked copies of these memos to the media.

Blais successfully appealed the Health department's charges and then negotiated a deal to resign. He didn't blow his severance flying south—he didn't even take a weekend off. Instead, he teamed up with Laval University's Robert Guidoin, a friend and sometimes research colleague, to focus on the Meme.

Guidoin had dismissed Kerrigan's report as "lacking depth" and "an embarrassment." Like Blais, he was itching to study the implant's make-up methodically.

The two chemists studied several samples of medically removed Memes and found that the polyurethane coverings had broken down extensively and pieces had become entangled with breast tissue. "I'm absolutely shocked at what we've seen here so far," Guidoin told me. "I had no idea that the quality of the foam material could be so poor."

By June 1990, Blais and Guidoin had completed studies of the polyurethane's breakdown chemicals. Using much milder methods to decompose the Meme's covering than those employed by Batish, they detected the presence of 2-4 toluene diamine.

The Federal Drug Administration

Late that month, I learned that FDA researchers were also turning up the chemical in their tests of the Meme. One of my contacts at the FDA said, "We've found preliminary evidence of TDA [2-4 toluene diamine] in the Meme's foam coating. We're finding what the Laval group is finding."

For several years, researchers at the FDA had been sharing their concerns about the Meme with Blais. They, too, were incredulous about the paucity of available research. Like Blais, they saw their bosses as inclined to protect the financial interests of manufacturers and doctors rather than the safety of patients. Indeed, for fifteen years, the safety concerns of the scientists were blocked by higher-level agency officials. The rift between scientists and managers at the FDA over breast implants was documented by a congressional committee, headed by the late Manhattan Democrat Ted Weiss.

In 1982, the FDA proposed that breast implants merely be categorized as having insufficient evidence to provide reasonable assurance of safety and efficacy. Even this timid move provoked strong lobbying by plastic surgeons: breast implants had become a cash cow for the cosmetically minded among them. The American Society of Plastic and Reconstructive Surgeons Inc., a lobbying group of several thousand doctors, even diagnosed small breasts as a "disease" in a memo to the FDA in the early 1980s.

The lobbyists must have had golden tongues—the FDA waited another six years before putting manufacturers of the implants on preliminary notice that they would be required to submit safety and efficacy data for review. By then, some two million American women had breast implants, and the breast-implant business was generating $400 million a year.

In June 1990, when I learned about the preliminary Meme tests at the FDA, the agency still had not finalized its ruling on safety reviews. My source said that, allowing for the usual FDA inertia, the day of reckoning was probably still six months to a year away. Once the ruling was published in the Federal Register, the companies would have time to prepare their test data for review. But if more elaborate FDA tests corroborated the initial detection of 2-4 toluene diamine in the implant's polyurethane cover—as everyone involved in the research expected—the FDA would be hard put to "keep an implant on the market with a carcinogen."

For all practical purposes, the Meme was dead foam. Even if the FDA agreed to review Surgitek's test data, the conclusion would be the same. "Given what we know about the Meme, it will be difficult to get it through our review," my source said. "It would take a miracle."

Because I deeply trusted my source, I went with the story.

It raised suspicions—and hackles—at the Health department, especially those of:

Margaret Catley-Carlson

On September 20, 1990, I met Margaret Catley-Carlson, the federal deputy Health minister, for the first time. She reminded me of Bette Midler. I almost expected her to break out in song. Also present for the interview in her large corner office were Albert Liston and Marcel Chartrand, head of media relations. The interview was taped, but no one sang. Instead, C.-C. badgered me about my source at the FDA. After all, if the FDA hadn't informed her people of any Meme tests or imminent action on the implant, then it simply wasn't true.

She was worried. This was good.

Now we all know that the information gathered in a large bureaucracy rises through several levels to the top. One way is via briefings, predigested synopses of events so bland that a minister questioned in the House can take one quick glance at the briefing and, by golly, there's an answer—of sorts.

Ask the Health Minister a question about the Meme and you'll get "Our scientists are studying the Meme." The minister may impart this information with confidence, even arrogance. (The briefing note may be referring to only two scientists, one with expertise in, say, medical test kits, and his relatively inexperienced assistant, but who would know?)

Or, you might get, with equal confidence, "We have no knowledge that the FDA has conducted Meme tests." (Of course, you don't, because your "scientists" don't have access to the inner workings of the FDA, or your managers are speaking to managers or scientists who also rely on briefings.)

I figured Bette Midler was badgering me about my source at the FDA because she was beginning to doubt the information flow in her department. (You'd be amazed at how little senior managers know about the goings-on in their own fiefdoms.) In this, at least, she had good instincts.

During the meeting, Liston mentioned that his "scientists" had conducted a study on the Meme's polyurethane covering. One was Irwin Hinberg, who excels in the study of medical test kits; the other was a subordinate, who had sometimes worked with Pierre Blais on an implant project, but who had neither

Blais's length nor his depth of experience.

Liston said that "the team" had found no sign of 2-4 toluene diamine. Catley-Carlson nodded in agreement. Now, it just so happened that I already knew the results of this study, and one thing was very clear: the scientists *had* detected signs of the chemical—not in all the test runs, but in enough to verify Batish's conclusion that an unstable polyurethane had been inexplicably and irresponsibly used to cover a breast implant.

Liston proved ill prepared to discuss the details of the study. The deputy was barely in the picture. How come senior managers in the Health department knew so little about the only Meme study their scientists had ever conducted? Simple. They hadn't been properly briefed.

Any briefing on the study probably would have originated with Hinberg. He would have commented on his own results and passed them up the ladder to his boss, Ernest Létourneau. Trained as a doctor, but no longer in practice, Létourneau would not have been the ideal reviewer of the study's chemistry or findings. Ditto for Liston and Catley-Carlson. (As we saw earlier, the level of technical competence at the Health department falls lower as you go up the ladder. It falls to zero when the Health minister delivers the usual filtered, rote response to a scientific question in the House.)

Not to worry, I'd go back to the bottom. I asked Liston to send me a copy of the study. He agreed.

A month later, he kept his promise. The study he sent matched the copy in my possession. But the study was now "public," so Hinberg was available for an interview.

He made two points: first, the Meme did release 2-4 toluene diamine under much milder laboratory conditions than those in the Batish study. Even these conditions, however, were not remotely related to those in the body. Second, an attempt to use body-like conditions to decompose the foam had failed.

So, don't worry. Be happy.

I ran through the Health department's test results with Batish. He said there was good reason to worry: "Their results under relatively mild conditions make me even more concerned about the long-term activity of the foam in the body."

Next I consulted Nir Kozzovsky, a pathologist and implant researcher at the University of California School of Medicine. He said: "The fact that the foam [breaks down] in relatively weak laboratory conditions when we compare the Canadian work with Batish's suggests to me that we should be seriously concerned about processes in the body that trigger production of chemicals that could break down foreign materials. There's plenty of reasons on principle to be concerned because the body's defence system triggers an extremely active biological factory to break down foreign materials, and don't forget, the Meme is being implanted supposedly for the long term."

Blais's take on the Health department's tests focused on the methods used to screen for 2-4 toluene diamine. He found that, in the test runs that approximated body conditions, the method of detection was too crude to pick up the chemical. "It could be there right in front of their noses, but they wouldn't pick it up," he said.

Scientists at the FDA who were conducting tests on the polyurethane would also find Hinberg's test methods, well, unusual.

Count Down

Here are the key events that led to the suspension of sale of the Meme by Bristol-Myers Squibb on April 17, 1991:

On March 26, a report from FDA scientists was made available to the agency's Toxicology Risk Assessment Committee. The report showed that decomposition of the Meme's polyurethane cover under body-like conditions led to the release of 2-4 toluene diamine. This information was leaked to me and published on April 10, the day before the committee was set to meet to begin its assessment of the Meme's cancer risk. That day, too, the FDA was to announce, at long last, that makers of any silicone-gel breast implants would have ninety days either to demonstrate that their products were safe or to remove them from the market.

The morning of the story's publication I received calls from two people who had read it, in Washington, a city where *The Gazette* is not a big seller. Each caller introduced himself as a public-relations specialist and attempted to coax me to divulge the name of my source. One caller was particularly aggressive.

The next day, I learned that the story had created quite a stir at the FDA committee meeting. The agency vowed to plug the leak. There was also serious talk that the FBI might tap certain telephones. My source and I worked out a contingency strategy that involved telephone booths.

But the biggest surprise was that Hinberg had showed up at the meeting at the Health department's request, to present Canada's official test data on the Meme. Suffice it to say that FDA scientists did not admire the study's methodology, and had difficulty understanding why tests were run with so little sensitivity to detect 2-4 toluene diamine. Even the committee noted that the Canadian analytical methods were significantly less sensitive than those of the FDA.

On Sunday, April 14, *The New York Times* caught up with the Meme story and weighed in with a strong piece on the implant's potential cancer risk. Citing sources close to the FDA study, the *Times* reported that, on the basis of preliminary calculations, the implant might cause cancer at the annual rate of two hundred to four hundred cases for every million users.

The story set off widespread speculation. Cancer-risk assessment depends on what you put in the formula. For example, if it dissolved completely within, say, five years, polyurethane would likely be a higher risk to the user than if it decomposed at a rate of 5 to 10 per cent over ten years. The FDA data suggested that decomposition of polyurethane under certain conditions might be completed within a five-year period, although this was far from certain.

According to my FDA source, the odds looked worse for women if the results of those early rat studies of the 1960s and 1970s were factored into the risk formula; but some committee members were reluctant to consider such old data.

For example, one study, published by John Autian in 1975 in the *Journal of Cancer Research*, was thought to be highly relevant by some FDA scientists. Autian, a toxicologist then at the University of Tennessee, implanted different polyurethanes in rats and reported that some behaved like "chemical carcinogens." The FDA scientists took these results into consideration in estimating the potential risk to be four hundred in one million.

I called Autian, now a private consultant, to gauge his reaction to the cancer-risk controversy. He hadn't seen the FDA report, but was amazed that anyone could be so stupid as to implant such a polyurethane in a human being, especially for the long term.

By the way, the Health department's crack toxicologist, Geoff Granville, had never heard of Autian's study, so I gave him the journal reference. However, he had calculated the Meme's cancer risk on the basis of Canada's official Meme study: it was negligible.

In April 1991, the Health department had been aware for at least one month of pioneering Meme research conducted by a three-member team at Foothills Hospital in Calgary. The researchers had detected the presence of the biological products of 2-4 toluene diamine—products related to the breakdown of the Meme's cover—in the urine of a forty-one-year-old Meme recipient. Rather than help the Calgarians do more research, the department waited for Surgitek to run comparable studies. So, for all practical purposes, the Calgary study was ignored, even though it was the only one of its kind.

As for Pierre Blais, he was concerned that risk assessment was not focusing on the potential of breast tissue absorbing large doses of 2-4 toluene diamine. The cancer risk, based on his calculations, might be between one in fifty and one in two hundred. At least FDA scientists involved in the Meme study agreed.

Surgitek crunched the numbers too, but somehow calculated that the numbers of cancers would be one in several million implants. The company's research consisted of studying ten implants that had been removed. Upon examination, their "structural integrity" was intact. Some of the cover had dissolved in the body, but the process had been very slow. As you can see, the assessment of cancer risk is more art—and perhaps the art of the possible—than science.

But on April 17, Bristol-Myers Squibb cited "unsubstantiated but widespread media reports" and halted shipments of the Meme, the leader among breast implants. The Meme had captured about 25 per cent of what was becoming an annual market of up to 150,000 implantations. Some 200,000 women, including about 15,000 Canadians, were already walking around with the polyurethane-covered implants.

On that day, some six years after concerns about the Meme were first raised in Canada, the Health department issued a release, asking doctors to cease using the product.

After thirty months on the story, I felt pretty damn good. For a while. The science history of the Meme told a chilling story of corporate irresponsibility. It wasn't time to cheer yet.

Cut and Paste

Think of a breast-implant manufacturing plant where there are inadequate safeguards to ensure sterility. Where there is no record-keeping of the raw materials used in breast implants. Where there are no records to indicate that implants are manufactured to established specifications. And where not all employees are properly trained. Welcome to the place where the Meme was made.

On July 11, 1988, FDA inspectors visited the Meme plant in Paso Robles, California. During the next sixteen days, they turned up these and other serious violations of the Federal Food, Drug and Cosmetic Act. Several months later, in March 1989, the FDA finally got around to warning Surgitek to clean up the place.

This was the least of Surgitek's problems. After acquiring the Meme from Cooper Surgical in December 1988, Surgitek had agreed to submit its safety and efficacy data on the Meme to the Health department. The first of several submissions arrived on April 4; by June, a review of the materials revealed huge gaps in the data. Crucial information was missing on, among other things, the short- and long-term effects of the polyurethane cover. Surgitek did not submit adequate data on how long the cover stays attached to the implant or remains intact in the body. Nor did the company provide adequate details on the chemicals in the polyurethane.

Speaking of chemicals, documents made available to me showed that Cooper Surgical, which took over the Meme from Natural-Y in 1987, learned that 2-4 toluene diamine could be released from the polyurethane only after Batish conducted his first tests, for a lawyer. The lawsuit heard in Florida in late 1987 spurred Cooper Surgical to ask for details on the polyurethane from its manufacturer, Scotfoam Corporation of Eddystone, Pennsylvania.

Tom Powell, a Cooper Surgical vice-president, called Ed Griffiths, manager of product control at Scotfoam, and asked if the cover could release 2-4 toluene diamine.

Yes, it could, Griffiths replied.

When I phoned in June 1991, Griffiths told me that he was surprised to learn from Powell that the polyurethane in question—which was used in oil filters, furniture, and carburetors—was being used in a breast implant. "They [referring to Natural-Y and Cooper Surgical] had been using our foam for many years and it was the first time that I or anyone else at the company had heard about it," he claimed.

While Scotfoam had conducted basic tests to show the polyurethane could release small amounts of 2-4 toluene diamine, the company had no data on the suitability of the product for long-term use in a breast implant or its relationship to "health effects."

In a series of letters exchanged between the two companies, dated from January 11 to August 3, 1988, Cooper Surgical indicated its desire to conduct basic studies on the polyurethane, which would characterize its chemical stability. To that end, Scotfoam agreed to provide Cooper Surgical with the polyurethane's ingredient list.

It all sounds very agreeable until you realize that women in Canada and the United States had implants inserted before its manufacturer knew its chemical composition. Without that knowledge Cooper could not possibly have conducted appropriate safety and efficacy studies.

When Bristol-Myers Squibb suspended sale of the Meme in April 1991, their studies of the polyurethane cover were barely under way. The studies of other breast implants were no farther along, as the Health department and FDA would soon discover.

By mid-summer 1991, the makers of breast implants had provided the FDA with most of their test data. There was so little of scientific value that some manufacturers were told that they didn't even have enough clinical data to qualify for a formal review. Surgitek was among the companies that didn't make the cut. A month later, on September 23, its parent company, Bristol-Myers Squibb, announced that it was getting out of the breast-implant business.

The following November, the FDA advisory panel on breast implants concluded that there was insufficient evidence to determine whether the products were safe. The panel, however, recommended continued sale of breast implants, claiming that they were an urgent health need for some women, particularly those cancer patients who wanted breast implants as an option for breast reconstruction after breast surgery. But there were conditions: Surgeons should obtain proper informed consent from their patients; companies were to submit more safety data on a strict timetable; and the government was to establish a national implant registry.

On January 6, 1992, David Kessler, the FDA commissioner, bypassed the panel's recommendations and called for a moratorium on breast implants. He had received information that raised further questions about the safety of the products, including additional evidence that they could possibly cause autoimmune or connective-tissue disorders. The main source of the concern consisted of internal memos from Dow Corning, the world's largest maker of silicone and silicone implants, which detailed staff warnings of potential side-effects. This information, going back to the 1970s, had been sealed in a lawsuit against the company and withheld from the FDA panel. Kessler was not pleased.

Two days later, on January 8, Benoît Bouchard, Canada's latest Health minister, announced a made-in-Canada moratorium. Bouchard gave the impression that the delay was caused by the department's own experts reaching their very own decision based on the available facts. Underscore the word "available" because Kessler had not shared the new information he had received.

In the United States, the FDA advisory panel was reconvened on February 18 to study Kessler's expanded file on breast implants and recommended limiting their use to women with cancer who required breast reconstruction and to select clinical tests.

It was almost twelve years to the day that my first documentary on breast implants aired, and the science behind the products was still in the Stone Age: There were scant data on the risks related to the implants, including cancer and autoimmune disease. There was little understanding of how the body's immune system reacts to silicone and the implants. There were few controlled studies.

More disturbing, the attitude of plastic surgeons hadn't changed much either. As a group, they showed little remorse. Instead they were whining about lost opportunities—for themselves and their patients. American plastic surgeons contributed $3.88 million to a large newspaper-ad campaign to protest what they still call a loss of choice for women. For thirty years, the American Society of Plastic and Reconstructive Surgeons Inc., has consistently downplayed published warnings about breast implants. Any library has scores of case reports and editorials that speak to the problems. Pity the doctors didn't bother to do their homework, for once the FDA awakened from its long sleep, Kessler issued guidelines to doctors on how to inform their patients of the benefits and risks of the surgery.

Jacques Papillon, the plastic surgeon who urged me back in November 1988 to investigate the Meme, surprised me by using the product and becoming one of its staunch defenders. He had privately chastised me and publicly denounced *The Gazette* for frightening women needlessly. And I would respond that my only alternative is to watch plastic surgeons ignore science and mislead women.

The Health department has certainly taken its lumps for its handling of the "Meme file," as Catley-Carlson referred to it, and breast implants in general. Politicians such as Joy Langan, Sheila Copps, and Beryl Gaffney have hammered away at the department.

It's clear to me that the Health department's actions reflected many things. One is a strong tendency in Canada and elsewhere to tip towards industry, rather than the public, in policy formulation. Some of this has much to do with the lack of technical expertise at top levels of management. The policy makers, who form friendly ties with industry, become slow to react to the concerns of scientists. In the march on deregulation, individuals like Pierre Blais, who make waves in the bureaucracy, are written off as "troublemakers." Catley-Carlson saw Blais as a throwback to a reformist era that was no longer viable in the modern world.

In my interview with Catley-Carlson and Liston in 1990, she was concerned that I was chasing theories of payoffs and conspiracies. She had heard rumours to that effect and must have known that the NDP and Liberals were snooping, too. I told her that I was checking things out. Sensing her unease that she might not have the opportunity to comment fully if I came up with some harebrained story involving her team or the Tories, I promised her that if I ever reached publishable conclusions, I would seek her out and divulge my information.

I still consider the "Meme file" open. And I do keep my promises.

In the meantime, I would tell her that the saga of the Meme boils down to more important things: It's about science gone awry, government negligence, medical stupidity, shattered faith, and increasingly—given the number of lawsuits being filed—the fierce determination of women to hold all the key players accountable.

The Last Word

The Health department still won't talk to me.

As you will recall, it accepted the word of the Meme's distributor in 1985 that the Meme was one of a line of implants available in Canada prior to the 1982 legislation; it was therefore an "old" implant, and exempt from government checks on safety and efficacy.

I learned that in November 1988, when David Johnson was inquiring about the implant's legal status. During the next many months I delved into the science surrounding the Meme, and found time to refocus my attention on the legal issue only in October 1991. The stimulus was a letter from Liston in response to questions I had raised during my meeting with him and Catley-Carlson.

I had specifically asked Liston to document how the Meme had received an exemption from the 1982 legislation. He wrote back that his staff had "verified that the Meme in its present form has been sold in Canada since 1982."

Checking through U.S. court depositions paid off. The record showed that the Meme was a spin-off of the Natural-Y, the implant that had been available early on in Canada. But the Meme was certainly different. While the Natural-Y was designed in 1969 primarily for use in breast reconstruction following cancer surgery, the Meme had a different design and was intended for cosmetic purposes. But U.S. court records show that Natural-Y Surgical Specialties Inc. sponsored the design of the Meme in 1981 and tests on some women in 1982. A concerted effort to sell the implant began in 1983.

I rang up the Health department's Meme spokesman, Marcel Chartrand. Could he please supply evidence, such as a bill of sale, that proved the Meme was sold in Canada as early as 1982, as Liston had claimed. Chartrand said he would try, which he did. He could find proof of sale only for the Natural-Y.

Could an error have been made by the Health department? Did it permit a "new" implant to be sold without the required safety review? Perhaps the Meme had not been sold in Canada until 1983, or later.

Yes, an error appears to have been made, Chartrand said.

All hell broke loose at the Health department after my story ran on August 17, 1991. According to my sources, Chartrand came close to being fired by a hot-under-the-collar Health minister. It was this event that led Benoît Bouchard to bar me from interviewing any of the department's employees.

In an effort to clear his department's name, Bouchard set up an internal review followed by an external audit of how the Meme file had been administered. They both show that the Health department erred in exempting the Meme on the grounds that it was essentially the same as the Natural-Y. But both reports present a neat twist on when the Meme was actually "sold" in Canada. It has to do with how the term "sell" is defined by the Food and Drugs Act, which governs the medical-devices regulations. The definition of "sell" includes "exposed for sale." The Meme was advertised in a U.S. journal in September and October 1982. This is taken by the Health department to mean the Meme had been sold in Canada prior to the new legislation.

A legal opinion commissioned by the firm conducting the external audit suggests that the courts mightn't see it quite that way.

7

TOO GOOD TO BE TRUE:

Migraine Headaches and Imitrex

THE THICK PRESS PACKAGE FROM GLAXO CANADA INC. arrived by messenger and then sat for several days. Curiosity didn't get the better of me, but I'm reluctant to trash PR without giving it a once-over before it sails into the blue recycling bin strategically positioned at my desk in the *Gazette* newsroom.

Occasionally, a drug company's pitch speaks to my personal interests and fears. (As I'm in my forties, materials on, say, prostate problems or heart attack command some passing respect.) Mostly, though, PR hype is so shamelessly contrived that a week's supply can be recycled in five minutes flat.

The materials from Glaxo, dated February 25, 1992, announced the availability of Imitrex, a new drug to fight migraines in injectable or tablet form. Now I sometimes suffer a bout of so-called common migraine. One side of my head throbs and pounds. Then come the waves of nausea. But I'm spared the visual disturbances, such as the flashing lights, that some people endure. And my migraines last only a few hours, not days.

Migraine triggers vary from person to person. They include food (particularly chocolate, caffeine, and aged cheese), hormonal changes, stress, bright sunlight, and lack of sleep. All told, migraines claim 5 to 10 per cent of the population. And although migraines have been fought with everything from aspirin to fungus extracts to beta-blockers, patients often experience excessive side-effects and inadequate relief.

Glaxo was coming to the rescue.

Call me a cynic, but I assume that a manufacturer will highlight a drug's good points and downplay its weaknesses, namely the side-effects. Glaxo's pitch for Imitrex made me do a triple take. Months later, I would fondly recall the auspicious moment when Glaxo included me in its PR plans.

Most PR packages touting a new drug have endorsements from doctors in some financial relationship with the drug company. Usually they conduct some of the research on the drug, and then become part of the company's stable of experts or "product champions."

Jacques Meloche, a neurologist and director of the Montreal Migraine Clinic, championed Imitrex in promotional literature. He was quoted in Glaxo's press package as saying: "It's very effective, easy-to-take and remarkably free of side effects, so people can use it any time during a migraine attack and carry on with their routine activities. It represents an important improvement over any migraine therapy available up to now."

Meloche's comment irritated me. Anyone with a modest knowledge of pharmacology and drug development knows that a convincing profile of a drug's side-effects requires years to complete. Early testing is usually confined to carefully selected groups of individuals most likely to benefit from the drug. As the drug is given to a more diverse patient population, side-effects often become more apparent and numerous. So why had Meloche been willing to jump the gun on Imitrex?

The polite answer is that doctors are like everyone else: they need financial security, and pine to be recognized as experts. Or they are easily manipulated by skilled entrepreneurs. Take your pick.

Meloche was not the only doctor to heap praise on Imitrex. Canadian Press covered Glaxo's Toronto press conference on the new drug. The story was carried in *The Ottawa Citizen* on February 26, the day after Glaxo went public with Imitrex. The headline read: DRUG OFFERS SHOT OF RELIEF FROM MIGRAINES. Okay, fine. The reporter then quoted Robert Nelson, head of neurology at Ottawa General Hospital: "[Imitrex] provides a vast improvement over any migraine therapy available up to now." The report then continued: "Nelson and other doctors at the press conference said they were enthusiastic about the drug because it was remarkably free of side-effects, such as nausea, vomiting, sedation and risk of addiction." The reporter even quoted a user of the drug. She said it was "simply terrific."

If you suffer from migraine headaches, how would you have reacted to this story? Probably with fierce determination to get your hands on Imitrex. Had the story described the rather unusual circumstances in which Health and Welfare Canada approved the drug for sale, it might have made you think again. Had the story documented that Glaxo may well be understating the potential negative impact of this drug on heart vessels, you would have cancelled that call to your doctor.

Granted, I'm getting a little ahead of the Imitrex saga here, but it's to show that a huge divide exists between a "report" on a new drug that amounts to PR and an in-depth look at the facts. All too often, however, PR prevails, and the consumer is the loser.

A Drug that Hits Only Targeted Blood Vessels in the Head?

In choosing my stories for *The Gazette*, I apply two simple rules: a story should have relevance to many readers and it should reveal valuable information to which they do not have easy access. The ways Glaxo appeared to be downplaying side-effects associated with Imitrex might have been such a story, but what fired up my interest was Glaxo's claim that Imitrex "works only on the painfully swollen blood vessels in the head." Though the exact cause of migraine is not clear, these blood vessels certainly swell during the course of the headache. Glaxo was claiming that Imitrex reduced symptoms by constricting these vessels. The company was even apparently convinced that the drug stimulated the "5-HT(1)" receptors found on the nerve cells of these vessels.

It sounded good, but it was "works only" that set off the alarm. It suggests a clear path to the target. It also implies that, by not affecting other parts of the body, Imitrex is likely to cause fewer disturbances than a more general drug.

"Hmmm," I thought. Several scientists whom I consulted also were sceptical. In drug development, there is a strong reliance on test-tube science and animal experiments, but very few life processes are as exact as laboratory science seems to indicate.

Glaxo Canada Inc. is a subsidiary of Glaxo Holdings of Great Britain. It is number two in international pharmaceutical sales volume and the thirteenth-largest public company in the world. It is a conglomerate that conducts research, and develops, manufactures, and markets prescription drugs for the treatment of everything from asthma and ulcers to heart disorders and infections. When such a powerhouse announces that it has put twenty years of research into a new migraine drug it will reassure most sufferers, doctors, scientists, and journalists.

And we sceptics? How do we take on Goliath? Uncovering solid information and making it public tends to level the playing field. Well-placed sources in the drug industry, the scientific community, and government sometimes help me bring drug giants down to my level, but this takes time and patience. The flow of information is usually slow and irregular, as it was with Imitrex.

One of my sources of information on Imitrex was familiar with Glaxo-sponsored studies on the drug, and was concerned that the scientific evidence backing the company's claim that the drug acted only on vessels in the head didn't stand up.

Evidence from laboratory research and the monitoring of people undergoing a common heart test showed that the drug could cause temporary spasms, and therefore possible harm, in heart vessels. Yet the company cited evidence from its pre-market clinical tests showing that Imitrex did not affect heart vessels. Perhaps, but these test patients did not have histories of cardiovascular disease or stroke. Given that this drug was being aimed at millions of diverse people, you'd expect the company would issue strong warnings about the potential of Imitrex to cause unwanted sideeffects in people who have some cardiovascular dysfunction, particularly those in mid-life. Glaxo's prescribing instructions on Imitrex notified doctors that the drug should not be given to patients with certain heart conditions, but didn't bother to warn about heart conditions in its ads and media hype, where such information would be most useful.

Research suggested that the marketed dosage of six milligrams of injectable Imitrex was too high for every patient. After walking through the Glaxo-sponsored controlled studies measuring the effects of various dosages of the drug, I grasped the point. An injection of three milligrams banished migraines in about 60 per cent of patients; the six-milligram dosage was effective in about 80 per cent of patients—as good as Imitrex gets. (There was very little additional benefit from an eight-milligram dosage.) Why, then, market only a six-milligram dosage? Isn't it standard medical practice to tailor dosage to a person's needs? After all, more than half the patients do just as well with half that dosage.

There was a particular reason to be concerned. Glaxo-sponsored research on the tablet form of Imitrex shows that subjects were placed at higher risk for side-effects—such as tingling and feelings of pressure and warmth—as the dosage is increased beyond the marketed dosage of 100 milligrams. In other words, the higher the dosage, the greater likelihood of side-effects.

In May 1992, I had enough information to ask Glaxo some pointed questions. Drug-company officials usually appear wary of reporters, concerned that the press will "sensationalize" problems associated with a drug and "needlessly worry" all those patients benefiting from their product. Sure, sure.

Most drug companies also require that reporters first contact their Corporate Affairs folks, so they can tease out the reporter's intentions. I just explain flat out what I'm looking for. Reactions to my direct approach differ, of course. Sometimes the phone lines freeze over, or there is a pregnant pause, followed by a cheerful "let's humour him" voice. On rare occasions, there is a real human being who behaves professionally and understands that the press has its job to do.

More often than not, an interview is granted, provided I present my questions in advance. This, I'm told, enables the company to be sure it will have properly researched answers to my questions. Unlike Health and Welfare, which continues to communicate with me by fax machine, drug companies usually have sufficient confidence in their officials to allow them to return phone calls and engage in a discussion or, at the very least, read a prepared statement and answer questions.

The day of my first contact with Glaxo Canada in regard to Imitrex, I was in a rush and decided to contact directly Grahaem Brown, vice-president of the Medical Sciences Division. Sometimes passing the PR office bears fruit, but not this time. Brown wasn't in. I left my name and number.

Brown didn't call. Michael Levy did. He is Glaxo's director of Clinical Research and Biostatistics. What was so special about Imitrex? Following the company line that the drug acts effectively on blood vessels in the head, he extolled its wonders: "The magic of this drug is that it's so specific." Could it perhaps constrict heart vessels in some cases as well? Absolutely not. So why warn doctors to avoid prescribing Imitrex for people with heart problems? "We do this because we have no test data on patients with these conditions," he replied, his tone suggesting that the company was merely tying up loose ends.

Levy was equally matter-of-fact when I questioned the six-milligram dosage of injectable Imitrex. "Imitrex administered in six milligrams has a huge safety margin," he said, adding that the dosage was based on numerous studies. He appeared reluctant to discuss the matter further.

"I'm sure I'll be talking to you again," I told Levy.

I was wrong. Brown returned the next call, which was made under very different circumstances.

A Warning from Britain

Glaxo had launched Imitrex in Britain in September 1991. Before long, the drug (named Imigran in Europe and the U.K.) was averaging 15,000 prescriptions per month.

On May 30, 1992, the *British Medical Journal* published a highly detailed letter from a group of doctors concerning a forty-seven-year-old man who showed signs on an electrocardiogram that an injection of Imigran (Imitrex) was affecting his heart vessels.

Back in May 1991, the man was admitted to hospital after suffering intermittent chest pain for about five months while on two older drug treatments for migraine. He was sent home after a physical exam, a series of electrocardiograms, and laboratory tests proved normal.

Seven months later, on December 15, he was readmitted, complaining again of chest pain. For ten days prior to his admission, he had experienced cluster headaches and felt no relief from his drugs. On December 11, he had been additionally prescribed Imigran (Imitrex), which he injected himself. He developed severe chest pain within minutes. His hospital tests proved normal.

His doctors tried an experiment. The man was given an injection of Imigran (Imitrex) while hooked up to an electrocardiogram. Four minutes later, he developed chest pain; two minutes after that, the machine indicated that his heart vessels were constricting. A laboratory test of cardiac enzymes—proteins that regulate the rate of chemical reaction in the heart—also detected some irregularities.

Twenty-two minutes after the injection, the pain had subsided and the electrocardiogram returned to normal. The enzyme levels were also normal again, indicating that no muscle cells had died. The doctors concluded that injectable Imigran (Imitrex) can cause at least a temporary heart-vessel spasm.

In June 1992, the U.K. Committee on Safety of Medicines, Britain's drug regulatory group, reported in *Current Problems*, its occasional newsletter, that Imigran (Imitrex) was possibly dangerous in patients with certain heart conditions because it might cause constriction of the heart vessels.

The committee had received thirty-four reports of patients who suffered pain or tightness in the chest after injection. In some patients, the chest pain was severe. Five patients developed similar reactions after being prescribed another injection of Imigran (Imitrex). However, the committee had no knowledge of whether any of the reported chest pain originated in heart vessels.

Meanwhile, back in Canada, I had learned that not everyone in the Health department was happy to see Imitrex approved. Questions about the drug's dosage and its effect on heart vessels had not been answered to the satisfaction of all. But no one would go public on this—yet—and I needed to get my hands on government documents that would tell the inside story.

This is where patience comes in. You can't force people to send you materials in brown envelopes before they are psychologically ready or morally committed to do so. Sometimes this day never comes; sometimes a source becomes privy to some other violation of public trust and suddenly comes across with the necessary documents. In the meantime, patience.

After reading the reports from Britain, I asked Health and Welfare for a rundown of problem reports it had received on Imitrex. I did this knowing full well that the voluntary reporting system of drug side-effects is so poorly organized that anything the government gets its hands on is serendipitous and a mere fragment of what is occurring. I suppose an inadequate program is better than none, so I telephoned Carole Peacock at the Health department and, as usual, dictated my questions into her tape recorder.

This time it took less than a week for a response (by fax). The department stated that fifty-two cases of side-effects associated with Imitrex had been reported for the first half of the year. Of those, thirty-seven were related to the injection form of the drug; some of those had to do with chest pain.

The rest of the information was typical. The Health department said it was discussing reports with Glaxo and with regulatory agencies in other countries. Very enlightening. The department downplayed the significance of reported side-effects. You see, based on Glaxo sales for the six-month period, the rate of side-effects was far below that listed in the company's prescribing instructions to doctors.

Now this assessment might well impress a product champion, but only because it wrongly assumes that the number of voluntary reports corresponds to reality. And to think it is this government bureaucracy we depend on to make intelligent policy decisions, such as the proper risk-benefit assessment of prescription drugs.

The fax did provide some heady advice for the consumer in the face of concerns raised in Britain about Imitrex: "Health and Welfare advises consumers that they should carefully read the literature that is supplied with this product [Imitrex]."

"Tell that to Robert Kaspy," I thought.

Robert Kaspy

In March 1992, thirty-five-year-old Robert Kaspy, a Montreal systems analyst, decided to have an Imitrex injection. He had studied Glaxo's information sheet for patients, in which he read that the drug could produce some mild side-effects, such as wheeziness; tightness in the chest, swelling of eyelids, face, or lips; skin rash; and lumps and hives. None appeared serious. He did note, however, that Glaxo warns patients to report chest pains and other side-effects to their doctors. Kaspy was concerned; he checked further on side-effects by phoning Glaxo representatives. He felt assured by what he read and heard: the drug produced only mild unwanted reactions, and only in a small number of people.

Kaspy asked his doctor to inject him. Within minutes, he experienced a crushing sensation in his chest and felt that he was choking. Chest, abdominal, and joint pain, and breathing problems, led to his hospitalization for one night. After one week of recuperation at home, he had no further symptoms. He vowed never to take the drug again, no matter how much pain he suffered from migraines.

Kaspy phoned me at *The Gazette* with the idea of making his case public. He wanted other potential users of Imitrex to know that serious side-effects could occur. He didn't trust Glaxo to spread the word, so we did. But not before checking back with the company.

I was curious to see how Glaxo's Michael Levy would explain the new evidence that Imitrex could affect heart vessels, but, alas, he was on vacation. Corporate Affairs told me that Grahaem Brown would call from Britain, where he was attending Glaxo meetings. And yes, I agreed to provide some questions in advance so that Brown could do any necessary research. For example, I told Corporate Affairs that the case report in the *British Medical Journal* would come up during the interview.

Brown quickly conceded that Imitrex could affect heart vessels. "We have to assume that 5-HT(1) receptors exist elsewhere in the body," he said. And yes, "the effect of the drug is not quite as specific as we had originally hoped. This new information came out of clinical experience."

Could the severe chest pain being reported originate in heart vessels? Not necessarily, Brown replied. Then where? He didn't know—maybe the oesophagus or chest muscles. Glaxo was looking into it.

Given this uncertainty, did the company plan to make any changes in the way Imitrex is marketed to doctors?

That would be determined with regulatory bodies, Brown replied.

Well, well, that's definitely not a yes and it's definitely not a no. Something may be brewing.

In September 1992, I received a fax from Health and Welfare in reply to several questions, including one that boiled down to: "What is the department doing about Imitrex?" I can't say that I was surprised to learn that Glaxo's prescribing instructions to doctors and its patient-information package insert were being revised. The new versions would inform doctors, pharmacists, and patients that severe chest pain associated with the use of Imitrex may occur. Doctors would be advised to take a careful medical history before prescribing Imitrex in order to exclude pre-existing cardiovascular disease. According to the department, a company letter to doctors and pharmacists would also accompany the new instructions.

The fax also informed me that, since June 30, twenty-two additional cases of side-effects associated with Imitrex had been reported: seven were related to "chest symptoms"; one was reported as "chest pain."

Back in Britain there was more news in September. A group of doctors reported in the *British Medical Journal* two cases of irregular beating of the heart soon after an injection of the drug. Another letter reported that of 1,881 patients followed up in an Imigran (Imitrex) study, the most common side-effects included chest tightness and discomfort, palpitations, and an "alarming" sense of impending doom. In 25 of the patients, the common factor had been chest tightness, from mild to "severe and terrifying." An "unprecedented" 2.2 per cent incidence of "nontrivial" reports of side-effects associated with Imigran (Imitrex) in the study group had led the study's director, Bill Inman, an expert in tracking drug side-effects, to warn doctors to be more cautious about prescribing the drug.

Inman told me that it would be impractical to monitor all patients on an electrocardiogram while they had their first injection of Imigran (Imitrex): but he "would certainly recommend it for patients who are suspected of having some heart disease."

Inman's study also included two reports of spasms of the bronchial tubes associated with Imigran (Imitrex). Inman said he "would be reluctant to prescribe Imitrex to asthmatics." Asthma constricts bronchial tubes and dams up the normal flow of air, sometimes causing death.

In reply to this latest round of reports of side-effects, Glaxo of Britain referred to the cases of irregular beating of the heart reported in the *British Medical Journal* as rare events, but said it would adjust its prescribing information to doctors accordingly. The company, however, downplayed Inman's concerns, contending that chest tightness may have been misinterpreted as being a sign of asthma.

Patience Pays Off

In late November, I finally had in my possession the complete set of documents that showed how Health and Welfare had approved Imitrex. In a word, the department rushed the drug through the review process despite strong warnings from its senior medical expert. A mere five days before this approval, Glaxo announced that it would construct a $70 million manufacturing facility in Canada and boost its research spending. For about a month prior to Imitrex's approval, Michelle Brill-Edwards, a medical doctor and then assistant director of the Bureau of Human Prescription Drugs, tried without success to convince her non-medical superiors that Glaxo's data on the drug was inadequate for approval. She was concerned that her superiors were about to approve the drug for the Canadian market, although the company had not documented its case that Imitrex would act only on blood vessels in the head. And she was dismayed at insufficient explanation of Glaxo's selection of a six-milligram dosage for the injectable form of the drug.

The documents also reveal that Glaxo Canada put pressure on Brill-Edwards and telephoned other employees in the hope of quickening Imitrex's approval. In a memo, dated December 20, 1991, sent by Brill-Edwards to Peter Jeffs, the bureau's assistant director of operations, she indicates that her suspicions about Imitrex have been aroused by the pressure put on one of her reviewers and other employees: She will consider the Glaxo submission herself. A request the previous day from her boss, Claire Franklin, for quick comment on the Imitrex file also had troubled her. Why the rush? In her reply to Franklin, also dated December 20, she writes: "Given the timing of your written note, it is my understanding that you consider even a few hours to review a new active substance which represents the first in its class to be an excessive time frame. Clearly this is unacceptable." As for the file itself, she writes that it "does not demonstrate evidence of adequate evaluation. No evaluation reports from the preclinical or clinical perspective are available on the file. The report of an outside consultant on cardiovascular safety issues is less than two paragraphs. There is no evidence on this file of adequate review."

Three days later, Brill-Edwards wrote a memo for the Imitrex file (no. 9427-G0003-149), indicating that she had returned Glaxo's submission to the reviewing unit "for further evaluation." She asked that attention focus on the company's inadequate information about the medical conditions for which Imitrex may be used, the drug's dosages, and warnings about heart side-effects. She notes that the "deficiencies are substantial. Progress [in approving the drug] at present is impeded by lack of available information regarding prior evaluation."

On January 6, Brill-Edwards wrote to Franklin, obviously worried that her concerns were not being heeded. She informed her boss, who is an expert in pesticides but not drugs, that the reviewing team had not discussed the file with her. As she had no line authority "to require attention to full resolution of deficiencies in the clinical evaluation of this submission, the matter is left under your responsibility."

The next day, Brill-Edwards received the file back from the

reviewing group and informed Franklin by memo that it was "a less-than-adequate response to the concerns" that she had raised. She also recommended to Franklin that the reviewing group "be required to remedy the deficiencies. . . . This action should be undertaken notwithstanding substantial pressure to the contrary from the manufacturer."

On January 15, Franklin sent a memo to Brill-Edwards advising her that the drug was about to be approved. In reply, Brill-Edwards urged Franklin to reconsider current drug-review practices, as exemplified by the Imitrex file. She added: "In my judgement, our methodology and organizational structure at present do not afford sufficient assurance of effective evaluation of new drugs prior to marketing for prescription use. Neither the Minister nor the Canadian public are well-served by inappropriate or inadequate application of expertise in the evaluation of new drugs. A discussion of this issue with you and senior officials of the Branch is required."

And what did Glaxo have to say about the concerns raised by Brill-Edwards when I telephoned to ask? Only the following: "Glaxo Canada follows the rules and regulations regarding applications and submissions for the approval of new prescription drugs. It is normal in the process to receive followup questions from the Health Protection Branch. We respond to those questions from the HPB and willingly provide the information for the Branch to make its decision."

Health minister Benoît Bouchard's response to my story on Imitrex in *The Gazette* on December 1, 1992, amounted to a rerun of his public stance on the Meme breast implant. He told the Commons that the side-effects of Imitrex were well known when the drug went on sale in Canada and were described in the manufacturer's directions for use. He either didn't read his cue cards correctly or was misbriefed.

In a question to Bouchard in the House, the NDP's Howard McCurdy said, "The whole situation stinks of government interference." Outside the Commons, Opposition health critics said they wanted Bouchard to investigate whether multinational drug companies are interfering with the safety review of prescription drugs.

South of the Border

On December 29, 1992, almost a year after Canada approved Imitrex, the U.S. Food and Drug Administration followed suit, but with some strong qualifications. The FDA warned that people with "underlying heart disease should not take the drug because of its potential to cause constriction of coronary arteries." Carl Peck, a medical doctor who heads the FDA's Center for Drug Evaluation and Research, said that the "FDA advises, as a precautionary measure in people who might have underlying coronary artery disease, that physicians consider giving the first injection in their office."

The FDA approved the six-milligram dosage for injectable Imitrex, but advised that lower doses can be given using a syringe and single-dose vial. The agency also noted that some patients experienced good results from as little as one milligram of injectable Imitrex.

To Be Continued

My interest in Imitrex began with the arrival of a press package. Since then, there have been important revelations about the effects Imitrex can have on the body—and about how little one can rely on a drug company's early claims for a new product. Yet, it is usually such strong early promotion via the press and medical journals that catches the attention of sufferers and doctors. Drug companies often whip up patient enthusiasm for a drug before it hits the market, thanks largely to journalists. (Glaxo was censured for heavy press coverage for Imigran (Imitrex) in France by the government before it had completed its safety review of the drug.)

Of course, if you're a patient desperately seeking an effective treatment, you might not care how the drug company conducts its business as long as you get their drug. One of my colleagues at *The Gazette* suffers from cluster headaches, intense and concentrated bursts of pounding. The pain is sometimes so severe that he's ready to ram his fist through a wall. He jumped at the chance to participate in an Imitrex study for cluster headaches and says that Imitrex eases his symptoms rapidly. So far, he hasn't had a bad experience and would probably fight to keep using it. But why should he have to take unnecessary risks?

Inman said that even people who do have bad experiences with Imitrex might want to continue using it as long as they know exactly what to expect. "This will require the doctor to spend a lot of time educating the patient about the drug," he said.

Such an approach to Imitrex may be of some use, but it hardly allays concerns about the drug. Explaining to patients that they should expect the possibility of severe chest pain or breathing difficulties after an Imitrex injection doesn't help science understand why they occur and what damage might be caused.

So, I'll be keeping an eye on Imitrex.

8

THOSE HALCION NIGHTS:

Sleep on a Tightrope

Aftertaking the sleeping pill Halcion, an elderly Ontario man became mean and unruly. He told his wife that he had never loved her. He verbally abused her. And he continued this treatment of her for weeks. But when the man's doctor withdrew him from Halcion, he returned to his normal, more gentle self and had no memory of the abuse that he had inflicted on his wife and other family members and friends.

A family member sent a letter to the Health department in October 1991, detailing the man's behaviour and requesting that Halcion be banned. The department's reply to the letter mentioned only several side-effects of the drug, including irritability and confusion, noted that Halcion is intended for short-term treatment of insomnia, and assured the family that government scientists along with six Canadian experts were reviewing the Halcion file.

Each year hundreds of thousands of Canadians end up in doctors' offices complaining that they can't sleep. Their insomnia may be due to the habitual downing of ten cups of coffee a day or to being a "regular" at Sally's Bar. Or they may be so stressed out that counting sheep or thousand-dollar bills doesn't do it. Depression and other illnesses also cause sleepless nights.

The effects of insomnia can be wicked. Some individuals can't function properly on the job; others are strapped into an emotional roller-coaster. Those deprived of sleep for longer than a month may even hallucinate.

Since the 1970s, more and more of these sleepless souls have been reaching for a benzodiazepine. These "sleeping pills" act on benzodiazepine receptors in the brain and calm excitable nerve cells. The result is a soothing or sedative effect.

"Benzos," which are used to treat mental disorders as well as insomnia, can have serious side-effects, including dizziness, light-headedness, coordination disorders, aggression, hostility, and concentration and memory problems. They can also be addictive, and sudden withdrawal can cause epileptic-like seizures.

Benzos are on the market because regulatory agencies believe their benefits outweigh their risks. But are consumers properly informed of the risks? Hmmm. Maybe the regulators don't want consumers to lose sleep over it.

Take the case of Halcion, the most widely prescribed sleeping pill in the world, a classic of regulatory disregard for consumer safety. Halcion has a checkered past. It was first introduced in 1977 by the Upjohn Company of Kalamazoo, Michigan, for sale in Belgium and The Netherlands. It moved immediately to the forefront of drug controversy and has stayed at the top of the charts to this day.

Halcion was highly touted for its speed: it could sedate people quickly and leave the body quickly. Therefore users experienced little grogginess the next day. This gave it a decided advantage over longer-acting benzos. The drug was available in strengths of 0.25, 0.5, and 1 milligram.

By 1979, Dutch authorities suspended the drug for six months after receiving more than 1,000 reports of side-effects, including depression, chronic anxiety, amnesia, hallucinations, paranoia, and verbal and physical aggression. Some of these reported reactions fit the profile of other benzos, but Halcion appeared to have unique—and downright bizarre—psychiatric side-effects. In 1980, the Dutch allowed only the 0.25-milligram dosage of Halcion back on the market, banning the higher dosages as too risky. Upjohn's response was to pull out of the Dutch market; but, by

1980, Upjohn had quietly removed the 1-milligram dosage from most markets, including Canada (where Halcion had become available in 1979).

Meanwhile, the drug was raising eyebrows at the FDA. One reviewer recommended against approval, saying the drug's benefits only narrowly outweighed the risks. But her bosses chose to approve Halcion anyway.

In 1983, the drug was launched in the United States at dosages of 0.5, 0.25, and 0.125 milligrams; but before long, reports cited problems such as personality changes and aggression. The FDA noted that reports on the drug outpaced those for Dalmane and Restoril, two of its competitors.

These reports and others led to the further lowering of the recommended strength of Halcion. In 1987, regulators in France and Italy forced the 0.5-milligram tablet off the market. Upjohn complained, but lowered the starting dosage worldwide to 0.25 milligrams.

In Canada, Upjohn sent a form letter to thousands of Canadian doctors in April 1988, advising them that it was ceasing distribution of its 0.5-milligram Halcion tablet, but retaining the weaker strengths of 0.25 and 0.125 milligrams. The letter made no mention of the thousands of reports worldwide of severe side-effects that regulatory agencies had received, including loss of memory, hallucinations, confusion, erratic behaviour, acts of violence, and attempted suicides.

Meanwhile, research at the Sleep and Research Treatment Center at Pennsylvania State University in Hershey suggested that the 0.25-milligram tablet was minimally effective; but its side-effects were similar to those associated with stronger dosages. In other words, there was little, if any, benefit to be derived from the 0.25-milligram dosage, but patients were vulnerable to the risks.

In early 1989, some researchers who track drug side-effects, including pharmacologist Pierre Biron of the University of Montreal, expressed concern that doctors were prescribing double the dose of the 0.25-milligram tablet. This was being somewhat encouraged by Upjohn. In its 1988 letter to Canadian doctors, the company implied this might be useful for "therapy-resistant patients." At the time, Canadian doctors were well on their way to their four-millionth prescription for Halcion.

In early 1989, I became curious about Health and Welfare's reaction to this apparent double-dosing pattern and called Thomas Da Silva, then head of the section for monitoring Halcion. Da Silva casually wrote off the need for further regulation in the matter, such as forcing Upjohn to write doctors a much more detailed letter cautioning them about the side-effects and proper use of Halcion. Da Silva thought the problem would sort itself out—doctors would magically find the right path out of the woods.

There is a large body of medical literature, mostly written by doctors, describing the great variety of errors commonly made in prescribing drugs, including unnecessary prescription and incorrect dosage. Some members of the medical profession have lambasted their colleagues for prescribing drugs like candy, particularly to the elderly. So one would think that senior officials at a regulatory agency would be doing more than crossing their fingers.

All attempts by agencies to change Halcion labelling, however, have been strongly opposed by Upjohn. The company says Halcion has been proved safe and effective, on the basis of more than two hundred clinical studies worldwide, and the company has been consistent in its defence of the drug against all comers. Upjohn has objected to any labelling that might indicate that Halcion causes some side-effects at a higher rate than other benzos. Halcion, Upjohn claims, has not been given a fair rap, particularly by the media. Spontaneous reporting of side-effects, it sniffs, cannot be trusted as a true measure of problems.

The FDA ordered the company in 1982 to warn in its package insert that Halcion can cause temporary amnesia; but the company's lack of more detailed public disclosure about Halcion's potential side-effects really caught up with Upjohn in Britain.

In October 1991, Britain suspended Halcion. A review of the drug by the nation's drug regulatory body found that Upjohn had not reported all known side-effects. It was Ian Oswald, a retired Scottish psychiatrist and sleep expert, who blew the whistle on Upjohn. Oswald had long been a strong critic of Halcion and had even called for its ban in 1989 in a letter to the British medical journal *The Lancet*. When serving as an expert witness at a trial of a woman who shot her mother eight times, allegedly when under the influence of Halcion, Oswald gained access to confidential Upjohn documents. These showed that serious psychiatric side-effects had been known to be associated with the drug as early as 1972; however, Upjohn had failed to report most of them to the FDA. The company has maintained it did not intentionally mislead the agency: the incomplete reporting was the result of a transcription error.

The British action moved other countries, including Canada, to re-examine Halcion.

By this time, more than 450 cases of side-effects associated with Halcion had been voluntarily reported to the Health department. Among them were 26 accounts of hostility and 9 episodes of violence. (As usual, of course, we must keep in mind that voluntary reports represent a small fraction of actual occurrences.)

On January 27, 1992, the Health department sent Canadian doctors a letter about Halcion and three generic near-copies. It explained that the Health Protection Branch had conducted a review of Halcion "with the advice of six prominent Canadian clinical experts" and decided that the drug could stay on the market, with certain restrictions. The prescribing instructions now include warnings about all known psychiatric reactions. The drug is recommended only for transient and short-term insomnia. The recommended starting dosage is 0.125 milligram for all patients, the maximum dosage, 0.25 milligram. Halcion use is not to exceed fourteen consecutive days (down from twenty-one days). The drug is now available in smaller packages, of seven pills; accompanying information for patients details its proper use and all potential side-effects.

A move in the right direction. Well done, Department of Health and Welfare.

But was this enough? No.

Meet Canada's "six prominent clinical experts"—four psychiatrists, a neurologist, and a family doctor. No leading expert in sleep laboratory studies was on the team, which met to review Halcion in October 1991; the meeting lasted one and one-half days. Perhaps they were asleep at the switch, but they reached a very peculiar—some might say half-witted—conclusion. Canada would keep the drug on the market at a recommended starting dosage of 0.125 milligram, at which level it is virtually ineffective against insomnia but can be powerful against peace of mind. Even Upjohn reported to the FDA in 1987 that the psychiatric side-effects associated with Halcion were pretty much the same, regardless of the dosage. Yet Halcion's effectiveness was given only brief mention at the meeting of Canada's "experts." But hey, Canada's regulators can feel confident in their decision because our neighbour to the south also decided that Halcion is safe and effective. This is not surprising. Experts in both countries are often hand-picked not to rock the regulatory boat.

In July 1992, eight U.S. experts advising the FDA approved continued use of Halcion; there was only one dissenting vote. The experts did concede, however, that the drug's label should have a stronger warning about side-effects.

Prior to the meeting of the experts, Upjohn had announced plans to conduct an eighteen-month study of 10,000 Halcion users.

Two months later, in August 1992, Britain reaffirmed its view that Halcion's benefit-to-risk ratio is narrow and upheld its ban on the drug. The controversy continues.

9

A CASE OF MISTAKEN IDENTITY:

Toradol for Pain Relief

EVERY TIME YOU SWALLOW A PILL, IT IS AN ACT OF TRUST. You trust the prescribing doctor to be well informed about the drug. You trust the drug company to test its product adequately for safety and effectiveness and to promote its benefits and risks accurately. You trust reviewers at Health and Welfare Canada to scrutinize this body of test information thoroughly.

Think about it—that's a lot of trust.

Advocates of increasing pharmaceutical deregulation tend to assume that all these parties—doctors, manufacturers, government reviewers—are trustworthy. Former deputy Health minister Margaret Catley-Carlson liked to say, for example, that it is in industry's best interest to do good. That a new day is dawning and industry must be encouraged to monitor itself.

The next time someone tries a "Catley-Carlson" on you, I prescribe the story of Toradol. (I've read up on it—trust me.)

In April 1991, the prescription drug Toradol became available in Canadian hospitals; four months later it could be purchased in pharmacies. It is prescribed as a short-term treatment, in intramuscular and tablet form, for sharp and temporary pain. Its Toronto co-promoters, Syntex Inc. and the Upjohn Company of Canada, began hyping the non-narcotic drug to doctors and the media as providing pain relief equal to narcotics, such as morphine, meperidine, and codeine, but without their potential for addiction and side-effects, which include confusion, sedation, nausea, vomiting, and constipation. Toradol acts on the site of the pain, whereas narcotics block pain by acting on the brain and spinal cord.

This was good news for our narcotic-ridden society—Canada has the world's highest per-capita consumption of codeine and ranks fifth worldwide for all narcotics use for medical purposes. This was a clever swipe at the competition, particularly the market leader, a Tylenol product that is much cheaper than Toradol but features acetaminophen with codeine. Toradol would free us from such enslaving narcotic painkillers.

Toradol was being aimed at a huge market, including hospital patients. Most in-hospital patients experience moderate to severe pain. Toradol, the promotional materials trumpeted, would keep patients more alert, cut their side-effects, and enable them to leave hospital sooner—a boon to the health-care system. Moreover, because Toradol can treat "a broad range of painful conditions," including post-surgical and gynaecological pain, it would also be suitable for prescribing by clinics and hospital emergency departments.

Well, Toradol is definitely a non-narcotic. And it kills pain. But Toradol, it turns out, is a non-narcotic painkiller with something extra.

Toradol is an anti-inflammatory that works on a group of chemicals in the body called prostaglandins, which contribute to fever, inflammation, and pain. This makes Toradol an NSAID—Non-Steroidal Anti-Inflammatory Drug. NSAIDs also have painkilling properties, and are therefore commonly prescribed for arthritis.

NSAIDs, which come in more than thirty varieties, are associated with serious side-effects, including ulcers, internal bleeding, and heart and kidney failure. According to some estimates, as many as two thousand Canadian NSAID users over the age of sixty probably die each year from such reactions. (The elderly are particularly vulnerable because their bodies take longer to excrete drugs.) Other common NSAID-related side-effects include skin, blood, liver, and central-nervous-system disorders; bone-marrow suppression; and salt retention leading to swelling. Because of their widespread use, mainly to fight arthritis and moderate pain, NSAIDs are estimated to be the source of up to 25 per cent of all drug side-effects.

Careful monitoring of patients on NSAIDs, particularly the elderly, is now a hard-and-fast rule in medicine. To monitor and prevent gastrointestinal effects, for example, patients are usually followed up in the first few months of NSAID use, tests are run for signs of blood in the gastrointestinal tract, and an anaemia check is done every six months. In short, a doctor must be extremely cautious and vigilant after prescribing an NSAID. One would therefore assume that Syntex and Upjohn would inform doctors clearly and concisely in their advertising that Toradol, the non-narcotic, is an NSAID.

Pierre Biron and Toradol Ads

Pierre Biron, a physician, is professor of pharmacology at the University of Montreal. His "pharmacoviligance" program at the university is widely respected by doctors and drug companies alike. Biron is fair and factual; his criticisms are based on careful research and cautious analysis.

In early April 1992, Biron mentioned Toradol during one of our periodic conversations. Had I seen the advertising for the drug? No? I should get a copy of an ad. The company had not been properly informing doctors that Toradol is an NSAID. The drug appeared to be doing well in the market-place, and Biron was concerned that doctors would prescribe the drug more liberally if they didn't know it is an NSAID. They might, for example, incorrectly prescribe it to a patient who is allergic to NSAIDs, including ASA (aspirin), the grand old originator of this product class. This could cause big trouble, possibly allergic shock and even death.

I told Biron I would check it out.

I found a Toradol ad running across pages 20 and 21 in the February 26, 1992, issue of *L'Actualité Médicale*, a French-language medical trade newspaper. Translated, the large headline shouted: TORADOL. NEW AND NON-NARCOTIC. THE EFFECTIVENESS OF NARCOTICS WITHOUT THEIR DISADVANTAGES.

The ad proclaimed Toradol to be a new idea in painkillers: its effectiveness compared favourably with that of narcotics and acetaminophen with codeine. The ad did not mention that the drug was an NSAID. Separate prescribing instructions in eye-straining type for doctors interested enough to turn back to page 19, did, but Biron was not impressed. For one thing, some doctors might not bother to seek out additional information, or would give it only a cursory glance. Moreover, at the very beginning of those prescribing instructions, Toradol is characterized only as a painkiller. True, the second paragraph reveals that it is an NSAID, but, according to Biron, this suggests a cat-and-mouse game that has no place in medicine.

By downplaying Toradol as an NSAID, Syntex and Upjohn were positioning the product more directly in competition with Tylenol with codeine.

By the following August, the advertising had been changed. The new ads mentioned the drug belongs to the NSAID family, but this fact was still dwarfed by claims for Toradol's non-narcotic painkilling properties. By then four Canadians—all elderly, two in the Maritimes, one in Saskatchewan, and one in Quebec—had died after taking Toradol. And the drug was suspected to have contributed in their deaths. At least eight other Canadians were known to have had extreme allergic reactions following the use of Toradol.

Here's why the ads for Toradol began to mention that it is an NSAID: Side-effects common to NSAIDs, particularly gastrointestinal problems, were being associated with the use of Toradol both in Canada and in the United States, where the drug was first marketed. Some of the reports that Syntex routinely forwarded to the Health department in January 1992 suggested that doctors might be prescribing Toradol to patients who should not have been given an NSAID, including those allergic to this product class. The department determined that the marketing information for the drug was inadequate.

In early February, the department requested a meeting with Syntex and the non-government Pharmaceutical Advertising Advisory Board, which reviews drug-promotional materials. At the meeting, revisions were made to the promotional material on

Toradol, including the information use by salesmen to pitch the drug to doctors. "Dear Doctor" and "Dear Pharmacist" letters noted that Toradol is an NSAID and detailed the positive and negative features of this product class. Syntex sent out the letters in March to doctors and pharmacists across Canada and issued its new promotional materials, including ads, in April.

So, the Health department was on the job and we all lived happily ever after, right?

Wrong. The new ads made no mention of any side-effects associated with the drug. Only the prescribing instructions did. Advertising for Toradol in the United States is very different. It includes a listing of the most serious side-effects. Doctors are referred to the prescribing instructions for more details.

U.S. advertising refers to Toradol as an "analgesic NSAID." As of mid-February 1993, the Canadian prescribing instructions still merely categorized the drug as an "analgesic agent." Biron's bulletin to health professionals referred to Toradol as an NSAID "being presented as an analgesic for short-term pain relief."

We have seen how creeping deregulation has led to fewer doctors holding key positions in the Health department, with negative consequences for drug review. It bears noting, then, that the department's central-nervous-system division, which helped to review Toradol—the same folks who handled Imitrex—lacks medical expertise at higher supervisory levels. If someone with Biron's medical understanding had been supervising the review of the submission for Toradol, it would have been tagged immediately as an NSAID and the companies would have been required to market it as such.

Instead, for almost a year, Syntex and Upjohn dressed Toradol up as a painkiller and sent it out to earn its keep, before it was hauled in for questioning.

When Toradol's true identity was revealed, Syntex tried to put a positive spin on the Toradol outing. When asked to explain why there was a change in the advertising, Rob Hamilton, Syntex's product manager for the drug, claimed that the company notified the Health department of problems and took "self-corrective action."

Evidently the Health department let the untruth stand—it

would rather be seen as unobservant than kick a drug company in the pants. It makes nice-nice and solves problems in a friendly, non-adversarial manner. Companies appreciate this team spirit and return the compliment, emphasizing how closely they work with the Health department. Evidently the companies never make mistakes; rather, they join with the department to refine knowledge about a drug. When I asked in September 1992 for its version of how the changes in its promotional material on Toradol came to be, the company (following in the department's footsteps) faxed me a statement. It began: "Syntex works closely with the HPB [the Health department's Health Protection Branch] throughout the drug approval process and in the postmarketing surveillance that follows the introduction of a new drug so that the best interests of the patient are served. . . ."

Then it got even more vague, maundering on about the changes in promotional materials while in no way answering my query, and attaching a PR pitch on the scientific basis for Toradol's safety and efficacy.

In contrast, the FDA sometimes gets tough with companies that mislead doctors. Back in 1988, the FDA objected to Syntex's promotion of Naprosyn, another NSAID, as the company had suggested that the drug could arrest and prevent joint deterioration in arthritic patients. Trouble was, they had no adequate scientific proof. Three years later, the FDA discovered that Syntex had expanded its promotion, claiming again, through its drug salesmen, ads in medical journals, cable-TV programs and ads, medical educational seminars, etc., that Naprosyn prevented joint degeneration.

On October 10, 1991, Syntex agreed to carry out "corrective action." They sent a letter by certified mail to approximately 250,000 doctors, acknowledging the FDA's findings regarding misleading promotion of Naprosyn and admitting that the drug has not been demonstrated to protect patients from arthritic joint deterioration. They also did some corrective advertising in medical journals.

More Bad News for Canadians about Toradol

If you botch a drug file the first and second time around, try again.

On November 27, 1992, the Health department issued its own "Dear Doctor" letter, indicating its concerns about the possible misuse of Toradol. And concerned it might well have been: two more elderly patients had died after taking Toradol, twenty-five reports had been received of non-fatal gastrointestinal bleeding, and severe allergic reactions had also been reported.

The letter to doctors explained that "the severe reactions were occurring primarily in patients known to be at high risk for developing such reactions to NSAIDs. They include the elderly, patients with histories of gastrointestinal problems and with known sensitivities to NSAIDs."

In other words, Toradol was behaving like an NSAID.

The letter didn't mention, of course, that, since April 1991, more than 900,000 prescriptions had been filled for Toradol in Canada. The rule of thumb is that only a small number of occurring side-effects are reported to the Health department, so this drug may well have negatively affected hundreds, if not thousands, of Canadians.

This stark statistical reality is understood by every regulatory agency. Yet, there was no attempt by the Health department to pressure Syntex and Upjohn to make further changes in advertising for Toradol. Why settle for half-measures? Biron wondered.

When I asked the Health department to answer this question, its fax passed the buck to the Pharmaceutical Advertising Advisory Board (PAAB), which "monitors and approves advertising for prescriptions drugs." As for Biron's concerns, the department wrote: "We would encourage Dr. Biron to direct his concern to the Commissioner of the PAAB with a copy of the correspondence to the Director General of the Drugs Directorate."

The last time I looked, in mid-February 1993, Syntex and Upjohn were still running ads for Toradol featuring its non-narcotic and painkilling properties and downplaying its NSAID connection.

3

STORM WARNINGS

10

WOMAN AS GUINEA PIG:

Pills for Menopause

MARY ANNE PARKHURST WAS BRIMMING WITH CONviction as she described a bold new form of drugcompany advertising. The campaign was for Premarin, the major estrogen-replacement pill for women in menopause: it has been available in Canada since 1941.

"We're travelling a road that is very unknown," she said in the spring of 1990. "And I take pride in the fact that we're travelling a road less travelled."

Parkhurst, the manager of women's health products at Ayerst Laboratories in St-Laurent, Quebec, was referring to the company's ongoing national advertising campaign entitled "I am Woman," which was running in *The Gazette* and sixteen other Canadian newspapers.

The ad pictured the face of a woman who was apparently entering menopause. The copy addressed women directly. They should be well informed about that phase of life, it advised. The ad, which mentioned the company name but not Premarin, suggested that anyone who was unsure about certain facts might take a minute or two to complete the "menopausal checklist." The fifteen symptoms listed included spotty menstrual flow, vaginal dryness, painful intercourse, changes in genital tissue, back pain, depression, anxiety, nervousness, irritability, headaches, and weight gain.

The completed checklist (if, in fact, a woman could really detect "changes in genital tissue") could then be taken to a doctor, who would provide information "about making life more liveable in the menopausal years. And after."

The ad caught my attention because medicine was a long way from understanding the biological and medical implications of the changes women undergo as they lose their ability to reproduce. Most "scientific" descriptions of menopause relied on subjective information gleaned from small samples of carefully selected women. In fact, there was very little available data on the extent to which women suffer from symptoms as their ovaries produce less and less estrogen. It was also very unclear whether some of the psychological symptoms usually attributed to menopause—loss of sexual feeling, irritability, depression, headaches, etc.—were, in fact, related to the physical changes comprising menopause. It was evident from a quick scan of the medical literature that hormone-replacement therapy was a vast experiment with unclear risks and benefits.

In the 1940s and 1950s, estrogen replacement was hyped to alleviate the symptoms associated with menopause, such as hot flashes and vaginal dryness; but in the 1960s and 1970s, replacement hormones were additionally touted as keeping wrinkles away and hair glossy, as well as reducing depression. In the 1980s, the drugs were pitched as a cure for brittle bones—osteoporosis—and all signs were that, in the 1990s, these hormones would be recycled as the solution to female heart disease.

In short, medicine was turning menopause, a natural process of aging, into a disease that caused other diseases. And there was the ad suggesting that a doctor could somehow make sense of a woman's menopausal complaints and prescribe accordingly. It particularly bothered me that Ayerst was making it seem as though a woman owed it to herself to visit her doctor, obviously playing up to new interest in women's health issues.

Drug companies are forbidden by Canadian law to advertise prescription drugs directly to the consumer. But this subtle approach of steering the public to the doctor's office was a sign of the times. The Upjohn Company of Canada, a Toronto-based drug firm, had started the ball rolling three years earlier by running radio, television, and magazine ads that told men that a medical treatment for hair loss existed; men concerned about hair loss should discuss the matter with a doctor. The hair ads didn't mention Upjohn by name.

I was naturally curious to see if Ayerst was pitching Premarin extra hard to doctors during its consumer campaign on menopause. It was.

Ayerst ads in medical journals informed doctors that Premarin (in large, red letters) could alleviate many of the symptoms that their patients could identify. The company informed doctors that a public-awareness campaign had been launched to urge women to get the "real story" on menopause from doctors, and that doctors were the best equipped to inform women about the need for therapy and choice of therapy.

Ayerst gave the doctors a checklist of the benefits that Premarin provides against some of the symptoms that were mentioned in the newspaper ads. Very clever.

The company also mailed bulky information kits on menopause and Premarin to nine thousand general practitioners and specialists in obstetrics and gynaecology. Included were several copies of a menopausal symptom checklist, similar to the list appearing in newspapers; patient-information booklets on menopause; a full-colour anatomical chart, depicting the process of female maturation; a list of treatments commonly prescribed for menopausal therapy, including Premarin products and several products from other drug companies, among them progestins (also hormones); several blank copies of patient medical-record charts, highlighting Premarin (in large, black letters); and, of course, the old faithful, a note pad, also calling attention to Premarin.

So there I was at Ayerst, having digested the full force of the company's strategy, and Parkhurst was waxing on about how the menopause ad was "the Bill of Rights for menopausal women."

Wouldn't some people think that this was one more crass attempt to exploit women?

Parkhurst defended Ayerst's approach: "Because I think that although one might argue that, well, they've only done it because they have a product that's used in menopause, I would counter with the fact that it's all the more reason for us to take leadership in reaching out to the public."

Sure.

The ad ignited reaction from social scientists and menopause specialists. Some were offended by its wording. Patricia Kaufert, a medical sociologist in the faculty of medicine at the University of Manitoba in Winnipeg, told me the ad's opening paragraph especially upset her. It read: "Today's woman. Woman of the nineties. Born of my mother's womb like generations before me." Kaufert, who studies how different cultures experience menopause, felt the company was co-opting feminist rhetoric. "It refers to a line of women, linking the generations—and feminists often use this type of image." She also criticized what she considered to be the ad's hidden message: "The woman in the ad is portrayed as serene, slightly sexy, and entering her aging years. The underlying implication is that if you don't use hormone-replacement therapy, your sexuality will be diminished and your body will get decrepit."

Kaufert also strongly disapproved of the checklist in the ad because it gave the false impression that the symptoms were scientifically related to menopause. "This can be very misleading," she said. "Many [non-menopausal] people could check off those items."

The ad angered others because it gave the impression that most women undergo menopause the same way. Margaret Lock, an anthropologist in the medical faculty at McGill University, has conducted studies that suggest a cultural diversity of responses to menopause. In a study of Japanese women, Lock found that women in Japan appear to ignore hot flashes because the experience of menopause in Japan is not strongly associated with ill health, but rather is seen as part of the natural aging process. She concludes: "Perhaps we should begin to examine some of the assumptions which are often made in connection with menopause and female aging in the West, namely that it is a debilitating time for the majority of women which is best managed through medication."

Because aging women are discriminated against in our society, which places a premium on youthful sexuality, menopause has been a target of overmedicalization. Millions of women take replacement hormones for decades—from onset of menopause through age eighty. Many, no doubt, are convinced that a replacement hormone will somehow keep the aging process—and its cultural agenda—at bay. Meanwhile, ovarian hormones, particularly estrogen (namely Premarin) have been linked to breast cancer in animal studies since the 1930s. Their use has also been linked to an increased risk of uterine cancer, stroke, migraines, and liver, heart, and gall bladder disease. More common side-effects include nausea, changes in body weight, increase in blood pressure, aggravation of migraine headaches, allergic reactions and rashes, nervousness, and dizziness. Estrogens taken in combination with progestins—as is commonly done—may neutralize the risk of uterine cancer; but it appears to increase the risk of heart disease and breast cancer. Progestins can also cause headaches, depression, acne, abdominal bloating, and, possibly, menstruation.

Given that Premarin is a top-seller among drugs in North America, many doctors must be downplaying the potential risks of hormone replacement. They likely reason that the risk data are inconclusive so it is better to err on the side of protection, namely the prevention of osteoporosis and heart disease. But, on the basis of available scientific data, replacement hormones may be vastly overprescribed—and downright dangerous. In fact, when a doctor tells a patient that the benefits of hormone therapy are worth the risks, he may be making a scientifically untenable claim. Let's take a closer look.

Poor Science, Hype, and Hope

First, brittle bones. Premarin is also sold as a way to help protect against osteoporosis. It's been known for several decades that this hormone is involved in the manufacture of women's bone. After menopause, when estrogen production shuts down, there is accelerated bone loss. More bone is lost than formed, particularly during the first seven or so years after menopause begins. This is why some doctors are quick to prescribe estrogens to menopausal women. The problem here is that lack of proper study data makes prescribing the optimal dosage of the drug for maximum benefit and fewest side-effects more a matter of luck than of science, as women lose bone at varying rates. Nor do doctors know if adding progestin is more beneficial than prescribing estrogen alone.

To complicate things, it is far from clear how much of a role estrogen deficiency actually plays in osteoporosis, says a 126-page report on menopause, issued by the U.S. Office of Technology Assessment in May 1992. Aging and genetics also influence its development.

Osteoporosis has been hyped by the media since the early 1980s as a major health threat, so it's likely that many women believe that all are at equal risk. They are not. Those who are include women whose ovaries were removed before age forty; with a family history of osteoporosis; on long-term steroid therapy; who suffer from conditions such as kidney disease and hyperthyroidism. There are millions of women on Premarin; obviously only a modest number of them can be high-risk cases. Doctors have probably prescribed the drug needlessly to hundreds of thousands of women who are now at risk for its side-effects.

There is also another issue here: can non-drug approaches do as well or better to prevent brittle bones? And for whom? There is precious little serious research on alternatives to hormone therapy—a symptom of a medical patriarchy. There has been very little focus, for example, on lifestyle factors that could help prevent osteoporosis. The best that science has done is to suggest that foods rich in calcium, such as fish and green veggies, and exercise, which can build bone, are likely to help reduce bone loss.

And rather than consider lifestyle factors that may be associated with debilitating hip fractures in older women, doctors instead reach for Premarin. They should take note of studies showing that people with fractures have the same bone density as those without fractures. Clearly, other things are going on: poor vision, balance problems, side-effects from various drugs, and poor living conditions. Medicine, however, has not bothered much to factor in such variables, being content to prescribe replacement hormones and leave the socio-economic problems to the politicians.

Now that we are entering the heart-disease era of replacement-hormone hype, doctors are likely to justify the drugs on cardiac-protective grounds alone, although there are no proper studies to support such prescriptions. The gold standard of science—the randomized controlled trial, which assigns subjects to study groups on an unbiased basis—has never been applied, so there are only suggestive data that replacement hormones can help prevent heart disease.

Moreover, studies claiming that replacement estrogen can have a protective effect on the heart (by virtue of its ability to metabolize fat and modify its concentrations) involved women who were on estrogen alone. Many women also take progestins, which may nullify any beneficial effect. But, in the absence of proper studies, who really knows? When medical scientists inject drugs in real guinea pigs, at least they observe and analyse.

Alice Rossi, a sociologist who presented a research paper on menopause to the American Psychological Association last August, in Washington, D.C., said doctors and drug firms are firing up the need for treatment because of self-interest. She also took a bead on authors of popular menopause books projecting their personal experience to the general population. Gail Sheehy, for example, writes in *The Silent Passage* about women lighting up the boardrooms of corporate America with hot flashes. Rossi countered that the scientific literature based on representative samples of healthy, middle-aged women shows that not more than one in ten experiences severe hot flashes of the kind that Sheehy describes.

Rossi also suggested that the danger in current popular attention to menopause is that its focus is off-target. In cultures where women have social, religious, and political power, there is no dread of aging. Therefore menopause is not the nightmare it is in our culture, where fifty-year-old women want to be twenty.

So, here's the dilemma: women are being encouraged to view menopause as some kind of baby-boom epidemic complete with debilitating hot flashes, heart attacks, bone fractures, and who-knows-what later on. Meanwhile, proper science on the subject is next to zilch.

When the Office of Technology Assessment reported last year that solid medical information on menopause is desperately needed, U.S. Congresswoman Patricia Schroeder (Democrat) said that if more data were not available soon, women "will be in the same position that we were in with silicone breast implants . . . millions of women taking it, but not enough data on safety or effectiveness."

But Shroeder's warning comes too late: women are in that very position right now. The disturbing similarity between breast-implant and menopause research is that there have not been studies that meet adequate design, duration, and sample-size requirements to determine the risks and benefits of both short- and long-term use.

I suppose the good news is that the U.S. National Institutes of Health are launching a $500-million decade-long study this year of between 60,000 to 70,000 older women who are at risk of a heart attack, cancer, or brittle bones. The study will determine the effects of diet, hormone-replacement therapy, calcium and vitamin-D supplements, and exercise.

Great. But another theory is begging for attention. It says that some menopausal women might become addicted to replacement hormones. British doctors Susan Bewley, a gynaecologist at University College, and her father, Thomas Bewley, a psychiatrist at St. George's Hospital Medical School, wrote in the journal *The Lancet* on February 1, 1992, of that possibility. (People have become addicted to other natural substances in the body, such as enkephalin, a brain peptide associated with the high that runners get.)

The Bewleys point to cases of women who have a need for more and more hormone therapy at decreasing intervals, thereby increasing the dangers with the dosage. How serious or widespread this phenomenon might be is not yet known, but the Bewleys are looking into it.

It's bad enough that drug companies such as Ayerst have been selling replacement hormones in the absence of solid research, but Wyeth-Ayerst even tried to monopolize the Canadian market by complaining to the government that generic versions of Premarin didn't work as well as the name brand. (Premarin is an old drug and therefore its patent had run out.) The Health department set up a committee (formed from two government standing committees) to look the matter over.

The committee met three times, between May 27 and November 15, 1991. Its report gave the generics a passing grade, but concluded that there were irregularities with Wyeth-Ayerst's Premarin. The report noted major variations in lots and dosage strengths of the drug.

Lo and behold, Premarin was also reformulated in 1991—without informing the Health department. (Until 1991, Canadian Premarin was a quick-release type of drug; now it's like U.S. Premarin, a delayed-release type.) Apparently the changes were not substantial enough to oblige Wyeth-Ayerst to report them to the department.

The committee also reported its concern that Wyeth-Ayerst was marketing Premarin for osteoporosis without having received Health department approval. Given the lack of data on the type of Premarin—Canadian quick release or U.S. delayed release—used in clinical studies in Canada, the committee advised the department to "clarify the situation." It also called for a standard to be set for the making of estrogens, including the release time of the drug into the body and the way it is absorbed.

In May 1992, Montreal-based ICN Canada Ltd., one of the manufacturers of generic Premarin, got tired of waiting and filed a brief with the Federal Court of Canada (which adjudicates disputes involving the federal government) to force the Health department to speed up its investigation of Premarin.

The generic companies were concerned that applications for other estrogen products would be held up until the department acted on the committee's recommendations.

Well, the court case hasn't been settled, and the department is apparently still addressing the committee's concerns.

What's me worry? It's only a pill for women.

11

NUTS AND BOLTS:

The Orthopaedic Hardware Store

I WAS ABOUT TO RELATE THE ENTIRE NATURAL HISTORY OF MY right knee, but I'll spare you the full treatment. Suffice to say that I cracked it up playing football in high school. In the years since then, my knee misbehaves on occasion—usually after a tough game of full-court basketball or chasing strong forearm blasts on the tennis court. No, let's be honest, it aches for days. After driving my car for long stretches, I'll limp for fifteen minutes or so.

There is a medical point to this autobiography. It has to do with miracles. Roughly fifteen years ago a sports-medicine specialist in Montreal announced that my knee was at least fifty years older than I was. I was shocked. Then he recommended that I take up swimming and give up basketball. He had to be kidding.

I was about thirty when this so-called expert tried to reduce me to wallowing in the chlorine stink of a pool. I figured that there must be a miracle, that medical science just had to have a simple and safe way to turn my knee into a bionic force, or supply a spare part that would allow me to play basketball well into my eighties.

I'm still waiting, and naturally, I keep my eyes open for any signs of real progress. I skim through the orthopaedic journals on my weekly visit to the medical library and take in the odd orthopaedic conference where all the gadgets and gizmos are on display.

You learn two things from journals and conferences. One, that the market for orthopaedic products, particularly implants, is huge. And two, which follows logically, that the variety of metal and silicone spare parts for the knee, hip, elbow, shoulder, chin, hand, thumb, finger, and so on is very impressive. Tens of thousands of Canadians have orthopaedic implant surgery each year: some 8,000 have artificial knees implanted; about 30,000 get new hips. With an aging population, you can expect a surge of interest in artificial parts.

Back in September 1990, I decided to look more closely at orthopaedic trends, to get a better handle on my chances of dunking the basketball at the millennium. The brochure for a Montreal conference promised more than 470 exhibits. Not bad, but then this was the eighteenth world congress of an international orthopaedics and traumatology society.

I attended some scientific presentations but spent most of the week in the exhibition hall, which looked like a humungous hardware store. Think of implant components as nuts, pins, bolts, sockets, hammers, and sophisticated winches and you'll get the picture.

Well, a week spent with the cobalt, chromium, titanium, and silicone set—the salesmen and orthopedic surgeons who carney for the manufacturers—turned out to be quite an education.

The Obvious Question

Yes, I'm fixated, but let's get back to knees, briefly. Knees are able to absorb six to eight times the force of your body's weight when you walk. Their workings are complex. You are likely to walk pain-free if your knee joint is smooth and its shock absorber—your knee cartilage—is in one piece, rather than spread around like hot peppers on a chicken burger. Strong knee muscles and ligaments create the stability to withstand the shake, rattle, and roll your bones go through every time you bend your leg.

Strong, yet delicate. That's a knee. Cartilage wears away. Bones rub together. Arthritis sets in, and the knee joint becomes inflamed and swollen. Ligaments tear with an audible pop. And orthopaedic specialists suggest swimming.

When a knee deteriorates even farther, metal and plastic may be called for. A doctor will announce: "You need an implant."

As I toured the exhibits, I couldn't help but notice that implants, each made of several metallic components, were not measuring up. The phrase "relatively primitive" crossed my mind. Granted, the salesmen made them out to be very sophisticated. Indeed, each company spokesperson, salesperson, or representative guaranteed his or her company's product to be the best and latest in a range of motion, mobility, and stability, and the least likely to loosen and require replacement. But they didn't seem to have much actual science on hand to support their sales pitches. Remembering how little research the manufacturer of the Meme breast implant had to back up its product, I wondered about the basis for the claims for knee and other orthopaedic implants. The obvious question was: What does science say about their safety and effectiveness?

The answer appears to be: science has only modest understanding of orthopaedic implant safety and efficacy. I quizzed some of the salespeople and surgeons at the exhibits, delved more deeply into the journals, and spoke with experts in biomaterials. The orthopaedic-implant field turns out to be more stylish than scientifically substantive. So much for slam-dunking into my twilight years.

But wait. This problem is larger even than basketball. In the past fifteen years more than one-half million artificial knees and about one million hips had been implanted in North Americans—not surprising, given that arthritis-related disease alone affects some forty million of us.

Why then are these devices so—well, primitive and poorly researched? It appears the villains are Sloth and Avarice. Rather than finance proper studies of their products, many manufacturers rely on short-term assessment by keen orthopaedic surgeons. There's another bad guy, too—Ego. It seems that a doc who hasn't designed at least one spare part might lack authority with the other orthopods. Can't you see it? Your name in lights? The Doctor X wrist! The Doctor Y shoulder!

The situation had become so troubling that the Academy of Orthopedic Surgeons in the United States actually discussed knee implants openly during a 1990 meeting in New Orleans. Biomaterials scientists and surgeons pointed out that the claims of knee-implant manufacturers are rarely substantiated by independent research and that the field is awash in anecdotal rather than scientific data. Clement Sledge, a past president of the academy, even suggested a surcharge of $5 per square foot for exhibit space during the academy's future meetings so that the hype on implants could be verified by actual research. Had the Sledge proposal been applied to that very meeting, about $750,000 would have been raised for research. Sledge explained that the necessary scientific assessment would involve complex engineering, biological, and surgical input, i.e., team work. Sledge's colleagues didn't take up his suggestion.

Albert Burstein was a participant in that discussion. He is the director of biomechanics at the Hospital for Special Surgery in New York City. Burstein was particularly concerned that lack of proper research was keeping the orthopaedic-implant field back, and that more dead ends were inevitable should the quick dash to fame and fortune do a fast break around the fundamental questions, such as how implant components transfer the pressure of everyday activity to the bone to which they are cemented. Some designs had allowed too much load to be borne by the bone, eroding the bone and loosening the implant. When I interviewed Burstein, he emphasized how perplexed he was about the focus on design rather than more serious matters such as testing and discovering new materials for implants. As a result, the rights of patients were being ignored. "The implication of these design fads for patients is that they are receiving poor informed consent," he said. "There is so little good data that can be presented to them."

Patients are certainly not being well advised about long-term implications of many orthopaedic implants because the data are virtually non-existent. Take hips, for example, which many surgeons and scientists say are the best performers of all orthopaedic implants. They certainly compare well to ankles, elbows, and wrists, which do not enjoy a reputation for staying in place and wearing well. Knees are probably in the ballpark with hips, which appear to last about ten years, but not necessarily without discomfort, pain, and inflammation. Now there are roughly twenty-five different models available. The older ones are cemented into the hip bone. Some new models—the current rage—are cement-free. They are designed to allow bone to grow directly into the metal. Trouble is, there is no reliable information to tell us whether these cement-free models perform better over the long run than those with cement. And this is why the Medical Research Council of Canada recently awarded generous funds to Michael Gross, an orthopaedic surgeon at Victoria General Hospital in Halifax. Gross will compare cement and cement-free hips. He will also try to gauge whether cement-free models may have some quirks that could lead to problems over the long haul.

Besides the inescapable fact that post-surgical recovery is long—about one year with total knee implants, for example—there are other concerns. The available scientific literature and surveys make it clear that implants tend to loosen and deteriorate. At least 10 per cent of the devices need to be reimplanted, and some 30 per cent of patients complain of pain and/or poor performance.

The bad news is the reaction of the body's immune system when it spots an implant. As detailed in the discussion of breast implants, the body furiously attacks the implant, which wears down and sheds particles that can migrate to other parts of the body. The result? Inflammation, blood clots, bone erosion, and, according to small numbers of case reports, cancer.

Moreover, this biological process is very poorly understood, although research is beginning to pick up. It was once thought that implant metals were inert, but now we know better. For example, silicone used in artificial fingers, thumbs, wrists, elbows, and shoulders was championed as being non-toxic and therefore tissue-friendly. But recent studies of biopsy specimens clearly show that silicone implants shed microparticles into nearby tissue. (You can bet the immune system takes note.) Some of this debris ends up causing such aggressive inflammation that it, in turn, eats up bone, causing fractures.

Studies also show that some of the debris lands in lymph nodes. Cases of malignant lymphoma have spurred a debate in the scientific literature as to whether implantation increases cancer risk.

You can't stop implantation on the available evidence; but surely it would be nice if more was known about the acceptable range of body responses to implants. Given our ignorance, on what basis do regulatory agencies allow these devices to be implanted in the body? The answer is familiar: on the basis of incomplete science and the assumption that manufacturers are doing their homework.

According to Pierre Blais, the scientist who dogged the Meme breast implant while working for Health and Welfare Canada, orthopaedic implants are given only cursory review attention by the Bureau of Radiation and Medical Devices. Implants with no movable parts are not considered worthy of full review. "Reviewers who look at orthopaedic devices that have movable parts are mainly concerned with whether the materials in the implants meet current materials standards and whether the mechanical properties of the devices make sense," Blais says, adding that some of the implants are considered to be mere variations of older ones that have been exempted from a full safety review. (Remember, companies are not required to provide detailed test data on implantable devices sold in Canada prior to October 1982.) In the United States, however, the FDA plans to review older types of knee and shoulder implants. I suppose this is a good sign, given the stakes are getting bigger.

Artificial hips and knees were first implanted mainly in the elderly, so even if they broke down after four or five years, the procedure was still good bang for the buck. However, people are living and remaining active much longer; so short-term implantation for the elderly is not the hot stuff it was.

In recent years, surgeons have been implanting more younger people. Emerson Brooks, an orthopaedic surgeon at Montreal General Hospital, says he finds it difficult to "tell a kid who is sixteen and can't walk to come back when he is older, like we used to. So, I'm doing more work now with teens." He admits, however, that some of his colleagues feel that, because the implants don't last, young people will be subjected to repeat operations. But Brooks counters that "some teens would be very happy to get out of their wheelchairs and go back to school if an implant will work well for them, say, for ten years."

He sees it as a philosophical issue.

But it is more than that.

12

SOFTWARE SAFETY:

The Neglect of Computer-Controlled Medical Devices

THE FAX DATED JUNE 23, 1992, WAS DROPPED ON MY desk. "It's a bit strange," the editor said, "but you never know."

It began with "To Whom It May Concern." The company, DLSF Systems Inc., of Kanata, a suburb of Ottawa, was offering an exclusive story on how and why Canadians were at risk from computerized medical devices. "We have selected four Canadian newspapers as our target," the fax stated. "The newspaper selected will be based solely on which one is first to respond and make a firm commitment to an article." It then went on to proclaim bluntly that "this tactic is being taken to avoid our wasting time and effort needlessly—a situation which has happened many times in the past." The newspapers—*The Gazette, The Toronto Star, The Financial Post,* and *The Globe and Mail*—had been sent the fax the same day.

I grinned. I hadn't seen a journalistic horse-race for a long while. The prize was presumably DLSF, a firm unknown to me. I figured from the tone of the fax that this was a consulting firm, offering its services to analyse the safety of computer software. True, more devices were becoming computerized—pacemakers, radiation therapy units, diagnostic scanners, and life-support equipment, among others—but chances were DLSF was not stirring up much business. The medical-devices industry, I had come to know, wasn't in a hurry to spend its cash on proper hazard analysis.

Nor was it being pushed hard to do so by regulatory agencies.

The Health department's Bureau of Radiation and Medical Devices lacked the expertise to judge the reliability of some of this complex medical machinery and therefore was content to rely on, and contribute its "resources" to, international efforts to standardize software safety, which included the International Organization for Standardization. The U.S. Food and Drug Administration wasn't faring much better. The FDA requirement that manufacturers of computerized medical devices submit proof of proper safety analysis applies only to new products. Exemptions are often granted on the grounds that a device is "substantially equivalent" to an old one. So anyone thinking that computer software for medical devices is automatically reviewed for bugs should think again.

I suppose you can't be too surprised that industry and governments don't get too excited about lapses in software-safety analysis. We do live in a world where commonplace horror is steadily displacing our sense of outrage. We eat our dinner before television images of people starving. We watch "live" coverage of war machines blasting away buildings, cities, and people.

Newspaper editors often resist emphasizing warnings in favour of blood-and-guts revelations. "I think we may be a little ahead of the story," they say. Translation: Wait until all hell breaks loose.

At *The Gazette*, I have been encouraged to pursue stories that might warn people about problems-in-the-making. However, the unusual fax from DLSF held a promise of blood and gore strewn over the landscape. So I began to research software safety. Well, the big news in the literature seemed to be that five cancer patients had been incorrectly zapped by a radiation-therapy machine named Therac-25. The maker was Atomic Energy of Canada Limited, a federal government-owned company. The first recorded ultrazaps were in June 1985, when a Canadian patient and one in Marietta, Georgia, were mutilated. Next spring at a hospital in Tyler, Texas, two patients received an excessive amount of radiation. One died; the other was paralysed. In 1987, a patient in Washington state received an overdose and was injured. At this point, the FDA suggested that perchance there was something wrong with the company's million-dollar zapper, and wouldn't the mystery of why people were being injured be solved before further use was made of the machine? Please. Thank you.

Eventually a defect in the software that guided Therac-25 was discovered: the culprit was the operation of an important switch.

Other software mess-ups are somewhat less dramatic. SRI of Menlo Park, California, a computer-industry think tank, tries to keep up on such things. They note that a system for keeping tabs on the vital life signs of patients mixed up the patients. A heart valve suddenly "froze." An insulin-dispensing machine delivered the wrong dose. An ultrasound machine underestimated foetal weight. Concentrations of oxygen and other vital gases in a ventilator dropped without warning. And so on. But nothing to knock the economy off the front page.

SRI also keeps a list of other types of software-related errors, about four hundred in all—such as bugs that affected flight plans of U.S. space shuttles, misfirings by war planes, deaths related to malfunction of industrial robots in Japan, and control failures in nuclear plants.

Now, few of us will ever make mission-control chief for Discovery 20 or pal around with potentially lethal robots in an industrial plant in Japan. And if we live near a nuclear plant or expect our airplanes and airport landing systems to bring us down safely, so what? We only rarely hear of problems.

When we do, they are usually handled with aplomb. In January 1990, a software error at Ontario Hydro's Bruce plant near Owen Sound released thousands of litres of radioactive water during a refuelling operation. But it's okay: no one was injured. More recently, a new radar system being tested out at Montreal's Dorval Airport failed for about fifteen minutes. There was no back-up, but hell, nothing happened. The air-traffic controllers simply paid attention until the machines took over again. And the system worked real well, without a sign of the software problems that caused it to freeze and to relay false information. An Air Canada 747-200 on "autopilot" went into a seventy-one-degree bank in September 1990. The crew regained control, and the jumbo was back on an even keel in no time flat. Not enough to cause me worry about software safety the next time that I fasten my seatbelt and put my seatback in an upright position.

Having completed such preliminary research on software safety, I sensed that perhaps DLSF was trying to horror-monger, and thereby scare up more business. I decided to call to see if I was still in the running for the exclusive.

Software Bugbusters

I was. No one else had showed any interest in DLSF.

DLSF was formed in 1984 to specialize in computer-systems consulting. President and computer specialist David Levan (DL) works mostly with colleague Susan Fraser (SF); they bring in outside expertise as needed. The company was looking for a niche in software-safety analysis. "We're living increasingly in a world where many computerized systems have direct consequences on human life, if their software behaves incorrectly," Levan explained. "We feel that it is also a moral imperative for companies and governments to get involved in this issue in a big way. And they are not."

Much of Levan's story was what I had expected: high ideals, high hopes. Some contracts to examine software screw-ups, and then not much. After being called in by Atomic Energy of Canada to look into Therac-25 software, and then by Ontario Hydro to find a way to protect its computerized system from further miscues, DLSF has gone from up-and-comer to nowhere. Not that its work hasn't been appreciated. Ontario Hydro has only good things to say about DLSF. They call Levan one of a very few individuals in the world qualified to set up procedures for software-safety analysis. (DLSF uses a step-by-step tree-branching walk through the software, developed over many years, to question how a system can fail.) But a business can't stay afloat when it is called in only after the fact, as in the case of Therac-25 and Ontario Hydro's radioactive spill.

"We've tried to interest hundreds of companies, especially medical-devices manufacturers, to let us come in and look over their software operations before any problems occur, but there is simply no interest," Levan says. "The companies are unable to appreciate the need for, or justify the expense, for performing safety analyses. In Canada, this attitude is particularly prevalent. There largely remains a false sense of security in many existing systems that have operated hazard-free for a time, and since governments are not pushing these companies, they don't bother. Some of these companies don't even seem to know what safety analysis is. We know this from our communications with them."

DLSF has also attempted to convince Canadian government departments, including Health and Welfare, Defence, and Transport, to take a greater interest in software safety. The reception has sometimes been courteous, but usually cool. Margaret Catley-Carlson, then deputy minister of Health, responded to Levan's approach by pointing out that her department is "an active participant in the development of internationally harmonized software safety standards."

This didn't impress Levan. "It will take five years or longer before any such standards are developed, and standards out there now are numerous, contradictory, and very confusing. The government should have set up its own standards by now and procedures for reviewing standards. It should at least be working on this now." (With DLSF's help, of course.) But Levan, rejected so often, now realizes that he has been dreaming.

What particularly bothers him is that there is considerable, growing interest in software safety among people employed in various government agencies, "but they are not given any support by their managers."

The Report

True enough. Back in April 1991, about twenty representatives from federal government agencies, including those involved in health, nuclear energy, and transportation, filed a report that warned of real danger to Canadians resulting from unreliable software. The group had met on at least eleven occasions over two years under the auspices of the National Research Council and had reached some strong conclusions. One was that there is an urgent need to formalize and coordinate standards for software and that a government agency is sorely needed to do this work—now, not later. The group also wanted a certification program established for computer programmers. There was a strong concern that anyone from a basement hacker to a PH.D in computer systems could claim expertise. The report stated: "Although computer programs are among the most complex artifacts built by humans, they are often 'built' and tested by haphazard techniques. . . ."

As for standards, the report said: "Unfortunately, although there are many existing standards in the international community, none are accepted widely as being adequate." Right. The report was shelved and ignored, and it was business as usual in computerland.

As of February 1993, DLSF is still in business—just. Further attempts to interest newspapers and television stations has produced no response.

"There is still no way to know most of the time whether a computerized medical device is less than thorough in software design, whether its programmers really had full comprehension of how the system was to be used, and whether incorrect assumptions about how systems elements in the device communicate," Levan said. "The companies —and government—are obviously playing the odds that nothing will happen, or that little will happen." And he added: "I predict that the next big medical fiasco will result from a software error. Maybe then, some people will wake up to this issue."

Well, David, you may be a little ahead of the story. And trying to frighten people doesn't make an exclusive. The real exclusive story is that not many people seem to care about what you are saying.

But I can tell you—I do.

13

THE 5-PER-CENT ACNE SOLUTION:
The Saga of Benzoyl Peroxide

WALK INTO YOUR NEAREST CHAIN PHARMACY AND you'll find aisles of food, perfumes, and school supplies. Somewhere near the back is the prescription counter, and in its immediate vicinity, near the condom shelf, are rows of over-the-counter drugs—cough and cold medicines, pain relievers, and acne medications. Some large pharmacies rent out space to foot-care specialists, dentists, chiropractors, and naturopaths. Some of these stores are open seven days a week, often from early morning until almost midnight. On weekends, paying for your Tylenol, Metamucil, panty-hose, paper towels, coffee, and bird seed can take half an hour.

At least once a year, and in apparent recognition of the fact that one can also buy pharmaceuticals in pharmacies, the organizations representing pharmacists have campaigns to encourage the populace to take advantage of their members' professional expertise. Want to know about a prescription drug's side-effects? ASK YOUR PHARMACIST. Need advice on which cold medicine to buy? ASK YOUR PHARMACIST. Well, maybe.

From my experience, which is often the result of researching a story on drugs, pharmacists have been helpful in answering questions on prescription products. Some pharmacists will sometimes even take exception to a doctor's prescription. A few will telephone a doctor and say something like: "You have prescribed much too high a dosage for this patient." Or, "I believe you made a prescribing error. This patient, who happens to be eighty-one years old, should never be given such a potent drug. It will blow out her kidneys."

Over-the-counter (OTC) medications are another matter. Whenever I've asked a pharmacist about a cough medicine or some pain remedy, the reply has usually amounted to: "They say it's good." On occasion, however, a pharmacist has discouraged me from using a particular product, usually by pointing to a competing brand and saying: "I think this may be better."

The truth is that the active ingredients found in some OTCs are about as effective against medical conditions as against cockroaches. Since the mid-1980s, regulatory agencies have been reviewing the efficacy of OTC products, such as cough and pain medicines and skin products, and finding that many of the ingredients lack efficacy, and, in some cases, may even be harmful, particularly when used in combination.

In March 1992, I navigated my way past the cans of mixed nuts, flea collars, and lipsticks in my local chain pharmacy to the large section of acne preparations. I had received a phone call from a former Health department doctor who suggested that I take an interest in the possibility that these ointments could contribute to skin cancer. One of his friends and colleagues at the department had first argued the case for cancer back in 1986 and retained his interest in the subject after retiring a year later. "George Frederick is a damn good toxicologist who got a raw deal in the department, like so many others," my medical contact volunteered. "Call him. He won't be afraid to talk to you about it. They can't do anything to him now."

Before calling Frederick, I thought I would take a peek at the various acne products. (If the story didn't work out, I'd still be stocked up on coffee and mixed-berry fruit juice.) So there I was, thinking of the thousands of adolescent hands that had reached out with a mixture of embarrassment and hope that a little dab would zap their zits.

Acne commonly begins in puberty and is caused by inflammation of the hair follicles and the sebaceous glands in the skin. The preparations claim to kill the bacteria involved in this process and then help to dry up the skin.

The active ingredient in many acne OTCs is benzoyl peroxide (BP)—most products contained a 5-per-cent concentration of this chemical that Frederick had wanted to ban.

George Frederick. The name sounded very familiar, but . . . Eureka! I had met George Frederick. He was the toxicologist who sat in on his Health department boss's two-hour soliloquy that answered none of my questions on Bendectin, a controversial anti-nausea drug. The event would have been the most boring two hours of my life, except that Frederick was yawning and fidgeting as much as I was, which cheered me up. When Frederick got in the occasional word, it was to sniff that as far as he was concerned, the drug was not causing birth defects and that if reporters knew something about science, we wouldn't be chasing the story.

Frederick's stiff telephone manner suggested that he hadn't changed his opinion of reporters and pointed out that he had been correct in his thinking about Bendectin, made unavailable to pregnant women because the media had trashed it. I'm convinced that the controversy over the drug has yet to be adequately resolved, but I bit my tongue. When I shifted the conversation to benzoyl peroxide, Frederick warmed a little.

The government had badly botched the case of BP, he said matter-of-factly, and with a trace of bitterness. His early retirement was prompted partly by the Health department's handling of the issue; but he hadn't quit on BP. He had written a technical report on acne preparations that he regularly updated. He promised to send a copy, and I said that I would get back to him after reading it.

I then decided to tap some of my sources, past and present employees of the Health department, to get a fix on Frederick. (Reporters do this type of background check to find out if there is a secret Hallowe'en party going on in the person's agenda.) Frederick was seen by all as a knowledgeable toxicologist, who had a tendency to "get involved" in issues. One of his former colleagues said: "George is solid, but he does go off on tangents." Another said: "George is really gung-ho on some things and he can be difficult when he gets his mind set."

I have no problem with gung-ho types, although I wonder how

they last in government as long as they do. Frederick had served for twenty years before he quit.

So what is this BP stuff, that was the last straw for George?

Benzoyl Peroxide

Benzoyl peroxide was first used in acne medications in Canada in the early 1960s on a prescription basis. In May 1981, products containing 5 per cent or less BP were permitted to be sold over the counter. The argument to allow a product to go off prescription typically runs as follows: It has stood the test of time. Its benefits exceed any known risks. Consumers should have the convenience of picking it off the shelf at a pharmacy. Visiting a doctor for a prescription unnecessarily adds to the nation's health-care bills.

This appears to be a reasonable argument—with one cautionary note: A product may have been around for a long time, but that doesn't necessarily mean that its long-term effects have been studied. In fact, research data showing BP has the potential to promote skin cancer (a process that may take two decades or longer) was first published the year that products containing it were allowed to be sold over the counter.

In the study, BP was given to mice previously treated with a known cancer-causing agent; the BP helped tumours to grow. As might be expected, one rodent study did not revolutionize the use of BP on humans; nor did several other similar studies pointing to the same conclusion. Reasonable questions crop up about studies of this type: Are the dosages of a chemical too strong? Are the test animals ultravulnerable to tumour-formation? Etc. The issue didn't begin to heat up until 1984 when a Japanese mouse study showed that BP not only promoted skin tumours, but caused tumour growth on its own. (Within a year, eight of twenty mice treated with BP developed skin tumours.)

The Japanese study eventually caught the medical eye of Ian Henderson, then the director of Canada's Bureau of Human Prescription Drugs. He wasn't especially concerned, but felt that a departmental effort should make sense of the available research data on BP. Henderson turned to Frederick, as he often did when in need of a toxicological assessment.

Frederick became convinced that BP was both a promoter and an initiator of skin cancer in animals. As acne is not a life-threatening condition, he argued, wasn't it senseless to allow continued use of BP products—whether OTC or prescription. Why take the risk? He recommended a ban on BP.

Henderson called in the department's advisory committee on dermatology, composed of dermatologists, pharmacologists, and pharmacists. As the committee lacked expertise in toxicology, Frederick was assigned to it as adviser.

The question before the committee was: Is BP likely to cause skin cancer in humans? The short answer was: Who knows? More studies were required. So the committee steered a middle ground. It recommended that BP be made available only on prescription until more data were collected.

Frederick was furious with the committee's decision. Why ban OTC sales of 5-per-cent concentrations of BP yet allow 10-per-cent or higher-level versions to be sold on prescription? Some committee members had faith that prescribing doctors would carefully monitor their patients. "By removing it from non-prescription sales, we figured that it would send a message to doctors that they should keep an eye on their patients and look for any problems," one said. Frederick countered, "There was excessive confidence that doctors can detect early stages of side-effects in their patients before these get serious."

Some committee members felt that Frederick was hell-bent on steering only one course—a ban. "His attitude," said one, "precluded discussion."

The committee's recommendation was made on April 20, 1987. Several days later, Frederick decided on early retirement. BP strongly influenced his decision, but he was also disturbed about changes in regulatory practice that increasingly favoured industry. For the drift towards shorter animal tests of the carcinogenic properties of new chemicals would inevitably allow potentially harmful products to slip through undetected. Industry was becoming much more aggressive, and government capitulation was not Frederick's idea of drug regulation.

So Frederick said goodbye to the Health department—but not to BP.

The Health department, as is customary, solicited reactions from health professionals and the drug industry to the dermatology committee's recommendation. The Non-prescription Drug Manufacturers Association of Canada and the Washington, D.C.–based Proprietary Association made a joint submission, dated July 9, 1987. The two lobbies cited the findings of the International Agency for Research in Cancer (IARC), a World Health Organization affiliate. In 1985, as part of its regular review of potential carcinogens, the agency had concluded that there was inadequate evidence on the basis of available research data for the carcinogenicity of BP, either to experimental animals or to humans. The lobbies claimed the IARC's routine reinvestigation of BP in 1987 was a complete update of the intervening years and that "the 1987 Working Group concluded that no change in the earlier evaluation was warranted."

Of course, that's not what the 1987 IARC report said. Rather, it made clear that its overall evaluation of BP "was generally based on the summary and evaluation of the most recent monograph on that agent [the 1985 report]." There it is, right on page 39.

Frederick got his hands on a copy of the non-prescription-drug industry's submission and immediately spotted the discrepancy. "Other studies on BP had been published in the interim and the IARC had not included them in their 1987 report," he said.

Angry and frustrated by what was, at a minimum, a stupid error, Frederick spoke to some reporters (and got a brief mention of his concerns in the January issue of *Canadian Consumer*.)

The Health department, however, sided with industry's view of the IARC BP review. A letter from former Health minister Jake Epp, dated June 29, 1988, to NDP MP Howard McCurdy, cites the 1987 IARC report as part of the evidence that led to the decision that "no action will be taken to restrict the nonprescription sale of products containing 5 per cent or less of BP." McCurdy, then

NDP health critic, had discussed BP with Frederick and had written to Epp asking that all BP products—prescription and non-prescription—be banned.

In a reply to Epp's letter, McCurdy wrote on July 27: "It is indeed unfortunate that members of your office, senior managers in [Health Protection Branch] and industry are providing you with such erroneous information."

But Epp didn't budge on the issue, and the controversy lost its legs. Frederick backed off from fighting via the media—until he heard from me, four years later.

After I read Frederick's detailed report on BP, I naturally wondered what the FDA's thinking was. I got in touch with Murray Lumpkin, an MD who is chief of the U.S. agency's anti-infective-drug division. Lumpkin was very informative, particularly about the agency's plans for products with BP. (In the United States, the concentrations of up to 10 per cent can be sold OTC.)

An FDA advisory panel met on April 10, 1992, to discuss BP. One of its concerns was BP's potential role in stimulating skin cancer initiated by sunlight. Lumpkin explained: "Teenagers are putting this stuff [acne preparations] on every day and going out into the sunlight. We know that sunlight is an initiator of skin tumours. We need to know whether benzoyl peroxide helps [sunlight] along." To this end, drug companies, prodded on by the FDA, were sponsoring studies to investigate this association, he said. They would be completed in 1995 or 1996.

To date, according to Lumpkin, there are no studies that can prove BP either safe or harmful. (A Saskatchewan population study sponsored by the Canadian and U.S. non-prescription-drug industry showed no association between acne medications and skin cancers. Lumpkin referred to the study, published in 1991 in the British *Journal of Dermatology*, as "helpful, but limited.")

The FDA committee voted unanimously to keep BP on the market, but asked the FDA to come up with wording that notifies consumers about the concerns. Lumpkin said the FDA was "working on this."

And what was the Canadian Health department working on?

House of Commons. June 18, 1992. Question Period. Howard McCurdy asks a question:

"Isn't it time for the Health department to act for the Canadian people . . . to protect those teenagers and young people who are using a potential carcinogen on their skin twice daily?"

Standing in for Health minister Benoît Bouchard, Barbara Sparrow, his parliamentary secretary, replies that BP concentrations in acne preparations are stronger in the United States. She goes on to say:

> *Ingredients are listed very explicitly and very carefully on all these salves and ointments sold within the retail business or indeed the wholesale business throughout Canada. There is not the cause for alarm in Canada, as indeed there might be south of the border.*

McCurdy:

> *Mr. Speaker, that is absolutely outrageous. We are talking about medicines used by teenagers for treating acne. They are supposed to understand that benzoyl peroxide means something. In fact, the concentrations the Hon. member is talking about are the same concentrations used for eliciting cancer in animals, the same concentration as used in mice.*
>
> *I repeat my question to the minister, Is this government prepared to re-examine recommendations made by its scientists and an external advisory committee that this stuff be banned from over-the-counter sales to kids?*

Sparrow:

> *Mr. Speaker, it is very serious and I take the member's question very seriously. I assure him that Health and Welfare Department will be monitoring this situation very closely.*

Maybe. But, if they don't, George Frederick certainly will.

4

OPTIONS

14

THE POLITICAL OPTION:

Swift Kick and New Think

Rethreading Canada's health-protection safety net will be a very difficult task. No simple formula can set things right.

Health and Welfare Canada's handling of drugs and medical devices has been negligent and near-criminal. Thanks to the Tory "laissez-faire" philosophy, the drug and medical-devices industries have been on a tear at the price of the safety of Canadians. Drugs are rushed on the market despite warnings from the Health department's own medical experts. Medical devices, including downright dangerous breast implants, are declared safe. The routine appearance of the Health minister as apologist for the status quo is a grotesque joke.

So, if we are ever to witness major change in health protection, we must begin with a thorough housecleaning in the Health department. Mere reform won't do. And we need short- and long-term ideas to make the system work for us, the Canadian people. We're tired of bureaucratic prescriptions that make only multinationals and their political toadies feel better.

And we can do it, for the fact is that the ability to reverse current trends rests with us. The politicians have to respond to public demand, even if it means whipping the bureaucrats into shape to restore a sense of duty to a system that is entrusted to protect us from the dangers of drugs and medical devices.

What is required to make the system work for us? The problems run much deeper than the money that flows to programs. Our politicians dance to the tune of a poorly conceived industrial strategy on drugs that is totally at odds with our most fundamental safety requirements.

We have managers in health protection who are not sufficiently schooled for the job—a pesticide expert managing a prescription drug bureau, heads of drug-review sectors who have no medical training, an assistant deputy minister brought in from the armed forces, who has never previously dealt with drugs or medical devices, etc. Cronyism and an emphasis on managerial skills have supplanted technical competence.

We have high-level government officials blithely claiming that industry wants only to do good by us. Are they merely in need of a vacation?

We have blatant conflict of interest in the review of drugs. Doctors and scientists with at least one body part in the drug industry are given large sums of taxpayers' money to recommend whether a drug should be approved.

Most amazing is the spectacle of a chief drug-industry lobbyist serving on a government committee that selects managers for the health-protection system. If this isn't the fox guarding the chicken coop, I'm not sure what is.

We have systemic harassment in the federal health-protection system. Nor is there a safe haven for public servants who wish to voice their concerns about public-health threats that are being ignored by their superiors.

No, mere money and new programs will not fix the health-protection system. Nor will merely replacing one set of politicians with another. Too much dirt has settled to be swept away by a new political broom.

Here's what we need to do, at minimum, for an adequate housecleaning:

1. Scour Management

In recent months, three senior bureaucrats at Health and Welfare have left their jobs. Margaret Catley-Carlson is no longer deputy Health minister. Albert Liston is no longer deputy minister for the Health Protection Branch. And Emmanuel Somers is no longer director general of the Drugs Directorate. All three had been mired in public controversy.

To scores of Health department scientists and doctors, their exit signified that there was a smidgeon of hope.

Then a bureaucrat from Agriculture took over Catley-Carlson's job and a career army officer was blasted into Liston's spot. The search continues for a permanent replacement for Somers: perhaps a ballroom dancer is available.

No sooner had the pesticides expert replaced Jacques Messier, the veterinarian, as head of the Bureau of Human Prescription Drugs than Messier took a job with a generic drug company.

Sooner or later, such shenanigans will prove so embarrassing that someone will establish a full, independent public review of the way Health and Welfare hires its managers. To continue to rely on individuals without appropriate technical skills to oversee the review of drugs and medical devices is to admit that politics—not science—rules the day. An open investigation would likely result in the demise of several fiefdoms and the rooting-out of some cronyism and harassment.

What is at issue is the integrity of Canada's largest government bureaucracy. Recent reports on drug review and medical devices, although they referred to the lack of morale among reviewers, paid no attention to the fundamental reasons for the turmoil.

2. Disinfect Against Conflict of Interest and Political Interference

The weakened safety system has little immunity to infection from the drug and medical-devices industries or the medical and scientific communities that depend on industry research funds. As we have seen, the Health department is content to allow a doctor conducting drug trials for a drug company to review its safety and efficacy submission on the same drug. And it thinks nothing of farming-out a drug submission to an outside expert whose wife is the medical director of a drug company. Even in the face of such evidence, department managers call for more farming-out of submissions for new drugs and medical devices to outside reviewers, many of whom either worked for or maintain ties with industry. Yet recent reports on drug review and medical devices do not even acknowledge that problems associated with contracting-out have been swept under the rug by Health department officials.

Denis Gagnon's latest assessment of drug review suggests that scientists in academe should be contracted to hasten the drug-review process. Can these scientists be sufficiently dissociated from industry? I doubt it, considering the huge industry funding that is funnelled into university science research and the industrial-academic loyalties thereby created. There are relatively few scientists totally free of this process.

Gagnon has also called for an arm's-length agency to take over some of the tasks of the Drugs Directorate. He also wants an advisory council on medicines to be staffed by "highly regarded Canadian professionals selected from outside the public service." In both recommendations, Gagnon fails to understand that the people least likely to fall under the spell of lobbyists are government scientists paid by the public. The lack of independence that has corroded health-protection research is a result of managers who have greater interest in the political pulse than in solid research. The Meme breast implant and anti-migraine drug Imitrex are particularly damning evidence of such interference.

Of course, farming-out reviews is totally unnecessary, the perceived need to do so is based on the false notion that delays in approving important drugs are harming Canadians. The Gagnon Report merely reiterates this industry-created bugaboo.

Assuming that reason will not prevail, and that more drugs and medical devices will be reviewed by outside doctors and scientists, strong and enforceable guidelines are required in order to prevent conflict of interest. Current guidelines, which allow some ties to industry, are unacceptable.

3. Scrub Industry Meddling with Government Operations

I was astounded. Judy Erola, the top-dog lobbyist for the multinational prescription-drug industry, was helping to select the head of the Non-prescription Drugs bureau. Yup, Erola actually sat on the board that reviewed candidates.

I was even more astounded by the response from Erola and the Health department. A mere shrug.

Should there be a formal investigation of this outrageous violation of public trust? Damn right. Will there be? Probably not. How was this ever allowed? Who is responsible? How much more industry interference goes on in government? I don't know, but I'm working on it.

4. Shine Up Rules that Prevent Government Scientists from Speaking Out on Urgent Health Matters

Over the years, I have spoken with many government scientists, sick at heart at being undercut or ignored after recommending that a product not be approved. Some were considered to be mere nitpickers or alarmists. Some probably were. But this book has presented dramatic cases of scientists who persisted in warning their bosses about a drug or medical device. There are more shocking stories of government neglect to be told, but I have learned to be patient, not bullying my sources into releasing documents necessary to deliver the story. They will come round—they usually do—and the truth will out.

Many individuals in government have a profound distrust of the media. They do not feel secure divulging information to someone who may not have control over how the information is used. I can understand that. Stories sometimes get trimmed or buried or botched.

Yet my own conclusion is that democracy suffers when individuals in government who wish to speak out on an issue do so only at their personal peril. There should be legislation to protect whistle blowers.

5. Air Undue Secrecy

The Health department functions like a secret society. Managers should be accountable for their decisions to parliamentary committees, not solely to the minister of Health. The occasional hearing or audit of operations is tokenism. Decisions on high-profile drugs or lack of action on controversial medical devices should be subject to rigorous, routine public review. Committees that advise the Health department should be required to hold open hearings on controversial drugs and medical devices. At present not only is the work done in private, but committee members are forbidden by the government to discuss their deliberations.

One member of the Halcion review committee asked the Health department for permission to talk to me, as I had requested. He then told me that he could be questioned on Halcion, but not on the committee's work. I knew from other sources that the committee's work was sloppy at best, which was not unexpected, as advisory committees meet infrequently and hurriedly. The committee that reviewed Halcion after the British banned it was thrown together by the Health department with little consideration of its technical competence to conduct a thorough and expert review. One witness to the proceedings said, "The eagerness to give the drug a good review from the start was deeply disturbing in the face of contrary evidence. And unfortunately, some committee members seemed predisposed to racing through that evidence."

Clearly, how the Health department selects committee members and how committees go about their business need serious scrutiny.

Any reorganization of federal evaluation of drugs and medical devices must be preceded by a wholesale housecleaning of the health-protection system. A good way to start the process would be for a special government committee, involving all major parties, to create a public forum for scientists and doctors in the Health department. With a guarantee of job protection, they could air their concerns about health protection in the open.

Focus of Attention on the Real Crisis

Canadians have been hearing a lot about how the approval of important new drugs is delayed and how the drug backlog has negatively affected the health of Canadians. The Gagnon Report is based on this fallacy. In fact, we are witnessing one of the greatest con jobs in Canadian health-care history. Even the opposition parties seem to have swallowed the drug-industry line.

It's time for the drug industry and its lobby, the Pharmaceutical Manufacturers Association of Canada, to put up or shut up. It is time for the industry to issue a list of drugs whose approval was untimely and to offer proof that these delays have affected the health of Canadians. Let's have a good look at the industry's case. Let the politicians who have joined this con game come up with lists, too. On what basis have they been mouthing off about the need to speed up drug approval? Let's make the process public. Let's have the evidence.

While we're at it, let the Health department make public a listing of all the drugs that have been approved for market since, say, 1980. The list should include all pertinent details about the drugs, such as the time it took for approval and whether reviewers considered them to be potential breakthrough products, i.e., significant improvements over older drugs or simply mimics of existing products.

Then let's set up a committee of pharmacologists and pharmacists that can assess the information and reach independent conclusions.

This issue is fundamental to health protection and to health care in general. New drugs are not necessarily better drugs. The same is true of medical devices. As health-care costs soar, and there is little evidence that more medicine means better health, non-pharmaceutical means to health, including assaults on poverty, malnutrition, poor housing, and environmental decay, are vital.

Before further reorganization of health protection occurs, the following issues must be addressed:

1. Policy on Pharmaceuticals and Medical Devices Must be Established in the Context of National Health Goals

Drug costs are rapidly increasing. Canadians now pay as much or more for pharmaceuticals than for physicians' services. New and more costly drugs are being touted to doctors along with mythology that anything new is an improvement. They are as vulnerable to ads in medical journals as TV watchers are to commercials.

One bright spot on the horizon is the possibility that federal and provincial governments will create a national drug agency to provide cost-benefit data on drugs and to seek out the most appropriate drugs for the most appropriate prices. But this is no substitute for a clear national health policy that creates a balance between the amounts we spend on treatment and on prevention of illness.

Despite all the hoopla you hear about prevention, hoopla is all it is. Back in 1975, Marc Lalonde, who then served as federal Health minister, issued a report entitled *A New Perspective on the Health of Canadians*. Lalonde concluded that any overall improvements in the health of the population will likely come about as a result of changes in lifestyles, social and physical environments, and biology—not from additional funding to treat illness.

Better sanitation and public-health programs have significantly reduced illness from infectious diseases. The new Enemy, chronic disease, has multiple causes, including poor diet, tobacco smoking, alchohol, and day-to-day stress.

Lalonde's work was endorsed by a wide range of health professionals in Canada, the United States and Europe. But, unfortunately, there was insufficient political will to draw funding from medical and hospital programs to the requisite social programs.

In 1986, Health minister Jake Epp introduced his Lalonde-like analysis and received considerable applause for his efforts, but the medical model of health prevails. Moreover, politicians are making it both easier and quicker for drug companies to drug us— and rob us. Agencies outside of government are focusing attention on the cost-benefit assessment of new medical technology, but there is little political initiative, apart from a few voices in the wilderness, to curb the medical arms race.

2. Loose Controls on Drug Advertising are Endangering Canadians

Federal legislation is needed to bring drug advertising under stronger control. The case of Toradol is but one example of why change is essential. Better balance is required in a product's presentation of its benefits and pitfalls. Monitoring should be done by a special unit at Consumer and Corporate Affairs, which should have strong legal powers to investigate suspected misleading advertising. Penalties should be stiff, and include criminal proceedings, if necessary.

Any system to evaluate the safety and effectiveness of drugs will be undermined if the drug industry is allowed to present doctors with unbalanced information on its products.

3. There must be Public and Political Debate on any Proposed International Agreements in Drug and Medical-Devices Review

Before we sign agreements to further limit safety reviews—such as reducing the time required for animal toxicology studies or for federal reviewers to respond to drug-company proposals for clinical tests—there should be ample opportunity to debate on these proposals. If scientists, inside or outside government, believe that animals should be followed for eighteen months rather than six months to detect signs of cancer, then they should have a public forum in which to present their cases. There is no good reason why Canada should become involved in some whirlwind harmonization of review standards. The only reason for doing so would be to bring music to please the drug industry's ears.

Some of my prescriptions for change border on heresy in a world where open debate is considered to be unnecessary by a bureaucratic élite habituated to unbridled power. I also know that there is no political advantage to opening up a can of worms.

But there you have it. If we can keep the can under their noses, and keep picking at the lid, sooner or later they'll have to sniff the contents.

In the meantime, there are some personal options—ways of dealing more effectively day-to-day in a world of growing deregulation.

15

THE PERSONAL OPTION:

Become Street Smart on Drugs and Medical Devices

RELAX. THIS ISN'T GOING TO BE SOME SILLY CALL TO futile action. If I have learned anything during my years of banging on the health-protection door, it is this: politicians may come and go, but bureaucrats drop anchor. True, the Americans have rid themselves of George and Dan, the twin towers of "deregulation." And low-rise Brian has followed the Torch of Wasted Time into the sunset. But fresh air is often insufficient to scrape the carbuncles off bureaucracies. This is particularly true of Health and Welfare Canada, and its culture incompatible with protecting Canadians from unsafe drugs and medical devices.

As we saw in the last chapter, with careful scrubbing, we can slowly eliminate some of the encrusted gunk, but patience is the watchword here. And beware, we are headed into a deregulated global economy without the balancing power of a global consumer movement. Battling solely for national improvements in health protection will prove futile in the face of free-trade pacts that supersede some national regulations.

There is no easy personal answer to this dilemma, of course. Much will depend on your level of commitment to seek out information and act on it, either alone or as part of an advocacy group. The first step is to become more acutely aware of the information around you.

Back in the 1960s, it was often claimed that media controls consciousness. This is still the rule, except perhaps for that of a hermit living without a cellular phone in the crater of an extinct volcano.

What actually enters your consciousness, is, of course, up for grabs. Hundreds of sales messages rat-ta-tat on the door to our psyche every day: from value-laden TV and radio advertising to billboards, to designer clothes emblazoned with endangered animals (or people), to newspapers, radio, books, and magazines. To dismiss much of this river of information as shallow, particularly as it applies to health, prescription drugs, and medical devices, is to miss the point. You can drown in only a couple of inches of drivel. The only way to protect yourself is to look before you leap. Sure, this is easier said than done, but here are some hints, anyway.

Media

Recently, I appeared with three other health reporters on *The Media Show*, a CBC Newsworld TV production. We discussed how the media handles health topics and unanimously concluded that far too many stories are generated by press conferences set up by drug companies or their public-relations factories. We also agreed that far too many health reporters for newspapers, TV, or radio have little or no technical expertise, so they are unable to raise critical questions. Or they are squeezed for time, forced to report quickly, without time to assess the validity of so-called medical or drug breakthroughs. Some reporters cite disappearing newsroom budgets that necessitate speedier and spottier coverage. They whine that their editors believe only hype sells. Of course, all reporters can say, "No, I'm sorry, I won't cover this story because it will be a disservice to our readers." Or, "Your concept of this story is bilge. I'm a reporter; not a public-relations specialist." They have nothing to lose but their jobs.

So you can expect very little investigative reporting on health issues in Canadian newspapers. Rarely do stories call to public attention the dangers and wasted resources in day-to-day health care. Few Canadian newspapers have even one reporter on the

Health beat full time. Usually, reporters on general assignment are handed medical or science stories. (In the United States, large newspapers have several reporters on the Health beat, but no more in-depth coverage. PR companies just strike gold more often, and conventional wisdom gets a more frequent airing.)

Television reporting on health is an even greater embarrassment, with its predictable focus on breakthroughs. If half the breakthroughs reported by TV in the past ten years were real we'd all be Olympic athletes at age one hundred.

Radio-news broadcasters tend to pick up some ditty off the wires or pilfer information from a newspaper. And beware of physicians who appear on radio talk shows. They may be knowledgeable in a particular area, but a medical degree does not automatically confer expertise on everything under the skin.

Radio talk shows are also the favourite playground for "product champions," physicians who tour the country on behalf of and on the expense account of drug companies. At some point in their exposition on a particular disease, these doctors casually slip in the name of the drug they are championing. Just once I'd like to hear a talk-show host asking a product champion: "Doctor, aren't you behaving unethically by shilling a drug to the public?" Hey, I can dream, can't I?

Doctors

The next time you visit your doctor, glance around the office. Note all the items donated by drug companies—scratch pads, pencils, pens, daily planners, calendars, and free samples. Even if you're not convinced that you're sitting in a drug-industry storage room, you might ask where your doctor's information on drugs originates: "On what basis are you prescribing this drug to me?" Or, "Did you learn about the drug from (A) a drug salesman or advertising, (B) scientific articles published in a journal, or (C) a colleague?"

If the answer is A, be wary. If it's B, ask for the journal references or an account of the research, including a detailed listing of potential side-effects. Think of a drug prescription as a form of "chemical surgery." If it's (C), ask if that doctor learned about the drug from (A) or (B), till you get back to the source.

If your doctor is not prepared to discuss drugs in these terms, you might want to shop around for more in-depth consultation.

But simply trusting any doctor's opinion about a drug or medical procedure isn't the answer. A profession allied with the drug and medical-devices industries cannot be taken at its word on anything. Informed opinions from people outside the medical mainstream are fundamental to your health protection. These may only be a telephone call away.

Consumer Groups

Several years ago, women's groups across Canada banded together and successfully pressured Health and Welfare Canada to hold off approval of Depo Provera, an injectable contraceptive manufactured by the Upjohn Company of Kalamazoo, Michigan. An advisory committee to the Health department had recommended approval of the drug, but the consumer umbrella group painstakingly highlighted the drug's inadequate testing and the scientific concerns that it had the potential to cause cancer. The protest showed two things: first, it is possible to affect health policy in Canada; but, second, an extraordinary effort is required in order to have an impact.

Unlike the United States, Canada does not have a strong consumer tradition in the health area. The Depo Provera issue created the makings of a network, but it lacks a cohesive and persuasive voice, a fact well noted by Health department officials who have little use for consumer input. (Appendix A lists consumer groups in Canada and the United States that focus on drugs and medical devices.)

The old standby, the Consumers' Association of Canada (CAC), is not geared to raise hell on health issues: instead, its representatives participate ably on professional health-care panels with groups such as the Canadian Medical Association and the Canadian Hospital Association. The CAC also joins the occasional government-sponsored committee, thus allowing politicians and bureaucrats to claim that the consumer's voice is heard in government deliberations.

This is not effective consumerism. What's needed in Canada are consumer groups that regularly monitor and challenge government regulatory decisions.

So you should also look south of the border for alternative information and advice on drugs and medical devices. At the top of the list should be the Washington-based Public Citizen's Health Research Group. Led by Sidney Wolfe, a physician, HRG is a perennial thorn in the side of the drug and medical-devices industries, and of the U.S. Food and Drug Administration. It has taken on such issues as breast implants and the sleeping pill Halcion. HRG publishes books, newsletters, and numerous position papers analysing FDA policy on specific drugs and medical devices. There is no consumer group even remotely comparable in Canada.

U.S. women's groups are also playing an important role in challenging health policy. Among them are the Boston Women's Book Collective (the group whose book, *Our Bodies, Ourselves*, revolutionized self-care for women) and the Women's National Health Network. During the height of the breast-implant débâcle, the Command Trust Network, a terrific source of information on breast implants, emerged as an influential voice. The information made available by these groups has been very valuable in my own investigations.

Government Committees

In Canada, occasional reports are produced by government committees digging into a particular health issue. (One such committee expressed concern about the lack of adequate treatment for breast cancer.) For the most part, however, the parliamentary system fails to oversee the performance of Health department bureaucrats. By contrast, U.S. congressional committees often hold hearings on health issues, during which high-level government bureaucrats are held accountable for their policy decisions. (For example, the House Subcommittee on Human Resources and Intergovernmental Affairs played a major role in rooting out some of the FDA's inaction on breast implants. The committee's investigators determined that the agency was not ensuring that breast implants were safe and effective. The hearings were public and reports were published.)

This type of information is invaluable in helping me to sort out issues in Canada. All it takes is a phone call to ask for a report or to speak to one of the committee investigators. You can do it too.

Voluntary Associations

Numerous national, regional, and local organizations represent the interests of individuals with cancer, heart disease, arthritis, AIDS, migraine headaches, and so on. These groups often do a bang-up job in fund-raising for research and providing support to those who are ill and their families. But I would not rely too heavily on these groups to provide full information about diseases and their treatments. Some of these voluntary associations are too chummy with the drug companies, which are delighted to provide financial assistance—and buy loyalty. Before you hook up with any association or support group, ask for a list of their sponsors.

Computer Access

It's remarkable what can be accessed by a computer, either your own or one at a library. Computer services retrieve a wide cross-section of articles. Some are "review articles," which sum up what is known on a subject, list the original studies, and analyse trends, often in language intelligible to the non-medical mind.

This is not something that everyone will care to do; but it is not as difficult as it may first appear. If it is informed opinion that you are after, there is no better way to get an excellent cross-section—and, no doubt, your fill of controversy.

No matter how involved you decide to get, remember the likelihood is that you're not getting the whole story. So, consumer—beware.

16

FINAL WORD

Looking Ahead

O N JANUARY 12, 1993, FEDERAL HEALTH MINISTER Benoît Bouchard finally extended a moratorium on the use of silicone-gel breast implants into a full-fledged ban. Their use now will be allowed only following removal of a cancerous breast or deformity, and any manufacturer wishing to sell this type of implant in Canada to women will have to prove it is safe and effective.

The department also released a survey of almost 4,000 women with breast implants, which revealed that one-third would not opt for surgery again and 23 per cent had some type of complication within two weeks of surgery.

Bouchard, true to form, maintained nonetheless that his department acted correctly in its handling of breast implants.

An *Ottawa Citizen* editorial three days later referred to the "too-little, too-late moves" as a "staggering dereliction of public responsibility over silicone breast implants."

Obviously, I can't agree more.

Silicone-gel breast implants have joined thalidomide and the Dalkon Shield as the major tragedies of health protection gone awry.

Will breast implants become an issue in the next federal election?

Probably. I know for a fact that the Liberals and NDP have been accumulating files for just that purpose.

Though hot politically, the breast-implant issue is, however, the thin edge of the wedge. Please, let's not forget this. In the last two weeks alone, I've set my sights on boiling issues that beg for more attention, and it's not surprising that some of the products of key concern are those used by women.

Look at fertility drugs, which may contribute to ovarian cancer and congenital malformations. For example, the drug Clomid has been prescribed widely to induce ovulation, but has never been methodically researched. It has been around for twenty-five years, yet no one has bothered to investigate how it works or to track the drug sufficiently to understand its range of risks.

Does this seem all too familiar?

Well, maybe I'd better call up Health and Welfare to see what is being done about Clomid.

And, of course, there's also the case of the . . .

APPENDIX A

Resources

The following health- and public-policy groups are the best in providing well-documented information on health issues.

CANADA

DES Action Canada
(National Office)
5890 Monkland Avenue,
Suite 203
Montreal, Quebec H4A 1G2
(514) 482-3204

Women's Health Resource
  Centre
790 Bay Street
Toronto, Ontario M5G 1N9
(416) 586-0211

UNITED STATES

(Ralph Nader's) Public Citizen
215 Pennsylvania Avenue SE
Washington, D.C. 20003
(202) 546-4996

Public Citizen's Health Research
  Group
2000 P. Street NW, Suite 700
Washington, D.C., 20036
(202) 833-3000

Command Trust Network
(Breast implants)
P.O. Box 17082
Covington, Kentucky 41017

The Boston Women's Health
Book Collective
240A Elm Street, Davis Square
Somerville, Mass. 02144
(617) 625-0271

National Women's Health
  Network
1325 G. Street NW
Washington, D.C. 20005
(202) 347-1140

Human Resources and
  Intergovernmental Relations
  Subcommittee of the
  Committee on Government
  Operations
Rayburn House Office Building,
Room 372
Washington, D.C. 20615
(202) 225-2382

APPENDIX B

On the paper trail of the Meme: a sampler

EXHIBIT ONE:
A covering memo and notes of a meeting held in the Research and Standards Division on January 6, 1989 to review polyurethane-coated breast prostheses. The memo is signed by David Johnson, Chief of the Division.

EXHIBIT TWO:
On February 20, 1989, Pierre Blais reported to his boss, I. Hinberg, Head of the Research and Development Section, that the Meme implant and its analogs "are unfit for human implantation and are potentially hazardous to users." This memo, summarizing the findings in the attached report, was received by Hinberg's office the same day.

EXHIBIT THREE:
On March 2, Hinberg directs Blais to alter his memo to incorporate "corrections" prepared by David Johnson, Hinberg's boss.

EXHIBIT FOUR:
A reproduction of David Johnson's handwritten alterations to Blais' report. (The complete text, as altered by Johnson, follows.) Hinberg's directive to Blais to alter the document (Exhibit Four) was attached to Johnson's revisions.

EXHIBIT FIVE:
On March 6, 1989, Blais unwillingly incorporated the changes demanded by Hinberg and Johnson, noting that they "significantly altered" both the record and the content of his findings.

EXHIBIT SIX:
The Health Department covers up Blais' recommendations in a March 8, 1989 briefing note to the Minister of Health.

EXHIBIT ONE:

Government of Canada Memorandum

To: Dr. E. G. Létourneau
Director, Bureau of Radiation and Medical Devices

From: David L. Johnson, Ph.D.
Chief, Research and Standards Division

Date: 189-01 13

Subject: RSD Meeting Re Polyurethane (PU) Breast Implants

Attached are my notes on a meeting recently held in my Division to review available information on PU coated breast prostheses. I suggest it be discussed at the next MDCC meeting.

Signed: David L. Johnson

attach: 1   Date stamped: Director's Office
cc: S. Mohanna, W. Welsh   Jan. 17, 1989

RESEARCH AND STANDARDS DIVISION
REPORT ON A CONSENSUS DEVELOPMENT MEETING ON POLYURETHANE (PU) COATED BREAST IMPLANTS

The meeting was held on Friday, January 6, 1989 in the Environmental Health Centre Boardroom. The meeting was chaired by Dr. David L. Johnson. In attendance were Mr. Louis Boulay, Mrs. K. Bedard, Mrs. H. Shahbazian and Drs. Ben-Simhon, Hinberg, Blais and Chawla. The following report summarizes discussion of the agenda (Attachment 1).

Introduction: Dr. Johnson noted that breast prostheses have been on the market for some 20 years. They are used for two distinctively different purposes; augmentation and reconstruction.

Within the last few years there has been increasing litigation in both the U.S. and Canada which is getting attention.

In June 1988, the Health Protection Branch announced publication of a booklet (developed in conjunction with the Canadian and Quebec Associations of Plastic Surgeons), which deals with augmentation (cosmetic) surgery.

In June 1988, the US FDA reclassified silicone breast implants into Class III – Premarket Review. (Breast implants have been subject to Premarket Review in Canada since 1983). On November 22, 1988, the US FDA held a panel meeting to review the available information on silicone breast implants. (Polyurethane (PU) coated breast implants were not included in this review.)

Over the last couple of years BRMD has been involved in research into the behaviour of polyurethane as an implant material in general.

This meeting was part of a continuing review by the Branch, of the effectiveness and safety of breast prostheses. The intent of this meeting was to focus on the particular benefits and problems of PU coated breast prostheses, to look at the net result of those, and to consider whether any further action is needed.

1) Mr. Boulay reported on the current market situation in Canada. Only one PU coated implant is notified, the Même prosthesis and its related models. As the manufacturer states that it is the same device that has been sold since 1981, this device predates Part V and does not need a Notice of Compliance. The role of BRMD regarding such "grandfathered devices" is to pay special attention to post market surveillance of their safety and effectiveness.

2) Mrs. Hripsime Shahbazian gave a review of the problem report history of breast implants. Only one of the ten or eleven Canadian reports

dealt with the Même breast prosthesis.

3) Dr. Blais reviewed the types of breast implant available, and sketched the history of the BRMD search for information on their performance. Problems with breast implants may occur as early as during the implantation, or as late as five years afterwards. Our research has not been specific to any particular implant, but has looked generally at adverse reactions, risks, long term effects, supporting creation of a reference sample collection and implant recovery program, some analysis of failed implants, and publication of results in scientific and medical journals.

In 1986, Branch asked the Canadian Society of Plastic and Reconstructive Surgeons to obtain some statistics on use of various types of implant. They reported that in Quebec and Ontario, some 300 to 400 women have breast prostheses removed annually. More than 100 women have the prostheses replaced.

The Branch has one contract, with Laval University, to characterize and study implants previously retrieved by the contractor. The contractor has recovered and characterized 107 samples. Despite suggestions that between 10% and 30% of implants sold may be PU coated, none of the 107 samples is PU. Dr. Blais expressed the opinion that the 107 were from a population implanted bedore the PU coated prosthesis became popular. He believes that since 1984, some 7500 PU coated implants have been sold in Canada.

4) Dr. Ben-Simhon reviewed the medical literature on PU coated implants. The PU coated breast implant was introduced in the early seventies by Ashley.[1] Since then, there have been several reports of severe complications associated with this type of implant.[2,3,4,6]

The complications include severe persistent infection and incorporation of PU into the surrounding tissue with severe difficulty in removing infected remains. The rough surface of the PU coated implant makes insertion more difficult and demands a larger incision.

It is difficult to explant a PU implant when it becomes infected. The PU foam, or its fragments can elicit a marked foreign body reaction.

There are reports in which infection has appeared as late as four months after insertion of the implant. It is unlikely that this infection could be related to contamination at the time of insertion.

The group agreed that patients should be told that implanting a PU prosthesis is a procedure that is not guaranteed and that problems can develop. Risks should be known by the patient so that the patient can determine for herself if they are acceptable.

Though there are occasional reports of satisfactory results with the PU coated implants[5] and favourable letters[7], the risks and severity of the complications seem to outweigh the possible advantages. Good plastic surgeons are aware of these concerns and most, at least in Ottawa, do not use the PU coated implant.

5) Dr. Chawla then reviewed BRMD and other scientific research on PU as an implant material, and the current thinking of the biomaterials research community. He noted that after implantation, collagen fibres will invade an implant and form a capsule around it. In 7-10 days the fibres will start to re-organize so that they lie essentially parallel to the implant. As the fibres continue to re-organize, the capsule contracts thereby making the implant feel harder. The collagen capsule is in a meta-stable state i.e., the capsule will disappear over time if the implant is removed.

It appears that PU coated breast implants are designed to elicit a foreign body reaction. Macrophages invading the implant could interfere with re-organization of the collagen fibre capsule thereby preventing the hardening of the breast implant. Unfortunately the macrophages may also attack the polyurethane and break it down. The degradation may result in "soft" (low molecular weight) segments disappearing leaving the "hard" segments of polyurethane in the vicinity of the implant. Physical stress on the foam is also a factor, and is probably the cause of the characteristic triangular shape of the PU foam debris, degradation of bubble walls leaving the triangular bubble junctions intact.

PU degradation may also induce adverse systemic affects. Should problems develop with the implant, it will be more difficult to remove it as tissue will normally have grown into the foamed structure. Furthermore, at the time of explant, small degraded polyurethane particles may be left behind in the host body and may continue to elicit foreign body reaction.

6) Dr. Hinberg summarized recent US FDA activity. The FDA has proposed (regulation 515b) that all manufacturers be required to submit information on the safety and effectiveness of breast implants, including those presently on the market. They would have 30 months to comply.

The CDRH panel convened November 22, 1988 made three recommendations:
1. National Registry to be set up for all silicone breast implants.
2. Implement mandatory patient information program to advise patients of potential risks.
3. FDA to keep public, physicians, industry and panel advised of new information received.

The FDA has undertaken to search their databases on the problem reports and produce an analysis for us. Dr. Johnson suggested that we participate in the FDA analysis.

7) Discussion. The meeting agreed that we can and should be dealing with the potential benefits and problems of PU coated implants distinct

from smooth silicone implants, while acknowledging that under the PU coating lies a fairly typical silicone implant.

The group reviewed the suggested benefits of the PU coated prosthesis, namely reduced early capsular contracture, and a possible niche for patients exhibiting recurrent problems (other than infection) with smooth silicone implants. The available evidence does not strongly substantiate the claim of reduced capsular contraction. Further, Dr. Ben-Simhon noted that after recurrent problems with a smooth silicone implant, many conservative physicians would recommend not a PU implant, but an external prosthesis. The great psychological benefit of a implanted prosthesis was noted.

Review of the risks and problems of the PU coated implant included the very serious situation arising in the event that infection should appear around the implant, and the obvious difficulty of cleanly and completely removing the prosthesis together with all fragments of degraded polyurethane from the implant site. Also noted were the unknown effects of disappearance of the low molecular weight fractions of the polyurethane, and the need (due to high friction of the PU coat) for a larger incision at the time of implantation.

The consensus of the meeting was that the net result of this review was significantly negative, and that acceptable alterantives to use of the PU coated implant were available.

Options for action were reviewed. Rejected options included the status quo. The group felt that all PU coated prostheses on the market before premarket review went into effect should be subject to the same scrutiny as other implants.

8) Recommendations. The group was unanimous in recommending that the Branch consider asking distributors, under Section 28 of the Medical Devices Regulations, to provide, on or before a certain date, evidence to establish the safety and effectiveness of the PU coated breast prostheses distributed by them.

The group also recommended that in the interim, distributors be asked to voluntarily stop sale of PU coated breast implants.

Finally, the group discussed communicating with the present bearers of PU coated implants. We confirmed that we still do not have any useful information to pass on.

EXHIBIT TWO:

Government of Canada Memorandum

To: I. Hinberg, Ph.D.
Head, Research and Development Section
Bureau of Radiation and Medical Devices

From: P. Blais, Ph.D.
Research and Development Section

Date: Feb. 20, 1989

Subject: Re: Même/Polyurethane/Breast Implants
(Your Memorandum of Feb. 13, received Feb. 17, 1989)

The above product and its analogs are unfit for human implantation and are potentially hazardous to users. They are fortuitously biodegradable implants with an uncharacterized composition, incorporating significant amounts of precursors to documented toxic chemical entities. Their history and their properties were discussed extensively at our Consensus Development Meeting of January 6, 1989.

In late January 1989, I reported to you that the prosthesis coating is made from a common class of commercial polyurethane foam available from various vendors for assorted consumer product applications. Industrial (nonspecific) applications of such foams allow broad compositional variations, elevated impurity levels and the incorporation of reactive intermediates of unknown biocompatibility. The safety, efficacy, and quality assurance levels of a medical implant based on these foams therefore cannot be demonstrated without testing each implant.

Additional processes in the fabrication of the coated devices introduce further uncertainties for each unit. Specifically, the need to bond the silicone shell to the foam layer using a reactive adhesive (hydrolysis of the polyurethane) and to heat-seal the seams on the coating (pyrolysis) are of particular concern.

Furthermore, evidence provided to the Branch in 1985 by the distributor but only made available to me recently confirms that the Même and its counterparts are only structural variants of the early Ashley Natural-Y breast prostheses using the same generic family of polyurethane foams.

The disappointing long term performance of these early 1970's products and their risks were described by Dr. H. Ben-Simhon in a review of the medical and scientific literature at our Consensus Development Meeting.

There are other areas of concern. It would take much more work and time to fully document the magnitude of the supplemental risk that these specific prostheses pose. Please note that my activities in that area ceased in compliance with directives from Dr. D. Johnson in his memorandum of February 8, 1989.

As requested in your recent memorandum, I address your questions in the Appended Report Supplement and I remain available at all times to discuss any area that may need clarification or elaboration.

Signed: P. Blais, Ph.D.
          February 20/89

Report Appended: p0001-0144, pages provided: 144

cc: D.L. Johnson   Date stamped: Received
    E.G. Létouneau   Feb. 20, 1989

EXHIBIT THREE:

Irwin Hinberg Ph.D.

Research and Development Section
Research and Standards Division

Chef
Recherche et développement
Division de recherche et normes

Bureau of Radiation and Medical Devices
Bureau de la radioprotection et des instruments médicaux

(613) 954-0392

Dr. Blais

89-03-02

[ ] NOTE AND FILE / NOTER ET CLASSER
[ ] AS REQUESTED / À VOTRE DEMANDE
[ ] NOTE AND RETURN / NOTER ET RETOURNER
[ ] APPROVAL / APPROUVER
[ ] COMMENT / COMMENTER
[ ] SIGNATURE / SIGNER
[ ] MAY WE DISCUSS / DISCUTER AVEC NOUS
[ ] INFORMATION / PRENDRE CONNAISSANCE
[ ] DIRECT REPLY / RÉPONDRE DIRECTEMENT
[ ] LABORATORY EVALUATION / ÉVALUATION DE LABORATOIRE
[ ] PREPARATION OF REPLY / RÉDIGER REPONSE
[ ] ACTION
[ ] FOR SIGNATURE OF / POUR LA SIGNATURE DE _____
[ ] ACTION BY / DONNER SUITE VERS LE _____ 19 ___

REMARKS — REMARQUES

Please make the corrections suggested by DLJ.

EXHIBIT FOUR:

Government of Canada / Gouvernement du Canada

MEMORANDUM "CORRECTED ...GIVEN BY I.H March 03, 1989..."

TO: I. Hinberg Ph.D.
Head
Research and Development Section
Bureau of Radiation and Medical Devices

FROM: P. Blais Ph.D.
Research and Development Section

SUBJECT: Re: Même/Polyurethane/Breast Implants
(Your Memorandum of February 14, received February 17, 1989)

IN MY OPINION, the above product MAY BE a biodegradable implant with an uncharacterized composition, incorporating significant amounts of precursors to documented toxic chemical entities.

In late January 1989, I reported to you that the prosthesis coating is made from a common class of commercial polyurethane foam available from various vendors for assorted consumer product applications. Industrial (nonspecific) applications of such foams allow broad compositional variations, elevated impurity levels and the incorporation of reactive intermediates of unknown biocompatibility. The safety, efficacy, and quality assurance levels of a medical implant based on these foams therefore cannot be demonstrated without testing each implant, or each BATCH OR FORM USED.

Additional processes in the fabrication of the coated devices introduce further uncertainties for each unit. Specifically, the need to bond the silicone shell to the foam layer using a reactive adhesive (hydrolysis of the polyurethane) and to heat-seal the seams on the coating (pyrolysis) are of particular concern.

(continued)
---2

DISCUSS WITH
DLT
PB
MAR 2

RECEIVED / REÇU LE
FEB 21 1989
Research and Standards Division
Division de recherche et des normes

Remove until you have presented the Dept with this guidance.

— 2 —

What evidence / Who had it?

Furthermore, evidence provided to the Branch in 1985 by the distributor but only made available to me recently confirms that the Mème and its counterparts are only structural variants of the early Ashley Natural-Y breast prostheses using the same generic family of polyurethane foams.

How did you get it / Why didn't you tell me about it?

The ~~disappointing~~ long term performance of these early 1970's products and their risks were described by Dr. H. Ben-Simhon in a ~~review of the medical and scientific literature at our Consensus Development Meeting~~ recent discussion with you.

There are other areas of concern. It would take much more work and time to fully document the magnitude of the supplemental risk that these specific prostheses pose. ~~Please note that my activities in that area ceased in compliance with directives from Dr. D. Johnson in his memorandum of February 8, 1906~~

As requested in your recent memorandum, I address your questions in the Appended Report Supplement and I remain available at all times to discuss any area that may need clarification or elaboration.

P. Blais Ph.D.

Report Appendix - no numbering. Points provided. Pages numbered 1–44.

c.c. D.L. Johnson
     E.G. Létouneau

EXHIBIT FOUR:

Corrected memorandum given by I.H. March 03, 1989, 10 a.m. with instructions to implement. P. Blais

Government of Canada Memorandum

To: I. Hinberg, Ph.D.
Head, Research and Development Section
Bureau of Radiation and Medical Devices

From: P. Blais, Ph.D.
Research and Development Section

Date: Feb. 20, 1989

Subject: Re: Même/Polyurethane/Breast Implants
(Your Memorandum of Feb. 13, received Feb. 17, 1989)

In my opinion, the above product may be a biodegradable implant with an uncharacterized composition, incorporating significant amounts of precursors to documented toxic chemical entities.

In late January 1989, I reported to you that the prosthesis coating is made from a common class of commercial polyurethane foam available from various vendors for assorted consumer product applications. No other polyurethane foams are available. Industrial (nonspecific) applications of such foams allow broad compositional variations, elevated impurity levels and the incorporation of reactive intermediates of unknown biocompatibility. The safety, efficacy, and quality assurance levels of a medical implant based on these foams therefore cannot be demonstrated without testing each implant, or each batch of foam used.

Additional processes in the fabrication of the coated devices introduce further uncertainties for each unit. Specifically, the need to bond the silicone shell to the foam layer using a reactive adhesive (hydrolysis of the polyurethane) and to heat-seal the seams on the coating (pyrolysis) are of particular concern.

Remove until you have presented the Dept. with this evidence.

The long term performance of these early 1970's products and their risks and benefits were described by Dr. H. Ben-Simhon in a recent discussion with you.

There are other areas of concern. It would take much more work and time to fully document the magnitude of the supplemental risk that these specific prostheses pose.

As requested in your recent memorandum, I address your questions in the Appended Report Supplement and I remain available at all times to discuss any area that may need clarification or elaboration.

Signed: P. Blais, Ph.D.
          February 20/89

Report Appended: p0001-0144, pages provided: 144

cc: D.L. Johnson   Date stamped: Received
    E.G. Létouneau   Feb. 21, 1989

EXHIBIT FIVE:

Government of Canada Round Trip Memorandum

To: I. Hinberg, Ph.D.
Head, Research and Development Section
Bureau of Radiation and Medical Devices

From: P. Blais, Ph.D.
Research and Development Section

Subject: Re: Même/Polyurethane/Breast Implants;
(Your memorandum of February 17, 1989).

As requested on March 2, 1989, the modifications that you and Dr. D.L. Johnson demanded with respect to my memorandum and my Report Supplement of February 20, 1989, have been implemented.

Please note that, in my opinion, the content of the original documents is significantly altered.

The deletion of references to our Consensus Development Meeting of January 6, 1989, which led to our recommendation to capture this product under provisions of Section 28 of the Medical Devices Regulations is of particular concern to me.

Signed: P. Blais, Ph.D.

Date stamped: Received Mar 6, 1989

APPENDIX B / 205

EXHIBIT SIX:

Briefing Information

Title Regulatory Status of Polyurethane (PU) Breast Implants.

Anticipated Question What is the Department doing to protect Canadian women from problems caused by Polyurethane coated breast implants?

Background On Tuesday, March 7, 1989, the Montreal Gazette headlined "Top officials ignore plea to halt sale of implant." The article alleges that at least five scientists in the Department have urged that the Meme PU coated breast implant be temporarily removed from the market.

Current Status The assertion is incorrect. The recommendations of scientific and medical staff were that 1) the Department should consider asking distributors to provide evidence of the safety and effectiveness of the device, 2) that patients should be informed (by their physicians) of the risks and benefits to be expected from a PU breast implant, and 3) further research should be undertaken on the behaviour of polyurethanes after implant in the body.

The Meme PU covered breast implant is distributed in Canada by Real Laperrierre Inc. of Montreal. The distributor has volunteered to provide the Department with information such as would be required in a premarket review submission. This offer was welcomed as a cooperative, non-confrontational means of obtaining the desired additional information.

Relevant Factors Laboratory research, and review of scientific and medical literature about the behaviour of the PU breast implant are supporting our earlier opinion that it has both unique benefits and unique problems.

Suggested Response Departmental staff have not recommended that the PU coated breast implant be temporarily withdrawn from the market. The Department does believe that additional information is needed, and that prospective implant patients should be informed of risks and benefits. Additional information is being acquired through a voluntary submission by the distributor, through continued review of medical and scientific literature, and through research in Departmental laboratories. The Department, in conjunction with the Canadian Association of Plastic Surgeons, has developed a patient information booklet on breast augmentation surgery. The booklet has been distributed by the plastic surgeons. Departmental officials are working with them to improve and elaborate this booklet, and to ensure that it adequately describes the risks and benefits of PU and silicone implants and implant procedures.

Health Protection Branch
March 8, 1989 10:00 a.m.
Dr. A.J. Liston 957-1804

INDEX

Academy of Orthopedic Surgeons, 151
acne medications, 162-68
Acnidazil, 23
L'Actualité Médicale, 131
advertising: breast implants, 73; drug industry, 51-53; Naprosyn, 134; Premarin, 139, 141; stronger controls needed, 178-79; Toradol, 131-33
Aequitron Medical Inc., 60
alerts: problems associated with medical devices, 41-45
Altschuler, Richard, 73
American Society of Plastic and Reconstructive Surgeons Inc., 94, 103
anaesthesia equipment, 41
animal drug testing, 68, 164-65
Annals of Internal Medicine, 51
asthma, 117
Atomic Energy of Canada Limited, 156, 158
Autian, John, 98-99
autoimmune disease, 102-03
Awang, Dennis, 33
Ayerst Laboratories, 139, 141, 146

Batish, Chris, 84-85, 96
Beatty, Perrin, 11, 21, 87, 92
Beauchemin, Guy, 16
Bégin, Monique, 11
Bendectin, 163
benzodiazepine, 124
benzoyl peroxide (BP), 163-68
Bewley, Susan and Thomas, 146
Bill C-22: licensing of generic drugs, 54, 56
Bill C-91: patent protection for brand-name drug companies, 54-56
Biron, Pierre, 125, 131-33, 135
Blais, Pierre, 42-43, 77-80, 82, 86-88, 90-93, 95-97, 99, 103, 154
Boston Women's Book Collective, 185
Bouchard, Benoît, 2, 5, 11, 25, 28, 46, 57, 102, 105, 119, 187
Bouchard, Jacques, 83
Boucher, Sylvain, 81-82
Brassard, Raymond, 1, 4, 82
breakthrough drugs, 19-20, 35-36
breast implants: carcinogen in Meme's polyurethane cover, 84-86; conditions at Meme manufacturing plant, 100-01; Health and Welfare Canada's policy, 86-93, 95-97; historical context, 78-79; Meme irregularities, 80-84; plastic surgeons, 103; silicone-gel, 61-63, 74-77, 187; U.S. Food and Drug Administration, 93-94; women's groups, 185
Brill-Edwards, Dr. Michelle, 27, 117-19
Bristol-Myers Squibb, 85, 97, 99, 101-02
British Medical Journal, 112, 116-17
Brooks, Emerson, 154
Brown, Grahaem, 112, 115-16
Bryant Medical Products Inc., 81
Burstein, Albert, 152
Bush, George, 64

Canadian Consumer, 166

Canadian Federation of Biological Societies, 54
Canadian Medical Association, 40-41, 52-53
Canadian Society for Clinical Investigation, 54
Capoten, 53
carcinogens: benzoyl peroxide, 162, 164-67; Meme breast implant, 84, 97-100
Cardiac Prevention Research Centre of Nova Scotia, 55
Carmen-Kasparek, Mary, 29
Catley-Carlson, Margaret, 1-4, 44-45, 95-96, 103-04, 129, 159, 172
Chartrand, Marcel, 1, 2, 95, 105
Children of Thalidomide, 9-10
Chopra, Nirmala, 46, 82
Chopra, Shiv, 30-33
Clomid, 188
cluster headaches, 120-21
Command Trust Network, 185
computer software: medical devices, 155-56
conflict of interest, 23-25, 173-74
consumer groups, 184-85
Consumers' Association of Canada, 55, 184
contraceptive device, 10
contracting-out drug submissions, 21-23, 174
Convexo-Concave (C-C) heart valve, 42-43, 65
Cooper Surgical, 100-01
Copps, Sheila, 103
Council on Competitiveness, 59, 63-64
Craig, Iris, 32

Dalkon Shield, 10-11, 39
Das Gupta, Agit, 39-44, 48
Da Silva, Thomas, 126
Depo Provera, 184

Dingell, John, 65-66
DLSF Systems Inc., 155, 158-60
doctors: endorsements for new drugs, 108; information on prescriptions, 183-84; on radio talk shows, 183; prescribing habits, 52
Dow Corning Chemical Corporation, 62-63, 74, 76, 102
drug industry: advertising, 51-53, 140, 178-79; clinical tests, 16-17; contracting-out, 21-23, 174; dealing with reporters, 111-12; financing of research, 55; international trade agreements, 56-57; list of drugs whose approval was untimely, 177; patent protection, 54-56; pressure to speed up approvals, 16-25, 57-58, 66-68; regulatory practice favoured, 165-66; review process, 27-34; safety review standards, 3-5, 12-13
drug spending, 49-51, 177-78
Duplessis, Suzanne, 78-79

Edwards, Charles, 64
elderly patients: NSAIDs 130-31; orthopaedic products, 154
Epp, Jake, 11, 18, 78-79, 166-67, 178
Erola, Judy, 29, 51, 174-75
estrogen, 143-44, 147
European Economic Community, 57, 68
Evans, Robert, 50

Fazekas, Atilla, 23-24
FDA. *See* U.S. Food and Drug Administration
fractures, 144
France: Halcion, 125
Franklin, Claire, 30-32, 118-19
Fraser, Susan, 158

Frederick, George, 162-67

Gaffney, Beryl, 103
Gagnon, Dr. Denis, 25, 57-58, 174
Gagnon Report, 174, 176
gastrointestinal problems: NSAIDs, 131, 132
General Agreement on Tariffs and Trade (GATT), 57
generic drugs, 54
Glaxo Canada Inc., 55, 107-18
Glaxo Holdings, 110, 112, 117
government agencies: software safety, 159-60
government committees, 185
Granville, Geoff, 99
Great Britain: Halcion, 126
Griffiths, Ed, 101
Gross, Michael, 153
Guidoin, Robert, 78, 93

Halcion, 123-28, 176
Hamilton, Rob, 133
Health and Welfare Canada: benzoyl peroxide, 164-68; Bureau of Human Prescription Drugs, 15-17, 20, 22-23, 26, 28-29;Bureau of Radiation and Medical Devices, 37-39, 44, 47, 154,156; changes required to system, 171-76; conflict of interest, 23-25; consumer groups, 184-85; drug-safety review system, 12-13; Halcion, 126-28, 176; Health Protection Branch, 2-3, 33; Imitrex, 114, 116-19; make public a listing of all approved drugs, 177; measures to speed drug through approval process, 17-25; Meme breast implant, 86-93; orthopaedic products, 154; policy on breast implants, 78-79; policy on Meme breast implant, 95-97, 103-05; Premarin, 147; safety concerns of doctors and scientists, 25-29; test on Meme, 95-100; thalidomide, 10; Toradol, 132-35
health-care policy, 50
health topics: media reports, 182-83
Hearn, Ambrose, 46-48
heart conditions: Imitrex, 110, 113-17; replacement estrogen, 145
heart valves, 42-43, 65
Henderson, Dr. Ian, 15-17, 164-65
Hickman, Roy, 44, 48
Hinberg, Irwin, 86-89, 90-91, 95-96, 98
hip implants, 152-53
Houle, Germain, 45
Hun-Medipharma Research Inc., 23-24

ICN Canada Ltd., 23, 147
Imitrex, 20, 24
immune system: implants, 153; silicone, 102-03
implants: breakdown of materials, 86; breast, 61-63, 73-105, 185, 187; hip, 152-53; jaw, 65; knee, 150-54; Meme breast implant, 77, 80-105; orthopaedic products, 149-54; registry, 66; silicone-gel, 74-77
infant respirators, 60
Inman, Bill, 116-17, 121
insomnia, 123, 127
International Agency for Research in Cancer, 166
international agreements, 179
Italy: Halcion, 125

Japan: animal drug testing, 68;
    menopause, 142
jaw implants, 65
Johnson, David, 80, 82, 86-89,
    91, 104
Johnson, Gordon, 27
Journal of Cancer Research, 98

Karpoff, Jim, 20
Kasper, Carmel, 33
Kaspy, Robert, 115
Kaufert, Patricia, 142
Kelsey, Frances, 10
Kerrigan, Carolyn, 92
Kessler, Dr. David, 59-67,
    102-03
Kevadon, 9
knee implants, 150-54
Kozzovsky, Nir, 97
Kroeger, Francine, 29

Lalonde, Marc, 178
The Lancet, 127, 146
Landry, Monique, 78
Langan, Joy, 103
Laperrière Inc., Réal, 81-82,
    84, 88
Letourneau, Ernest, 44-45, 48,
    89, 96
Levan, David, 158-60
Levy, Michael, 112, 115
Liston, Albert, 19-21, 26, 41,
    42, 44, 45, 88, 91-92, 95-96,
    104, 172
Lock, Margaret, 142
Lomas, Jonathan, 50
Lumpkin, Murray, 167
lymph nodes, 153

Marion Merrell Dow Canada
    Inc., 55
Marketplace, 89
Markham, Jacqueline, 85
McCurdy, Howard, 119, 166-68
media, 182-83

medical devices, 36-48, 65;
    breast implants, 73-74;
    computerized, 155-56;
    policy on, 177-78
Medical Research Council of
    Canada, 55, 153
Medicine: A New Vision, 35-36
Meloche, Jacques, 108
Meme breast implant, 1-2, 43,
    77, 80-83; cancer risk, 84-86,
    95-100; conditions at manu-
    facturing plant, 100-01;
    Health and Welfare Canada,
    86-93, 103-05; memos regard-
    ing, 192-206; suspended
    sale of, 101-02; 2-4 toluene
    diamine, 84-86; U.S. Food and
    Drug Administration, 93-94
menopause, 139-40, 142-46
Merrell Company, William S., 10
Messier, Jacques, 26-28, 173
migraine headaches, 107
Monteith, J. Waldo, 10
Montreal Gazette, 4, 82-84, 91,
    103, 109, 115, 119, 156
Montreal Migraine Clinic, 108
multinational drug companies, 3, 5

Napke, Dr. Edward, 17
Naprosyn, 134
narcotics: pain relief, 129
National Research Council, 159
Natural-Y Surgical Specialties,
    81, 85, 100, 104-05
Nelson, Dr. Robert, 24-25, 108
The Netherlands: Halcion, 124
New York Times, 59, 63
Nickel, Anne-Kristin, 23
Non-prescription Drug Manu-
    facturers Association of
    Canada, 166
Non-Steroidal Anti-Inflamma-
    tory Drug (NSAID), 130-35
North American Free Trade
    Agreement (NAFTA), 57

INDEX / 211

Ontario Hydro, 157-58
Open Reality, 73
orthopaedic products, 149-54
osteoporosis, 143-47
Oswald, Ian, 126-27
Ottawa Citizen, 27-28, 108, 187
over-the-counter (OTC) medications, 162

Pagtakhan, Rey, 20
pain relief, 129-30
Papillon, Jacques, 76-77, 80, 103
Parkhurst, Mary Anne, 139, 141
patent protection, 54, 56-57
Patented Medicine Prices Review Board, 55
Peacock, Carole, 2, 24, 114
Peck, Carl, 120
Pfizer Inc., 42-43
Pharmaceutical Advertising Advisory Board, 52, 132, 135
Pharmaceutical Manufacturers Association of Canada, 16, 29, 51, 53-56, 177
pharmaceuticals: policy on, 177-78
pharmacists: professional expertise, 161-62
plastic surgeons, 83, 94, 103
polyurethane: decomposition of, 85-86, 93, 97-100; used in breast implants, 100-01
Powell, Tom, 101
Premarin, 139, 141, 143-44, 146-147
prevention of illness, 178
product monograph, 13
Professional Institute of the Public Service of Canada, 31-33
progestins, 143, 145

Proprietary Association, 166
prostaglandins, 130
Public Citizen's Health Research Group, 15, 60, 68, 76-77, 185
public relations, 35-37, 108, 182
Public Service Commission, 31, 32

Quayle, Dan, 59, 60, 63-64

Renaud, Marc, 50
replacement hormones, 139, 143, 145, 146
Replicon breast implant, 81
research and development, 55-56
Ritter, Len, 29
Robbins Company, A. H., 10-11
Rossi, Alice, 145

safety and efficacy: breast implants, 187; Meme breast implant, 76-82, 101-05; orthopaedic implants, 151-54; over-the-counter medications, 162; review standards, 3-5, 12-13, 173-74; software, 155-60; testing harmonization, 68; tighter advertising control, 179
Schroeder, Patricia, 146
Scotfoam Corporation, 101
Sheehy, Gail, 145
Shiley Inc., 42-43
side-effects: benzodiazepine, 124; breakdown of implant materials, 86; Halcion, 123-28; Imitrex, 108-18; NSAIDs, 130, 132; Premarin, 143; reporting, 13; silicone-gel breast implants, 74-75, 102

Silent Passage, 145
silicone-gel implants, 74-77, 102-03, 153. *See also* Meme breast implant
Silimed Inc., 81
skin cancer: acne preparations, 162, 164-65, 167
Sledge, Clement, 151-52
Sleep and Research Treatment Centre, 125
sleeping pills, 123-24
Somers, Emmanuel, 19-21, 25, 29, 30, 32-33, 40, 42, 44, 48, 172
Sparrow, Barbara, 168
Squibb Canada Inc., 53, 82
SRI, 157
Sullivan, Louis, 61
Surgitek, 85, 99-100, 102
Syntex Inc., 129, 131-35

Talimol, 9
thalidomide, 9-10
Therac-25, 156-58
Toradol, 129-35, 178
trade agreements, 57
Transplantation/Implantation Today, 77
Turner, Chris, 22, 29
2-4 toluene diamine, 84, 93, 96, 97, 100-01
Tylenol with codeine, 130, 132

United States: consumer groups, 184-85; government committees, 185; speeding up review, 66-68

U.S. Environmental Agency, 85
U.S. Food and Drug Administration, 10, 15, 51, 60, 63-68, 76; benzoyl peroxide, 167; computerized medical devices, 156; Halcion, 125, 126, 128; Imitrex, 120; Meme breast implant, 93-94, 97-103; Public Citizen's Health Research Group,185; review of orthopaedic products, 154; Toradol, 134
U.S. National Institutes of Health, 146
Upjohn Company, 124-28, 184
Upjohn Company of Canada, 129, 131-35, 140-41

voluntary associations, 186

Wake Carroll, Barbara, 28
Walker, Robert, 1
War Amputations of Canada, 10
Weck, 82
Weiss, Ted, 62-63, 94
Welsh, William, 45-46
West Germany: thalidomide, 9
Williams, John, 53
Wilson, Linda, 86
Wolfe, Dr. Sidney, 15, 185
Women's National Health Network, 185
Wyeth-Ayerst, 146-47

Zuckerman, Diana, 62-63